MacArthur Park

MacArthur Park

ANDREW DURBIN

Nightboat Books
New York

ISBN: 978-1-937658-69-4

Interior and cover design: Familiar
Cover art: Thomas Eggerer, *Fence Romance*, 2009
acrylic and oil on canvas, 177 × 204 cm | 69 ⅔ × 80 ⅓ in
Courtesy Galerie Buchholz, Berlin/Cologne/New York

Cataloging-in-publication data is available from the Library of
Congress

Distributed by the University Press of New England

One Court Street
Lenanon, NH 03766
www.upne.com

Nightboat Books
New York
www.nightboat.org

For Jacolby Satterwhite and Stewart Uoo

... She was inside a story ... parts of which felt like stories she'd lived through before: the expression of a face she couldn't quite place, a word or phrase spoken by someone she forgot a moment later, a detail of a room, a stick of furniture, the pattern of a curtain, the color of wallpaper, part of a doorway: it was not a story, really, not a narrative at any rate that moved from A to B to C, but rather a shower of moments, all out of order, trying to cohere in some manner, trying to show her something: some lesson, or crystallization of many things she had missed the logical connectives of: that she was herself outside this "I" the story seemed to be about ...

—Gary Indiana, *Depraved Indifference*

For awhile, I hadn't actually been writing but doing a transcription that fell in the deep space between drawing and landscaping.

—Renee Gladman, *Calamities*

Two years after Hurricane Sandy made landfall in New York City, Klaus Biesenbach, the director of MoMA PS1, posted to his popular Instagram account an image of the Statue of Liberty overrun by a tidal wave from the film *The Day After Tomorrow*, with the caption: "2 years ago #Sandy hit making clear how vulnerable the city is." One of his followers commented: "Great screenshot from The Day After Tomorrow. Funny people believe it's real."

Biesenbach countered: "I picked the picture because pictures from movies often seem more 'real' than documents." Then he wrote: "The days after the hurricane felt very much like in this movie." And finally: "I will post a pic a day this week, but felt it was good to start with a constructed image as we all didn't know what was really happening the day/night of [the hurricane] until the floods and fires took their devastating toll." Several other users continued to criticize his choice of image for the start of his series. He responded that the film still was a reminder that fiction can be made real: "I was evacuated from Rockaway Beach (in the midst of planting trees) and went to the city and spent Sunday/Monday indoors until the storm was over, watching TV and the news until the electricity [blacked] out. What did you do?"

Housesat in the West Village for Chris H., an art collector whom I had been assisting part-time, my first job in the city after college. In advance of the storm, he'd gone to his second home (the smallest of three) in Connecticut with his husband, a landlord of skyscrapers, and asked me to watch their apartment for them while they were tucked away in storm-free Greenwich. On the eleventh floor of a building at the edge of evacuation zone C, his place would be safer than mine, he argued over email, which was in zone B, in Brooklyn. (After the storm, the city would redraw these borders, increasing the number of vulnerable neighborhoods within a new, six-tiered zoning system that would mark the sites of disaster without devising any new response to protect them.) "We'll pay for groceries," he wrote. Subject: "Mine during big storm."

Picked up groceries (tortillas, two chicken breasts, a can of black beans) and a few frozen dinners at the scuttled Whole Foods in Union Square, weed from a scattershot and severely nervous dealer in the East Village, and kept awake through the hurricane as the wind gathered speed and the waters of the Hudson, the East River, and the Atlantic surged over the boroughs, into Battery Park and the tunnels between Brooklyn, Queens, and Manhattan. As the harbor inundated the Financial District, I rolled a joint and watched, through a cloud of sweet-smelling smoke, CNN's chatty cluster of pundits fret amongst themselves in a split-screen alongside unedited storm footage until the power plant by the East River exploded in a concussive burst of intense white light in the east-facing window of the apartment. New York, or at least my part of New York, went dark, full dark, a dark you could brag about, if you had someone to talk to. I was alone.

I stood up, and with requisite paranoia wondered aloud if it had been a bomb, since any blast in see-something-say-something New York had to be an *attack* by someone seeking to take advantage of the storm of the century. What would the tv be saying if the tv weren't dead? I knew I'd smoked too much, though in my mind's eye rows of Manhattan skyscrapers were suddenly imploding amid plumes of smoke swirling devilishly in the hurricane wind, end-of-days-like to a soundtrack of death wails. But out the window, there was no evidence of distant fires against the darkened skyline of the Village, no scream of sirens, nor any telling signs of some enlarging crisis, though the uneasy, creeping sense of one lingered in the nippy air.

The city fell silent in the blackout. I tried to check the news on my phone, but it had died while I was stoned on CNN's rolling coverage of the end of the world. I slid the windowpane up and stuck my head out above Fifth Avenue, into the throttled calm of what I took to be Sandy's lopsided eye as it squatted overhead. A blast of salty, cold air shot through the apartment. Candles, flashlights, and whatever else was available to whomever was awake, lit the windows of nearby apartment buildings. Far below, NYU students emerged from a dormitory across the street to play in the drizzle. They ran about, enthralled with the novelty of this dent in the city's armor, rapt with dumb joy as a chilly mist spritzed the turbulent October air, ignorant of whatever it was that was happening at the frayed edges of Queens and Brooklyn and Lower Manhattan, until the hurricane wind gained strength again and the students returned to their rooms for the last act, whatever that would look like. Wrinkled sheets of rain darted across the city like huge flocks of birds, threaded between buildings and down the avenue. Far downtown, the Goldman Sachs building, a Tower of Gold buried in the velvety black of the storm, glowed obscenely amid its shadowed neighbors, powered apparently by its own generators. We, though apparently not they, were in for it.

With the power out, the wi-fi down, and my phone dead, I spent the next day in the apartment as the little dry food I had (varieties of crackers, mostly) ran out, wondering what had happened and who was injured and if anyone I knew had been killed. I paced the small guest room, moved back and forth between the window and the double bed. Outside, a few neighbors stood dizzied in the wreck of tree branches and stray garbage that had been flung down the avenue by the storm, seemingly dazed in the first gray light of this new world, which was probably the same world, only of a different, less Sotheby's International Realty-approved mood. Below, Fifth Avenue was like a scene from a film I hadn't wanted to see let alone appear in: its plant life ripped apart, with branches scattered across the asphalt. Overhead the sky had resolved into the color of wet concrete. I kept to the bed for the rest of the day, trying to read a bad novel, until I couldn't take the isolation of somebody else's apartment with somebody else's things anymore, so I left and found a taxi.

We flew through the manic, cop-directed traffic of Manhattan without its streetlights, past the fallen trees and piles of trash and the dispersed and ugly detritus of buildings and vehicles, chunks of plastic and overturned garbage cans, until we crossed the empty Williamsburg Bridge and headed toward South Williamsburg, where I arrived home almost in tears, though I couldn't explain to my roommate at the time why I felt so terrible since I was OK, "we," everyone I knew, were OK. My distress was ridiculous, even to me, and felt all the more so whenever I had to explain the feeling to him—or to anyone, for that matter (outside of New York, it seemed that the storm had had no effect on the rest of the world). In the disaster the city had become me, or I had become the city—a one-act drama that, even in previews, gained little sympathy from its would-be friendly audience. Things proceeded, online and elsewhere, per usual. My parents said it was fine. A one-night fling shrugged his shoulders. I couldn't quite place this feeling in my catalog of previous melodramas, only that a city-me had been dealt some awful blow and I was struggling, on this makeshift stage of poorly defined grief, to get back up to monologue nobly about my or anyone's resilience. I allowed the luxury of my passing victimhood to take its indefinite, blob-like shape in me. I would suffer, and make of my suffering a performance that somehow managed to ignore both the fact that I was unharmed and that the consequences of this new world with its new climate extended far more dangerously beyond the city.

"It's fine," my roommate said.

"I know it's fine."

Had I been in danger? Never once. And yet the storm's vengeful spirit continued to haunt the edge of my reality. What would the city become now, and who would we become with it?

In the following week, my grandparents sent me a chain email with images from movies that were being passed off on the internet as photographs from the real hurricane (almost all of them were from disaster films), including the one from *The Day After Tomorrow* that Biesenbach would post some years later to his Instagram. Composite images of tornadoes over Manhattan, a supercell storm system from the Midwest or some other flat, sky-scraper-less place Photoshopped over Midtown, sharks cruising the flooded Financial District. My paternal grandparents, cozy in their far-from-the-sea suburb in Nebraska, were happy to hear that I wasn't hurt, but they wanted to know if the Statue had survived the storm. Subject: "FWD:FWD:FWD:FWD:FWD: You won't BELIEVE what Sandy did to NYC!!"

Ed Halter, writing for *Artforum* online about disaster films of the 2010s, notes that these films propose a day after tomorrow in which we no longer overcome or survive disaster but rather enter an age of its permanent management:

> These are cynical films at heart, allowing us to fantasize about negotiating survival within a failing system rather than letting us hope to replace it with something

better. Their anxieties mirror the just-in-time logic of networked economies, in which a typical day of work consists of the management of multiple crises, thrown onto the laps of multitaskers thanks to the unfettered spread of instant connectivity.

Halter concludes his essay by quoting Susan Sontag's "The Imagination of Disaster," her prophetic 1965 essay on atomic-era films where she writes that these works "are only a sampling, stripped of sophistication, of the inadequacy of most people's response to the unassimilable terrors that infect their consciousness."

In recent disaster films, the crisis frequently results from the strain on—or collapse of—those networked economies as their multi-taskers go offline once the power is cut off, the city has flooded, and the fires have spread across the bleak urban and suburban landscape. Scientists, realizing all too late that the seismograph has recorded the first tremors of an earthquake of an unprecedented magnitude, or that a global superstorm is booming in the Atlantic and scurrying toward the northeastern megalopolis, fail to alert or convince the sluggish authorities of the coming disaster that unfolds faster than the under-funded, understaffed response system can react, leaving ordinary people, played by extraordinary actors, to their own means of escape into this new world.

"I picked the picture because pictures from movies often seem more 'real' ..."

The Day After Tomorrow ends with a frosty New York lost forever to the tundra of a New Siberia, an icebox in the Acela corridor, its streets buried in untouched snow. Exiled to Mexico, the United States government sends a helicopter rescue mission to scoop up the remaining survivors in the Northeast, knowing that few—if any—have survived the weather no one believed would come. The future is here, the grave, sullen president acknowledges. Finally, really, here. After all these years of saying it wouldn't happen, it has, a cinematic comeuppance in a world unwilling to face a changing climate. That is, ours. With much of the United States uninhabitable, unseated permanently from its metropolitan kingdom, the film ends in an absurd prophecy of crisis management that concurs with the doomsy mood of the eco-disaster films of the past few years.

"What did you do?"

Susan Sontag concludes:

> There is a sense in which all these movies are in complicity with the abhorrent. They neutralize it, as I have said. It is no more, perhaps, than the way all art draws its audience into a circle of complicity with the thing represented ... The films perpetuate clichés about identity, volition, power, knowledge, happiness, social consensus, guilt, responsibility, which are, to say the least, not serviceable in our present extremity.

Not quite a form of PTSD, not attributable to any direct confrontation with actual disaster, a protracted exhaustion came over me once the power returned a week or so after the storm, mostly indefinable except in sleeplessness or, when I did fall asleep, in long-winded, talky nightmares in which neighbors discussed other storms, or storms loomed up over ominous dream-horizons deckled with the shards of broken cities, torched palm trees, erased beaches. Sensing, in my clipped, typo-ridden emails, that I was out of sorts in this disheveled New York, Chris wrote, "Why don't you take a vacation."

He had already decided to spend the month in Greenwich, wary of returning to the semi-operational city.

"Sure," I replied. Where to.

He insisted I go down to Miami, a city that I had never been to before, to stay with a friend of his named Robert, whom Chris had known since they were children, growing up on the Upper East Side. "Robert is a sweetheart," he explained, and he's also rich, and "with a guest house. He's out of town, I think. I'm sure he'd let you stay at his place. It's right on South Beach."

Robert, who never wrote to me directly, said yes without question. Chris purchased me a weekend ticket to Florida.

Miami, like much of South Florida, was built on porous limestone consisting of two distinct layers called "facies," per the United States Geologic Survey: an upper oolitic facie that is "moderately indurated, sandy … with scattered concentrations of fossils" and a lower bryozoan facie that is "white to orangish gray, poorly to well indurated, sandy, fossiliferous."

The rock's Swiss cheese-like in form, encrusted with shells and punctured through with holes of varying sizes that make the entire area, anything built on the limestone (so, all of Miami), particularly susceptible to flooding from the Bay of Biscayne, the Atlantic, any nearby body of water for that matter, and which render any known efforts to stem the floods—sea walls, levies, pumps—mostly useless. Local politicians and scientists stand in public dismay, shortchanged by the state and federal governments: what to do about the half-trillion dollars sitting on a sponge? By the early 2010s, the state began to build a $206 million, wholly inadequate pump system to protect the city from the rising sea. As it stands now, the system can't withstand the projected rise for the region. Not even close.

Since the mid-nineties, the sea level has increased nearly four inches. By the end of the century, the oceans are predicted to rise nearly eight feet globally, meaning a slightly higher level for south Florida due to its unusual closeness to the North Atlantic Current, which pushes more water up against the state than the rest of the East Coast. Sometimes there's also what's called a king tide, an abnormally high tide when the Moon is at perigee with the Earth and the gravitational force it exerts on the planet (and so the tides) is strongest. Hot, salty Florida water, muddied and green, gushes up over land to flood the city. This happens often, and more and more often.

In late fall 2012, I didn't know the full extent of Miami's predicament, or if I knew it I wasn't paying much attention to what was happening in Florida because I'd never been to the state before, and, in any case, Florida was Florida, a rolling social calamity, ensured by legislated idiocies, with a keen preference for spectacles of racist absurdity and violence. That was the news. I decided to spend my first long weekend there in the temperature-controlled water of Robert's pool or at the beach, refusing to think about Sandy, or the fact that I was vacationing in the heart of the heart of hurricane country.

The plane touched down at Miami International in early evening, just as the sky's sunset amber cracked and flooded with veins of deeper shades of purple. Taxiing to the arrival gate, I watched dusk give way to a dense blue speckled with tropical starlight. I collected my things at baggage claim and exited into the warm evening outside arrivals, where I hailed a cab to Robert's on South Beach. Once inside his many-windowed home, I dropped my things in the guest room and promptly collapsed on the bed.

I dreamt of crossing the Williamsburg Bridge in a cab under a cloud of thousands of seagulls, all of them squawking out the hungry misery of bird-life, a misery that formed a language I couldn't understand but must have drawn from some ur-tongue I had once belonged to. They flocked to the cab as we crossed the bridge. The cab driver slowed down, terrified that they might peck through his windshield. "Keep going," I shouted, as birds gathered on the hood of the car, their beady, dark eyes boring into me throughthewindows.Onelargebirdopeneditsmouth,widerandwider—

I startled awake. These were the dreams I couldn't shake. Half past midnight, I got into my swim trunks and jumped into Robert's pool, which was enclosed in a tall privacy fence of hedgerows. A fat lizard posed on a small white stone bench near the deep end, where the concrete met a narrow strip of grass before the bushes loomed up, and it eyed me with mild concern when I swam over to get a better look at it. I splashed water its way but it didn't move. "OK," I said aloud to myself. It turned at the sound of my voice, cocked its head, and fled into the grass. I hadn't wanted it to go, I realized. What I needed was a drink.

I found Robert's stash of booze under the silverware drawer—vodka, tequila, and a new bottle of rye whiskey. I opened the whiskey, made a mental note to replace it before I left (did not, in the end), and poured myself a glass. The oven clock blinked two a.m. I went back out and stood by the pool, stretched in the fresh air while holding the glass extended over my head. Overhead, larger and larger bands of heavy clouds, under-lit by the city lights across the bay, began to roll across South Beach, promising rain.

Is this the future.

In the present there was not only the question of the porous limestone, but also of "beach nourishment," another way of asking what to do about erosion. Ocean currents had begun to slough off

South Beach much quicker than the city or the Army Corps of Engineers had anticipated and the sediment normally deposited by rivers as they meet salt water had been cut off by harbors and dams, meaning that the seafloor sand deposits that the state usually harvests for its beaches were becoming scant to nil. With dwindling reserves, the city was eventually forced to admit that it didn't know what to do about its beaches, didn't have a plan, and had resolved to import from elsewhere since the narrow continental shelf around Miami had been nearly exhausted.

"Would it still be Miami Beach with foreign sand?" the *Christian Science Monitor* asked in 2007. In the next decade the question no longer mattered: only that sand had to get there, from some more stable elsewhere, since it wouldn't be Florida. In 2009, the Miami-Dade County Department of Environmental Resources Management released a report on the state of Miami Beach's coastline that called for a renewed focus on beach nourishment, not only for purposes of tourism, but for hurricane safety, too. All but one "borrowing site" for sand had been permanently depleted, they wrote, and "new sources need to be identified" or the beach would revert to the pitiful, slender state it had reached before the first major nourishment that began in 1975 and ended in 1981.

But the beach had not always been there. The land on which Miami and Miami Beach now sit first appeared more than a hundred thousand years ago, shortly after the warmer, interglacial Eemian period ended and the oceans drained as the ice caps boomed again.

If I were to have taken a walk on South Beach during the Eemian—which many scientists don't see as the best model for thinking about the immediate future of the climate (say, the next ten thousand years) despite its warmer temperatures and its popularity as an example among the commentariat, but humor me—there would be nowhere to walk, of course, so instead if I were to have sailed about the ocean around where Miami is now, I would have found only choppy, warm waters, a big stretch of open ocean that'd go on for about six hundred miles—to what's now Macon, Georgia. The tropics were wetter and warmer than they are now and, below your boat, the waters would have teemed with strange Paleolithic sea life, giant squid, and swarms of unrecognizable fish.

Even if it won't quite look like that, Miami's future will be something close to it: its slim sliver of land will vanish into the waves, returning to the seafloor from which it emerged when the water last crept up into the ice caps.

A lizard in the late evening.

I wasn't sure why I'd come all the way down to Florida to think less about a hurricane, except that it was paid for by my boss, which was good enough for me. I wasn't sure why I needed to get away since I had gone unharmed by Sandy's ugly path while so many hadn't. Outside of the city, in Miami and elsewhere, no one seemed to care much about what happened to New York and New Jersey. It was not clear if the government would provide the necessary funds to assist either state, despite a much-discussed photograph of a brotherly embrace between the president and the adversarial governor of New Jersey. But in the week after the storm, when downtown's power had yet to be restored and the subway remained offline, the malignant spores of a citywide malaise seemed to pollute New York's air, sticking to everything, every neighborhood, like gray mold across the stripped facades of apartment buildings. Had I been infected, too? My chest was heavy. Having lost nothing, no one, I nevertheless felt I'd already lost a world. I kept a notebook of writings about storms that I would later shape into an essay, one of the first pieces that I would publish as I struggled to become a writer, though at that moment, it felt entirely shapeless—and, in that way, this writing resembled me.

"You're being so dramatic," a boyfriend I'd picked up on a dating site told me at the time, right before I left for Florida.

"How do you mean?"

"I mean you're acting like this is the end of the world when it's not the end of the world. It's obsessive."

I swam over to the other side of the pool and finished the whiskey.

Around two in the morning a drizzle began to lightly patter against the surface of the water, slowly at first, before thickening into hectoring waves of fat, warm droplets that fell in infrequent sheets, until the sky boomed and a crack of thunder shook me out of the pool. Within minutes a large storm moved in, clouding out the remaining starlight, and deluged the city with a late fall's flood. The heavy downpour began to lull me to sleep on a white wooly sofa chair in Robert's living room while I finished another glass of whiskey.

A large oil painting of cranes occupied the wall opposite the chair. I couldn't figure out Robert's taste. (Who was Robert, for that matter, this missing person who'd invited me to his home on the strength of the recommendation of my employer? The home, decorated in the generic style of the West Elm wealthy, offered no idea about him. Later I realized, with occasional exposure to New York's wealthy elite, that their absence is the condition that defines them.) In the painting, three cranes—one in the water, one in mid-liftoff, and another in flight—are framed in a wide view of a swamp, maybe the Everglades, and are detailed with a Whistler-like attention to the abstract qualities of living things: their feathers flushed with light and wind, they blur in an illustration of the stages of motion. It was a dull, nearly pointless painting, probably held over from some dead relative to whom it mattered in sentimental terms. Oddly, there was no other art in the apartment. Perhaps Robert liked its image of departure since he himself was apparently never home. Cranes are a symbol of vigilance, protectors of stuff for those absent. I stared at the birds, stuck in paint, until I fell asleep.

At ten a.m., it was still raining, though the storm was beginning to taper off, with a few stray beams of sunlight managing to break through the cloud cover. Out front, the streets, lined with tall palms, were flooded and dark water had risen over the stone patio, all the way to the bottom of a squat grill under a shaded alcove. *Should I call someone?* I thought. Obviously, there was no one to call—and I didn't want to alarm Robert, who was in China. Who could do what? This happened all the time.

Stop, I told myself.

What if it floods.

It wouldn't flood.

I borrowed Robert's bike in the late afternoon, after the storm broke to improbable blue skies and the streets drained of floodwater, and took a long ride from his apartment in the 30s down to the lower tip of South Beach, where I peddled around the construction sites for the new condominiums that were gradually rising along the bay, turned on Washington Avenue in a sweep of sunlight and sped past the lines of crummy pizza restaurants and two-star hotels until 11th Street. From there, I crossed over to Meridian and rode along a park where I had heard men went to cruise for other men, then made my way up again until I hit the Holocaust Memorial with its fist of defiance or anger or what, the rage of history, then curved along the park and golf course until I hit west 34th Street, where the streets gave way to a full suburb that looked nothing like the other neighborhoods that lined the beach only a few blocks away, just square houses and square houses and palm trees and square houses and a man in a white t-shirt mowing his lawn, a cigarette dangling from the parched corner of his mouth. I circled the block a few times. Everything looked the same. A woman stood in her driveway yelling into her phone. She threw it in the grass. "Fuckit."

Miami's existential risk is calculated in terms of real estate. The commercial broker CBRE, for example, reported in late 2015 (so, three years after I first went to South Florida) that $366 billion in real estate was vulnerable to coastal flooding and that the entire region would face up to $672 million in annual losses from environmental catastrophe, whichever one came first. They're talking about the hotels along Ocean Avenue and, to a lesser degree, the less glitzy neighborhoods I rode around in aimlessly. I couldn't quite understand this measure of worth: it seemed an absurd redoubling of the economic logic that allowed for the crisis in the first place, especially in its privileging of the land's value vis-à-vis its location over whether that land was truly safe and would be there in a century or so. But the idea that maybe something wasn't worth so much if you included its future in your estimation of its "value," e.g., its future under water, wasn't going to work with developers. How do you calculate loss, as in the loss of place, encompassing those whose "investment" in their home was not simply economic but who had nowhere else to go? How do you calculate the loss of a place, not only its real geography but the geography of its imagination?

I read about the floods and about the sea-level rise and what was at stake—everything, really—and what could be done. The entire social system that had established the community, like many other precarious communities in the United States, was premised on an erroneous assumption about the long-term stability of those landscapes with a great view. In fact, in the worldwide upheaval of a changing climate, those places—beachside, cliffside, or on the precipitous crack between two continental plates—are rarely a good place to set your foundation. But we are too late: you cannot turn your back on $366 billion.

And in any case this is Florida, the American zero: its cultural event horizon, over which remaindered life passes into an oblivion that is not so much defined by its lawlessness as it is by a giggly sense that life is meaningless, an object—usually someone else's, usually someone who isn't white—that may be traded with death freely and without consequence. Go to Florida and you don't come back. Toss the phone in the yard, fuckit. There is no real "return" once you've resigned yourself to it; instead, there is balmy, endless, unregulated sunshine, pouring through palm fronds onto the half-empty parking lots of 7-Elevens.

I sat down on the sidewalk with my notebook and tried to define the emotional and visual coordinates of this place in hopes that it might prepare me to do more writing on these jeopardized landscapes. Wrote in my notebook everything I saw instead: woman mowing her lawn; eleven palm trees; several bushes, though I didn't stop to count them; twenty houses: most seemed empty, but surely weren't; my iPhone, resting on my thigh, playing Donna Summer out loud since I'd unplugged my headphones; my notebook on my lap; two Hasidic men wandering in the light; a bland description of the weather: humid, sticky, and thick enough to have winded me after the long bike ride; the fist, somewhere outside of my view; the promise of Europe, in these quasi-tropics, no promise at all; my great grandmother on my mother's side, who fled that promise, also to Florida; tiny droplets of sweat on the asphalt.

I couldn't fix an answer as to what I wanted to write down, what description would make the most sense for the block. I scribbled, crossed words and sentences out.

"Do you need help?" a woman asked me. A leashed dachshund stood patiently by her side. She stared down at me. Her beady eyes were perched at the top of an aquiline nose that defined the gravity of her expression: "You dehydrated?"

"Oh, no, sorry." I got up. "I was just, just writing some things down."

"You want to be careful," she said, stepping around me. "You could get burned sitting in the sun like that." As the dachshund was licking my ankle she yanked its leash with a "Come on, now." It yelped in tow. The dog looked at her with an expression of obvious shock, betrayed by its protector. It had wanted to say hello, was all. "Stop that," she said. "Let's go." The dog whimpered, then trotted on, goodbye.

Another dream: There is a city that is not destroyed by the tomorrow that approaches it, tomorrow as storm country, the storm that makes landfall everywhere at once and engulfs you. Over the city, gulls idle in the hurricane wind, aloft without moving forward or falling back to land below, surrounded by the "local," which in this case equals apartment plus sky plus the neighborhoods that have boarded themselves up, local birds over a local city under a local storm. Other images of avian vigilance. Nothing is destroyed.

In "The Imagination of Disaster," Sontag writes that a deep anxiety underlies science-fiction films (particularly sci-fi involving an alien invasion)—not simply the anxiety of total destruction (the Bomb), but rather "the negative imagination about the impersonal": the aliens, typically humanoid, resemble us in most ways except in their emotional response to events and other individuals. While humans fret and resist, hide in fear or struggle admirably to communicate before they're vaporized at the welcome-to-Earth ceremony, the aliens in these films remain cold, indifferent to the fluctuation of emotions that define first contact. Instead, they frequently leverage disarray to their icy, inhuman advantage. This fear, Sontag argues, rests on the belief that aliens will impose a "regime of emotionlessness, of impersonality, of regimentation," like that of the Soviet Union. In ecological-disaster films, the source of fear is reversed: it is not the threat of a new regime of impersonality, but rather an emotional chaos of pure personality, where survival depends on the strength and tenacity of individuals who resist group safety or survival efforts—Jake Gyllenhaal in *The Day After Tomorrow* (2004) or The Rock, a decade later, in *San Andreas* (2015)—amid the tumbling wreck of American civilization.

In these films, love of family trumps (and triumphs over) the emotionless bureaucracy of the rescue effort, of government-protected "higher ground," FEMA and its conspiracy of trailers. The storms roll in, destroy what they can, whom they can, especially those who follow the lead of others, into the fire, the epicenter, the flood zone, the imploding skyscraper. We do not witness these deaths with horror when the faceless group diverges from our hero's advice and collectively miscalculates the stability of that shelter, that road, that path through the woods. Rather, we pity their foolishness, and are relieved that The Rock did not follow them.

On screen, no one believes the various Cassandras who insist that global catastrophe is drawing near, that a superstorm will destroy the United States, not even the protagonists tenacious enough to go against prescribed safety to survive. They survive because they refute the premise of the prediction: life will go on and will never end no matter what the clear and consensus-based science says. A catastrophe is an opportunity. San Francisco will be wiped out, but it will carry on for those who keep it within them, for those strong enough to rebuild.

And us? We now abandon theory for practice, weather forecast for weather event. The email arrives with a series of images claiming to show the devastation of the storm. A wave overtakes the Statue of Liberty. Cars lift up in eight feet of floodwater in an underground garage in Lower Manhattan. Standing in the rain, anonymous guards keep watch over the Tomb of the Unknown Soldier. Scuba divers shine a light in the 42nd Street–Times Square station. A McDonald's is flooded to the counter, the brown water littered with branded trash, a statue of Ronald McDonald floating facedown amid the debris like a mob hit. A great white shark attacks a rescue helicopter rocking in the stormy wind above the East River, the EMT dangling by a rope in reach of the animal's jaws. Lightning bolts tear through Midtown Manhattan. I'm pacing an apartment that isn't mine, smoking a joint I eventually flick into the fire when it's finished. A strong wind beats the windows. The doorman calls up to recommend that I unplug any electronics, especially the computers, in case of a blackout that might cause a power surge when and if it returns. The power plant explodes within minutes of the call, and the apartment goes dark. I run into the kitchen to fetch a flashlight or candles, though I don't know where to look for either. I rummage through the drawers of Chris's home, but find nothing but plastic forks, birthday candles, Citarella receipts. In the film version of this scene, Jake Gyllenhaal plays the character based on me. In it, he calmly manages to locate a self-generating flashlight and a set of candles in a closet that he uses to relight the apartment, only to find that much of the city is on fire and that, eleven flights below, water is beginning to rise across Lower Manhattan. Somewhere his fellow protagonist is trapped in a taxi slowly filling with river water. The music begins to swell. Anxious violins. How to save her, he wonders, thinking nothing of himself. The lighter's flame fades. A supercell hovers over Queens. The Brooklyn Bridge is inundated by the East River, which isn't a river, but a tidal estuary. A flashlight. A siren. Traffic, snarled on Fifth Avenue, vibrates with the tumble of water raging up the street. Everyone slowly gets out of their cars to look south, where a hundred-foot wave is headed toward them. Flee, push aside fellow commuters, cabbies, strangers, Jake Gyllenhaal. Go under. A Burger King is destroyed. Water rises.

PART ONE

1

The room where we gathered was pink. Or the first dusk light that filled the room was pink and everything in it—a table, walls of books, several handsomely framed antique maps of New York State, even the members of "the project," each tottering in their expressive blankness and dressed in uniformed shirts and shorts of white linen—was bathed in a soft pinkness. We were late. Simon, my sort-of boyfriend, and I had pulled into the small New York town at the base of the hill, near where the project lived, about half an hour after we were due. We parked the car in the town's small, crowded municipal lot and followed hand-painted signs to a path dimpled with orange salamanders that wound into a thick stretch of trees, and continued for about quarter mile up, into a clearing at the hilltop. There, the steel face of the central building of this project—an imposing, Brutalist cube, designed by the artists Helen Hunley Wright and George Wright in the early 1990s—stopped us at the end of the path. It stood in defiance of its otherwise rustic surroundings, glinting meanly at dusk.

The building was divided into three distinct parts, with each section built of a different material (brick, steel, and wood) that formed a capital T-shape. The back of the house opened onto a porch elevated by stilts fifteen or so feet off the ground with a generous view of a weedy field that ran down to the Delaware River between the hydraulically fractured counties of Pennsylvania and the untouched ones of New York, and where a small number of dumpy cottages lurched in the grass for the residents of this artists' colony. In summer the field was thick with gnats.

Inside, we joined the other guests and residents in the living room, where Helen was midway through her introductory remarks, after which she welcomed us into her large kitchen that opened onto the porch. The dinner, Helen explained to all of us who were gathered around her, would be held here, under mosquito nets in the prettiest evening you'll find outside of the city. "What a story this place will tell," she said.

Near an array of copper pans that hung from the back wall, an old astrological chart of the Sun and its nine planets (including Pluto), each celestial body's orbit traced in a dotted line, distracted me from what Helen was saying. In it, the Earth was a grim, faintly blue ball on yellowed paper, the Moon nothing more than a small thumbprint-sized smudge to the upper right of our sphere. Helen was saying something about how happy she was to have us in her home. Also, that this place, whatever this place was, was a different kind of art community.

I want to show you that. To Simon and me: Good evening, boys. And hello.

She spoke with the rehearsed confidence of someone who knew a routine that would never change. Guests, pink light, sunset. She was smaller in person than she appeared in the images of her that I had found online, though her features were kinder, less hardened than in the black-and-white photographs that were taken during her East Village years two decades ago, when she lived on east 11th Street and "knew people," mostly people who were now dead. Her hair— speared by two silver sticks—jiggled in a tidy, gray bun at the top of her head as she talked about what she and her project did. Clapping her hands together, she outlined for us, in brief, the rich history of what she called the "project" or the "community," which was not "her" project or "her" community, she clarified, but one that belonged to many, "so many." Founded in 1992 with her ex-husband, the artist George Wright, the project has provided artists, writers, and musicians with a space to broaden their practice beyond the art studio or the writing desk for some twenty years: instead, they farm, harvest crops, churn butter, build. She explained, in slightly dated artspeak, how the artists at the project work with each other and the materials of the earth in "open space" rather than the studio, the gallery, the museum. She talked about moving beyond "normative" art production, with a requisite, if odd, reference to Bourriaud. Then she concluded this speech with a smile, wide as the view behind her: "And we are so glad you're here. So. Let's have a quick tour while there's still some light."

We toured, trekked across the campus, trooped behind her through the gnat clouds, and trudged toward cabins and workshops and farming sites and other makeshift structures that evinced various green initiatives. Ever a host, she made small talk with each of us, including me:

Why are you here? Who do you know? Are you interested in applying to work here? How long have you and Simon been friends?

"Oh not long, six months." Helen wore all white, too, though her uniform differed in kind from her monkish residents in that it appeared to be a custom if incredible zoot suit, the ankles discolored with mud. No, I didn't plan to apply.

Presenting the project's well, she told us that the community had taken an active, let's even say aggressive, stance against fracking. They organized and attended protests on both sides of the state border. In Pennsylvania, it was legal; in New York, not—and they hoped to keep it that way. They wrote and distributed pamphlets about climate change, the problems with natural gas, and the benefits of green-energy efficiency. These efforts had been met with both

27

frustration and success. Yoko Ono tweeted her support. The Governor of Pennsylvania did not. She snapped her fingers when she made a point about water rights. She liked to make points, and spoke with the self-assurance of someone who had always made points, good points, even if the meaningful context of peers in which making such good points mattered had long ago dissolved around her into a force field of nodding residents. Her charm, buoyed by her enthusiasm for an issue I felt strongly about myself, lulled me into an appreciation for the thoughtfulness with which she addressed her relationship to the land, her knowledge of the composition of the soil that enabled them to grow the modest crops they did, her attention to the health of that crop yield, her earnest love of people, all people, the people here, the people there, the people who did things, the people who did nothing at all, such that I didn't question her or her project's authenticity—or integrity. Doing this, living on a mountain somewhere in New York's woodsy upstate, seemed like the right move, if not for me, then at least for these activist-artists who had long wearied of the studio and lack of sales.

"This is great," I whispered to Simon, though I couldn't say what it was that I found so great: only that Helen, play acting the fearless leader, made a good case for paying attention to her and her cottony crowd. He gave me a look of really? "It's funny. I don't know about *great*, though," he said. As he'd made clear in the car ride over, he had misgivings about the project, but after years of visiting the mountain for dinner parties, concerts, performances, and bonfires, he thought of Helen as a friend, as his neighbor, and as an important part of his stretch of the state, even if she remained to him, this boy who spent most of his time in the city, a rural curiosity.

Tiny field of legumes after tiny field of corn, "But it *is* hard to imagine the appeal of this to artists, really," I admitted to him.

"Sort of. 'Relational aesthetics,' is what they call it."

"So crazy that she just ... That that's it." The term and its aesthetic prerogatives—art composed out of (and into) public social relations rather than the privacy of the white cube—had long since fallen out of fashion, at least in New York. And, in any case, I didn't think anyone had ever used that term with any seriousness, except for the critic who coined it.

"I know."

He nodded to Helen, who was coming over to us to give Simon a hug, hi, sweetie. He introduced me again: "You know Nick's a writer," he said. "He writes about art."

She smiled. "Do I know your work?"

"I don't think so." I was too obscure, responsible for only a few reviews here and there, and nothing substantial.

"Who do you write for?" she asked, with a stiff smile.

"Oh just some art magazines. *Frieze. Artforum.*"

"Well, now," she said. "Tell me about it." In fact, I had been trying to write an essay about the sculptor Greer Lankton, who, based on some cursory research into Helen that I'd done on the ride over, I suspected she had known in the eighties since they showed at the same gallery, Civilian Warfare. Lankton, who died in 1996, was best known for her strange doll-like sculptures of celebrities and downtown personalities. They were arresting in photographs but I had yet to see any in person since they had fallen into relative obscurity.

I jumped in: "You showed at Civilian Warfare ... Did you know Greer Lankton?" I asked. "I'm actually writing about her work. Or at least trying to."

"I did, I did. That's so wonderful! Greer was a great artist," she said, walking us down the field toward what would be the last part of the tour, a visit to a large compost heap surrounded by chicken-wire fence. "One of the best artists I ever met, someone who really focused, loved what she did." She ticked off a few biographical lines about Lankton: that she had lived with the photographer Nan Goldin, had struggled to sell her work (and relied on David Wojnarowicz to do so early on in her career), her long-term relationship with her partner Paul, who now manages her estate. I'd read about most of this before, but Helen added new, personal weight to Lankton's story. They were facts, facts that didn't just come from the few books or essays I'd tracked down that mention her, but were spoken by a person who had known her, who had been her friend and who had had dinner with her, gone to her openings. But she offered little else: "Did you know her in the nineties?" I asked.

"I didn't, no."

The pink light, waning into the steady, dark blue of night, consumed us. Simon grinned as I got hooked on Helen's line. "You going to move here?" he asked as we arrived at the Big Compost. I elbowed him. With her back to the heap, Helen told us that the humid pile behind her was the most essential part of the entire project, though she didn't clarify quite how so, except that it provided both a literal site of recycling and a kind of metaphor for life on the mountain. I watched Simon as he listened intently, this pretty, half-French (through his mother), EU passport-carrying, though thoroughly Americanized boy with black curly hair, someone I didn't really know all that well in the end, someone whom I'd met at a party, though now we were sleeping together fairly regularly and so we did sort of know one another, at least in the sense that we knew one another's desires, but was that enough to be up here, visiting him—for the first time—at his parents' upstate house? It felt serious. Was serious. I ran my eyes up and down him while Helen went on about rotten vegetables decomposing in un-fracked earth. Life eats itself up. The lumpy mound was flecked with bits of food, plants, much of it smeared among the piles of dirt shot through with grass and weeds, like streaked sprinkles baked into a cupcake. I turned away from Simon to stare at it. "Without this we're nothing," she said. She got animated as she gestured toward it, Mickey conducting the mops. Sure we got it.

That weekend, Simon and I had gone up to his parents' place in Phoenicia with two of his closest friends, Zachary and Julia. In the car, we rarely strayed from the surface of our lives, and our conversation dwelled on the easy politics of pop and film. Julia liked Taylor Swift. Zachary did not. Julia felt Taylor's celebrity was premised on the emptiness of white feminism, which was funny to her. Zachary didn't understand. I nodded along in nervous agreement with both, unsure what position to stake among them (Simon, who was driving with strained focus on the road, had no opinion); I still didn't know the three of them very well. Or they didn't know me. To break the ice over lunch, Simon suggested we go to Helen's place. "What is that?" Zachary said.

"It's an artist's residency." Seeing Zachary's drawn face, "But different. They're having a dinner tonight that we're invited to. It's run by this woman, Helen Hunley Wright. She started it with her husband, George. He's an artist." He turned to me: "Do you know his work?"

"Sort of," I said, though I didn't know much at all, only that he was semi-famous, and that his practice consisted mostly of complex installations: a series of tar-coated pinwheel-like structures on which he hung also-tarred objects so mangled in their production as to be unrecognizable, though occasionally they took the form of animals (cats, crows, a pig split in half); elegant arrangements of reproductions of furniture from the colonial period; excavated trees he deposited in the gallery; cabinets of organic detritus he'd collected on a beach in the South of France—all of it intelligently defended in press releases and in articles written by critic friends. Nineties stuff. He was an artist whose subject was "the environment." I'd never heard of Helen.

"Anyway, they have these lecture nights over the summer. It's like $30 and it comes with a meal and a party afterward. You can even stay over, if there's room, so it might be fun. Cute boys, Zachary." It wasn't that Simon was interested in art—in the city, he had nothing to do with it except at those moments, usually in nightlife, when it intersected with parties and his own vaguely defined career as a stylist—but, up here, there was seldom anything to do. Helen's was the closest to fun in the area, and the only place that attracted anyone in their mid- to late twenties.

Zachary rolled his eyes. "We'd rather go swimming," he said, and so he and Julia did, about twenty miles up the road in a cold river near an abandoned lodge for summering Jewish families in the mid-century. Julia had wanted to go with us, she told me upstairs after lunch while we unpacked, but she'd agreed to accompany Zachary and ease the burden that his foul mood would've otherwise placed on Simon if he'd been dragged to Helen's. "Are you sure?" I asked.

She lied: "Yes, of course."

"Get ready, Nick," Simon called from downstairs, where he and Zachary were putting away the dishes.

"Wish you would," I said to Julia, whom I wanted to get to know better.

"Next time. You and Simon will have fun."

Are you sure? "It's really fine." I conceded: she would go to the river.

Julia had been to Helen's before, anyway—but, yes, loved it. "What?" Zachary said when she admitted that she'd visited in the past and even liked it, characteristically envious that she and Simon had gone and done a thing without him. "Well, I never get invited to anything, so that's no surprise, I guess," Zachary said before pulling away from the remaining dishes he was cleaning in the kitchen to fume upstairs, bitter until Julia escorted him out of the house for their swim. His jealousy was absurd, even banal, and he knew we knew that, which made him firmer in his belief that he had to feel this way about it. This, I had learned, was what he always did. He was captivated by his own emotional impermanence, that he entered and left the room as present as smoke unless he focused himself, usually through the prism of his sexual desire, long enough to condense into simpering human form. What little enthusiasm he could ever muster for himself or others was usually short-lived, and disappeared as he inevitably devolved back into a kind of ongoing self-loathing. He was, moreover, a frequent liar, someone who loved to lie, even if the lie was unnecessary: "I used to sleep with him," Zachary told me once about someone on tv. Julia shook her head and mouthed No because no.

Julia too seemed ever poised to vanish before us, as if the lines that distinguished her from the world around her were fading. She was lanky, with long black hair that framed her pale, triangular face, and she often appeared distant, even indifferent to the conversation around her, though this remove lent her a certain liquidity, in speech and movement, like that of an octopus quietly spilling across the sand as it jettisons itself forward, tentacles and voluminous head billowing in the current. In this, she was ever the escapist—quite literally, sometimes, as at night she was always the first to leave the bar, disappearing before saying goodbye to any of us. Likewise she was stone quiet most of the time, giving her the necessary space for thoughtfulness (contra Zachary's usual, talky rush to poor judgment) when she expressed an opinion, and both Zachary and Simon hung dutifully on her every word.

Her mother had apparently survived a small plane crash in Canada early on in her pregnancy, and the shock of their tandem survival revised Julia's family into tentative life, as if they lived only by chance—and without much certainty as to the longevity of their stay on Earth. Three years ago, her father went out the windshield on the freeway in Michigan. Bad luck follows some with remarkable persistence, and it did so with Julia, all the way to a would-be love life that she skirted through a devotion to Simon. They spent much of their time together. (She had boy-friends, though she committed to none with the same intensity as she did to her friendship with Simon.) He kept her as his clos-est confidant, but she read this intimacy as some more funda-mental connection, one above friendship—and perhaps even romance, though she was no fool and knew that he would never "fall for her" (and I don't think she ever fell for him either). Rather, she seemed to view their friendship as a sibling-like alli-ance, truer than one conditioned by sex and desire. Love of Simon purified her and, in a way, her love purified him. They believed, foremost, in one another. For Simon, we all fell into a disorganized line that began with her, then Zachary, and then me, though my place was peculiar since I was the one who was sleeping with him. I was no threat to her, or at least not in a way that led her to any animosity toward me, and we got along well.

She wanted to become a writer, did write, or at least was making various much-discussed attempts to do so. What do you want to write about? I asked. "My friends." I understood: but what do your friends look like in fiction? She wasn't sure what I meant by the question. "I'll send you a story sometime," she said.

I was curious so I pushed her to do so since I imagined she might possess, in her fiction about her friends, a skeleton key to Simon. She stalled for months, but eventually sent me the draft of a novel that began: "Our friendship was over." Whoever it was that she included in this "our" was not entirely clear, though the primary character besides the narrator seemed to be based on Simon, and the book wobbled along a narrative arc that carried him from café life in New York to South Carolina, where the narrator retreated to a small coastal town for some unclear reason. She had never been to South Carolina whereas I had, since I was from North Carolina, and when I pressed her on why she had chosen to write (unconvincingly) about the low country, she balked and said, "Let's talk about the ending instead." It concluded abruptly, with the Simon character appropriating a small fishing boat that he took out into a storm in a quasi-suicide attempt, though what would become of the character was unclear. Before that, not much happened, which didn't bother me as a reader, though the flicker of events that composed the book never achieved a clear picture. Perhaps that wasn't what she wanted. She asked me for my thoughts, but we never got around to talking about them. Her prose was flinty, coldly pretty, and smart.

Zachary and Julia were, in a sense, two runaways. Both refused their pasts and rarely discussed what their previous lives, the ones before New York, had been like. Zachary was dopey, though he was from an "upper middle-class Republican" family in New Hampshire, people who were "big on Romney" in the 2012 election, so I always wondered how lost he could be given his northeastern pedigree and the financial security his "big on Romney" parents provided him. Simon, who knew much more about them than I did, wrote off their reluctance to divulge anything personal to me as nervous insecurity.

"They don't know you yet," he said. "Let them get to know you."

Simon was "wealthy-ish," his word, but he minded that people suspected that he was well-off, as I had when we first met, and so he often downplayed his background by constantly mocking "rich taste," which was, at bottom, his taste. Despite assurances that he was like everyone else who was "struggling," he never managed to lose his prim, boarding-school manners nor his upright and boyish tone, which he often deployed with me early on in our relationship. This moneyed affect irked me, the performance of a class difference between us that seemed to cryptically matter to him. (My parents were what passed for working-class in the postindustrial south, my mother a school teacher and my father an accountant.) I'd roll my eyes, and eventually he took the hint, dropping the attitude, though certain vestiges remained several months into "our thing." He called me "darling" in that obnoxious way gay men sometimes do. Rather, he forced himself to call me darling, appending a smile to each use of that word like it was a gift he was offering me, a quarter he placed in my open hand that I could finally spend. For most others, he repressed these tics with charm and good looks. He was handsome and smart and I liked him, whether I was his darling or not. When I said stop calling me that he said OK, and did. He went with honey.

With them, I felt like no one, a flat type that they could fill with their ideas of the person I ought to be, the person Simon ought to date. For Julia, this meant I was an upwardly mobile writer who might someday be responsible for some decent novel (that I was, up to that point, a poet who sometimes wrote about art, "like Frank O'Hara," seemed not to factor into her picture of me), and therefore a Person of Interest, someone to know. Zachary, who was much more suspicious in general, allowed me to be even more of a blank, a harmless fuck that Simon used to bide his time until what, he wasn't sure, but not someone who would alter Simon in any meaningful way. Knowing this, I wondered what Simon was to them. And who they were to him. I had hoped going upstate would allow us to clarify ourselves to one another.

Simon's house was a modest two-story built in the early forties. It sat on top of a hill amid tall, uncut grass. It had never been renovated, and it sagged under its own weight, accumulating dust and grime with each passing season. While the house technically belonged to his parents, who had needed somewhere to park cash in a real-estate holding, they never visited (they lived in, and never left, the Upper West Side of Manhattan)—and so it was mostly Simon's. He had convinced them that a house in upstate New York—far from the flood zones of the coast—was the safest bet for their money. After the purchase was completed, they spent a weekend at the house and never went back.

The floors sloped oddly with the land. The appliances, held over from the previous owner, were long out of date and no longer practical, almost comically old, but Simon kept them because he couldn't afford not to. A total modernization was out of the question, his father had insisted, mostly because they never went there—and even Simon's stays were too infrequent to justify the amount it would cost to start over. In any case, Simon maintained his faith in things, especially old things, including the house, and he thought of it as a gift he liked to honor by sharing it with friends whenever he did make the trip to New York. Zachary, who came infrequently, was flippant and complained about the cold water. Julia considered any home of Simon's hers.

"Bye, bye," Zachary said. Julia rolled her eyes and followed him out. They would borrow Simon's car, and we would take the Jeep his father kept at the house.

Simon went upstairs to change before we left for Helen's project. I sat on the porch and waved Zachary and Julia off.

I could not make myself belong to them. Though we were "dating," Simon and I didn't fit easily into the mold of a couple. We went out a lot, but he didn't like books all that much, especially poetry, and only seemed to care about art because it was something that one was supposed to care about, while they were things that I liked because they were what I did, write poetry, write about art, so he refused readings, openings, dinners. We went instead to clubs and gay bars, Julius, the Cock, Spectrum. Drugs made him horny, made him break the code of indifference we swore to one another in public, want to kiss me whenever we passed each other at the bar or the backroom. He had mentioned, after one speedy night of a vial of "good" cocaine from an uptown dealer who prided herself on "blending in" with the local set—her local set, so the man-or-born of Madison Avenue—that he thought of me as "his" boy-friend. His real boyfriend. I hadn't at all.

"Really," He said. "You don't? Why not?" I couldn't say, mostly because I refused to allow my feelings to cohere for him into some notional, if provisional love. To do so would have been to court a calamity. I just wanted to have fun. He was crushed but high enough to carry on fine without my agreeing with him. We were sitting in front of his computer as dawn set loose its pale colors against the dark silhouette of the city. A video of David Bowie and Cher from sometime in the seventies played on YouTube. It was an improbable but gorgeous duet, their two wraith-like figures flickering in the bad transfer on the screen, rumored to be so high on "good" cocaine themselves as to have no memory of their performance once it was done and yet, in Bowie's steady can-ter, there was an almost totalizing sense of the memory that he had performed this before, that this song, like all the events to which a song belongs, was an act of memorializing a previous song that had already been sung, a past performance, the last rosary bead before the next he threaded through his fingers, all the same, so what was remembering it, it's a continuous, unending loop. There was no song outside that song. Bowie had the sharpest teeth it was like he was sucking the blood out of the air. Cher was crowned with a dome of orange hair.

"Not really," I said. "But I like you a lot."

The project, conducted with a steady rotation of artists who lived on Helen's land (some for only a few weeks, some for a few months), worked along the line of relational aesthetics, as Simon said, insisting that anyone who lived there discontinue their normal work or "practice" for the benefit of the community, which was never ours or mine, but was itself to be considered a work of art (though Helen didn't use that phrase, "work of art") that had no single author, and so none of the artists who greeted us were actually artists anymore. Instead, they were farmers, cooks, cleaners. They said this with a pride I admired but didn't believe. A few told me they were writers, but no one wrote anymore since there was so little time to do so. "I used to write experimental poetry," this guy told me. He'd relieved himself of that burden by cleaning toilets. I got it. In any case, it didn't seem, as we peeked into the almost bare living quarters of the residents, that there were even any pens or paper or computers, only a scattering of science textbooks and magazines, including predictable stacks of old copies of *National Geographic* in several cabins. They were cut off. Everyone had the cheerful daze of a member of a cult, their zealotry betraying no expression other than radiant pride for the gorgeous landscapes they'd worked themselves into, together, the tripartite home, the cottages, the white linen, Helen, the food, the view of Pennsylvania, the visitors, all of whom were to gather in a barn set off about fifty yards from the big house to listen to lectures on art and a climate that we would someday no longer recognize as our own. It was all so much for them, these true believers in the cause of not-making-art. In the cause of stopping. And they appeared to want nothing else. A man conducted Simon and me to the barn after we'd strayed from our tour. Pointing to the entrance, "The lectures," he said, "will begin shortly."

2

After Miami, I returned to New York. Fall progressed to unremark-able winter. At a party someone said, "What do you do?"

"I don't know."

"Right."

Nearly everyone I knew asked everyone they didn't know, "What do you do?" This is one way to account for the days, by what you do, and everyone seemed to want to know what I did, when-ever they met me. The truth was not much.

In the waning intervals of winter daylight I retreated to my windowless room in my railroad-style apartment to read and write, lounge bored with books I couldn't finish, fiddle with sex apps and chat with strangers whom I'd meet after several vodkas, wait for spring, the spring that would force some change, whatever that might be, though that January and February were warmer than usual and everyone was always out, elsewhere, and so it was always a kind of spring, and no change ever came about other than weather. I some-times temped at an academic publisher near Central Park and spent my lunch breaks eating near Columbus Circle, on the rocks just past the memorial tower to the merchants who guarded the southwestern entrance. With time, the subway returned to reduced service. One tunnel would be closed until the following year.

Except for work I rarely went out during the day. I tried to write a novel—my first—titled *The Shopping List*. It was no good, and mostly concerned unappealing losers who scammed rich uptown families by shopping on their behalf, and eventually I con-signed it to the trash bin on my laptop. I didn't know if I could write. *The Shopping List* suggested that I couldn't.

I climbed into bed with anyone. Climbed into bed with too many friends, too many strangers, and two different men in my building, one of whom had a boyfriend who was always away, though I suspected, finally, that there was no boyfriend and that he was just lonely but incapable of admitting it to strangers. Climbed into bed with a poet who was married and who later divorced his wife because he realized he'd liked men all along. I wanted to climb into bed with her, too, or at least with him while she was there, but neither of them would have the ruin I wanted to make of their lives. Their separation was amicable, though its spirit was greatly improved by an agreement, brokered a month into their separation, that I had to go from the poet's life, and in their goodbye to me they both said how much they loved each other. I was another matter.

Went to poetry readings at night, tiny gatherings of the cul-turally dispossessed in the back of outer-borough bars with cheap beers and sometimes long-winded poets, each more hopeful than the next that their otherwise private genius might finally captivate an audience of ten to fifteen that, should the night be a good one, might also include a friendly small-press publisher who would print their first, second, or perhaps third chapbook.

Fourth reader of the night: "Hi, I'm going to read from a manuscript I've been working on, a project about ..."

I loved it, that we would come together and not only listen to but believe in poetry as a real thing, as a thing worthy of all our inexhaustible gossip, hook-ups, friendships, the poems usually being somewhat secondary to all of this, an excuse to get drunk, extraordinarily drunk. I often stumbled home from the readings alone because I couldn't afford the subway, cab, or bus back, and, in any case, I wanted to see who I might run into on the street. We were not so great at what we did—or at least I wasn't—and I liked it that way: that no one seemed to care about the quality of any of this, any measurable greatness. We were tiny people, but our tininess was at times formidable.

I rarely read my own work during these events and lost confidence in what I did bring to the microphone as soon as I rose to whatever stage was available that night.

Fifth reader: "I'm going to read … it's this new poem. I think I've. It's."

I didn't go far. Often jobless or between jobs, I assisted Chris in his slow accrual of art when I could, moved expensive things between his lavish homes, until finally that became too much as the steady stream of these objects, what I had thought I loved, rendered art a gray, administrative task, one devoid of feeling. After a friend introduced me to another "patron of the arts" in need of someone to help him write a collection of stories, I took up ghostwriting in addition to temp office work. I wrote for other people: the unpublished collection of short fiction; grants; ad copy; two science-fiction stories (both about mutant abortions) for an anonymous client, a pervy right-winger from Oklahoma, whose only encouragement was to "get more graphic re the details re the MUTANT ABORTION," which I did, happily, all these alien guts bursting from women and men (in the much more complicated second story the narrative required that a cruel man be impregnated by a gentle, kind alien female, his rejection of their child being some kind of nonsensical statement on baby life as an issue of universal importance, and not strictly a "women's issue"); and about thirty exactly eight-hundred-word introductions to policy papers for an NGO in Lower Manhattan. All of it amounted to an anti-poetry that made poetry better when I heard it.

We, and by we I mean everyone I knew then, poets and artists, nightlife people, itinerant fags and whoever else wandered between clubs at night in search of a social and chemical fix, used to dance at 59 Montrose Street in Bushwick where there was an illegal nightclub called the Spectrum on its first floor, in what looked like an old dance studio. I never knew what it was or had been. I only knew that someone named Gage, who was from San Francisco, ran it as a "platform" for queer performance and dance. Was that the word they used, platform? I can't remember, but that was the word people often used to describe these alternative spaces, at least in the thinky, jargon-littered prose of the occasional writing that emerged about this side of New York, usually in arriviste art publications: a platform, to balance upon. What did we call it? Mostly, it was for dancing. It had no word.

From the nondescript entrance of the building, which you couldn't queue in front of in case the police came by to break up the illegal bar, you followed a long hallway that opened at its midpoint into what passed for a bathroom, or at least the remnants of a bathroom, semi-flooded with piss and mud, a room that stank of those two fluids as they combined into a shit-colored estuary on the tile floor, with two ceramic artifacts to urinate into on either end of this quite literal water closet, both broken and perhaps once workable toilets, and then on to the larger room, where people danced. Rank with the strong smell of human musk, sweat, spilled beer, two of the room's walls were mirrored, and covered with finger- and hand-prints from all the dancers who had been pressed up against the glass at some point in the middle of the night or who, suspended in a turbulent and self-reflexive high over some subjective vacuum, had pressed their faces to the glass and had, in that same high, traced their features with their fingers on the mirror in an attempt to reorient themselves upon the permanent axis of their faces. The glass was always condensed with sweat. Scratched, scuffed, it was a recombinant mirror where the stains of others overlaid one's reflection.

You could smoke inside so everyone loved it, a rare place to do so under Bloomberg's anti-smoking sanctions, and by everyone I mean mostly radical faeries, non-gender-conforming performers, women and men of color, trans people, some artists, a few writers, loners, the ignored, poor, thrifty, otherwise-didn't-fit, all of them cute or beautiful or strange, mostly strange, which itself represented a category of the beautiful more important than any other I knew then, and while the Spectrum was only open every other Saturday or so in the early days, in 2011 and 2012 that is, it ran the clock from ten p.m. to the afternoon the next day. I'd dance, get drunk, occasionally take ecstasy offered by strangers, do whatever with strangers, "whatever" being, for a long time, this operative performance of any number of listless actions, sexual or otherwise, which I would mostly forget because "whatever" usually occurred on the extreme end of some befogged blackout, the wobbly edges of any capable vision of "whatever" usually involving the confused closeness of bodies, mine and others'. There was nothing very romantic about this place, romantic in any downtown sense of a New York retrieved from its wilder past and reconstituted among a newly fashionable set. I liked it because it was near my apartment, I knew people who went every time it was open and who DJ'd there, and, importantly, it was very easy to find someone to take home.

I often met people on a torn couch near the bar.

(Eventually, this couch would disappear and a new wing of the club would open in the back, greatly enlarging the available space for hanging out (as bigger crowds did as we headed into the mid-2010s). In the end, we crowded ourselves out—and the Spectrum closed, though a newer, but quite different version later materialized in Ridgewood, Queens a few years later. But we're far from then right now. At this moment, let's say it's the very narrow moment right after Sandy and before I meet Helen Hunley Wright, the Spectrum is still very small, tight-knit, without much attention from the coming retinue of curators, gallerists, and European art tourists from Berlin on some kind of cocaine tour of how the other side lives, not so many straight people, and few if any pretensions to anything other than its own convenience as a place, or perhaps a platform, to dance and do what you want among others like you.

You, and by you I mean me, could also not dance: you could sit on a couch, smoke a cigarette, and wait for someone to talk to you and tell you what they wanted to do with you.)

A hot cloud of cigarette smoke hung in the air, up near the paneled ceiling, and the room had grown stuffier as we clocked past three a.m. People, mostly shadows that assumed brief human form between rotating lights, had begun to undress. They stuffed neon mesh shirts, things hung together by plastic or leather straps, faded jeans, shorts, anything they were wearing into corners, beneath tables, wherever you could hide your clothes, and these piles began to accumulate like soft sculpture. I was already hoarse from the smoke and alcohol, a bit dizzied from a joint someone had passed me in the half-light, at least three bumps of cocaine, and my head rolled on my shoulders.

"Hi," a boy said. He dropped onto the couch and wrapped his arm around my shoulders like he knew me. He was handsome, thin, a little tattered by whatever he had done that night, with faint gray rings around his hawkish eyes, and a long, ovular blotch of red skin where someone must have sucked on his pale neck.

"Hey," I said.

"I think we've met before?" He was shirtless, and he tightened his modest chest muscles as we spoke, drunkenly admiring his skinny body, his long, brown hair hanging over his shoulders. He wasn't someone I remembered, but I would have had we met.

I shook my head: "Maybe?"

"No, for sure." He was barely audible over the bass of the speakers behind us. At the other end of the room, the DJ blared driving remixes of songs by artists I didn't recognize into a pulsating throb that shook the walls and floor of the club. I shook, too. "Definitely did," he insisted.

"Yeah, maybe," I said. "My memory's terrible."

"I'm Zachary. Do you want to dance?" I said sure.

He escorted me to the dance floor a few feet away by hand. The Spectrum was close to capacity—whatever capacity was, since no one enforced any clear rules governing the space. Most had worked themselves into a heavy sweat that, in the un-air-conditioned hotbox of smoke, drugs, and dancing, soaked everything, flooded down into the world itself with the run-off of all these friends and strangers so that the only remedy to the near-unbearable heat was to take almost everything off, as Zachary did, and what that slippery world wanted me to do, too.

He pulled my shirt off, threw it into a corner behind the speaker system, and then shimmied out of his pants, into his briefs before trying to unbutton my jeans. He slid his fingers under my waistband, but I pushed his hand away and said, "Later."

"Later, OK." He smiled and nodded. He glowed in the neon light, his sweat beaded in a band across his forehead like a liquid crown. The lights changed, from purple to blue to yellow to cold white, then back to purple, blue, yellow, cold white again. I glanced at myself in the mirror: my vision refused to sharpen into a clear view, but I was recklessly drunk. In the blur my features swam up in the smudged glass—my large, slightly hooked nose, full lips, cleft chin, green uneven eyes, with the skin around the left one's lower lid a bruised, sleepier shade than the rest of my face. My short brown hair was slicked back. I was not so far gone that I didn't recognize my own reflection, but I wanted to refuse it, give it back to the mirror, to whomever had appeared there. The dancers around me organized their clutter into a second portrait behind me, one that my face eased toward as Zachary tugged me back into their embrace. Maybe I was too stoned, too high on coke to dance with someone, I thought. Or it was too late.

"I'll hold you to that 'later' later," he said.

We went along with the crowd, sometimes with others who joined us, sometimes alone. I went and got us beers, then came back and found him making out with someone else. I turned to retreat to the couch, but Zachary caught me and dragged me over to the front of the club with his new friend. I opened the beers, handed one to Zachary, but he waved it off. The three of us started to make out while I held the two PBRs awkwardly behind their backs, fumbling with the cans while moving with the new boy, but who shot his tongue into my mouth as soon as I arrived. Eventually, I managed to untangle myself from them long enough to set the beers down on the floor, before their four hands ferried me back to our threesome.

We were locked in a flat, endless no-time in the growing throng that swelled on the dance floor, distorting space and any sense of the hour. With the crowd, we pushed toward the right wall, up against the glass, into a pit of other dancers who closed in around us, tightening into an iron maiden.

In this we had no choice but to go at it, at one another, our mouths in hungry competition for attention, with Zachary's hard-on pushing up against my stomach while the new boy, who was already just some other boy and no longer very new now that I'd been on the inside of his mouth with my tongue for what felt like a half hour, pushed his hand down into my pants and began to play with my cock. Out of the corner of my eye I could see our reflection in the mirror up close again, Zachary's thin profile and the other boy's darker eyes, which clicked into mine as he looked over, too, and together our features arranged and rearranged themselves in a collage of flesh tones lit in brief by the colored lights before plunging back into shadow. In the dense cloud of smoke, I felt this big, wolf-like hunger hound up my spine with each kiss.

Zachary abruptly dropped away. "Should we follow him?" I asked the other boy.

"No. Take this," he said. His features were briefly illuminated as he opened his palm to offer me a pill, and I could see that he was handsome, with a square jaw and bushy eyebrows that he had studiously trimmed, before we were sunk back into blackness. He told me his name was Simon, though I couldn't make out anything he said except an occasional "How are you?" as though that question mattered at all, could be in any way answered to a satisfying degree in the swamp of our surroundings, goodbye, I thought, goodbye, and slipped further into myself, away from him, "It's molly, is that OK?" Perfectly OK. I'm fine, into it, I said, I'm always fine. He had thick, curly black hair that I kept running my hands through. I looked at the pill in my hand. I hadn't taken it yet.

"Then do it." I did it.

I woke up naked, rolled over to cover my face with a pillow that wasn't my pillow and shield my eyes from the sunlight that poured into the room like concrete, burying me in the thick sludge of day.

Remembered almost nothing, but noticed when I'd come to that the window across the room from me was not my window, didn't look out to Brooklyn, but instead to Manhattan.

It was snowing. Or it was not snowing.

My head ached, and words refused to form into coherent sentences when I opened my mouth. Move your jaw and tongue, talk, *what, where am I*, but even the simplest question, *what time is it*, halted—and directed to whom, anyway? no one was in bed next to me—at the *what* that crept up on my tongue and stopped there like a nervous child standing at the deep end of a pool. (After the no-time of the Spectrum, time always re-enforces its regime with characteristic force: all that remains the morning after is the clock, ticking through a hangover like a wagging finger.) Where was I? Not home, but somewhere else, Zachary's maybe, whoever Zachary was, or perhaps I was at the other boy's place. That was where I was, at this boy's apartment whose name warbled back as ... Simon?

"You were pretty fucked up last night," he said.

I pulled the pillow away from my face. Squinting, I could see his outline opposite me, the sunlight behind him. He was fully dressed, with a big water bottle in his hand. "Water?"

"Yes ... Is this ... Where is this?"

"We're at my apartment," he laughed. "We went back ... to my place." Recognizing my puzzled look: "Oh, well, maybe you don't remember. I'm Simon. We came back here after the Spectrum. You wanted to. You said your place was a mess."

"Yes. Right ... right." Simon. The boy with the pill who lives on Ludlow Street and who must be rich, as I had said to him in the cab ride over the Williamsburg Bridge. ("Do you obsess about other people's money?" he'd asked. "I just want to know, well, your politics," I said, the last of the molly still coursing through my blood in a supercharge of emotions.) We'd paused mid-make-out to watch the sun rise over Lower Manhattan as the car clipped along the empty bridge until we met a brief wakeup snarl on Delancey Street. It might have been snowing. All winter I kept thinking that it was snowing, though it was often too warm to stick or seemingly too cold to snow, and so the silver-gray clouds, like the underbellies of fish, kept their close, mindful distance, always refusing to break out of their steady overhead stream into an event. The weather did not like to make itself understood.

"I'm not rich," he had said, though he was. That was his politics, to the extent that he had any. I said sure and went back to kissing him. My hands, on their own journey across Simon's body, found their way into his pants as the driver eyed us in the mirror, neither offended nor interested but something else, a twinkling, passing curiosity that I thought meant he might want to join.

"Simon, right. Right. I'm sorry. It must be so late."

"It's four."

"In the afternoon?" I couldn't believe it. "Oh, god."

"I know. You were out. It was like you'd died but you were breathing so."

I grunted, tried to laugh, went into a coughing fit, then managed: "I definitely died."

I leaned up in bed to look around. The room was small and oddly shaped, with the bed pushed up against the wall near two doors—one that opened to a kitchen with a shower in it and the other to a bathroom (or, really, to a closet with a toilet but no sink). From the bed, you could see the entire apartment.

My eyes finally adjusted to the afternoon. It *was* snowing. This *was* Manhattan. Simon extended the water bottle to me. Tangles of his curly hair hung across his forehead, down nearly to his eyelids. I could see him better, finally. He had serious, cold eyes set in a thin, serious face and a nose that was scarred at the tip, like it had been cut. "So," he said.

I slid the comforter off. I was naked, and my arms were marked with dark bruises. I ran my index finger over the blotches, unsure of how they got there, and then looked up at Simon. "Last night was crazy?"

"Yeah."

Simon. I rolled this name around in my head. *Simon from the Spectrum.*

"What do you do?"

"I'm a stylist," he said without much confidence. I knew several stylists but never knew what they did.

"Oh OK," I said.

An uncomfortable silence fell over us. He broke it with a funny smirk: "You should come up to my house in the country. We'll have more fun."

"Up where?"

"Upstate, duh."

"Do you live upstate?"

"No. Well, yes, my parents have a house there. But you were telling me last night you went to school near Kingston. You apparently *love* going upstate." He laughed.

I couldn't remember what he seemed to recall effortlessly: whatever conversation we'd had, in the last few hours at the Spectrum, hadn't produced any strong memories through the blitz of drugs and booze that had erased nearly everything else in my head save a few flickering seconds of the cab ride, jump cuts of us kissing, stripping, my hips pressed against his rear as my cock found his ass, his right hand reaching back to grab my thigh, squeezing it tightly, before he ejaculated all over the sheets and apologized for it as though we were at my place and it was my mess to wash out. My confused, "No, no, I'm sorry, actually."

I wanted to dip my head in the fountain at Washington Square Park. I wanted to jump in the river, stick my head out of a cab, scream off the headache.

Simon turned to look out the window as I struggled out of bed and began to search for my clothes in the pile of his laundry on the floor. As I leant forward to pick up my socks my brain imploded between my ears. "Worst. Hangover. Ever," I said. I felt slugged, maybe still drunk, maybe even a little high. I waited for him to say something but he kept quiet.

"But sure, I'd go upstate one day," I told him, not recalling our conversation about it.

I would like that, he told me, "Let's hang out again soon." Sure, definitely. We will. My head throbbed. I should stop doing this, I thought, in what passed for a fleeting acknowledgment that I needed to course-correct in my life, though I knew I didn't mean it, not yet at least, and that I'd be out again later that night, at some party, having already forgotten the brutal hangover of the afternoon, which, when I stood up in Simon's room, fully seized me in its awful grip, like it would never let me go. "I'll see you later," I said, trying my best not to throw up. Do I have your number? I did.

3

I woke up halfway through the third (and final) talk—delivered by a somber Canadian environmental activist-artist, a de-feathered buzzard draped in a large anti-fracking t-shirt, whose latest project involved dropping bags of an invasive, destructive ant species into the ventilation shafts of branches of Deutsche Bank, thereby shutting them down for days at a time—and went out for a cigarette I bummed from the woman sitting next to me. "I'll come with you," she whispered.

Outside, she moved to the other end of the barn to call someone. I was drowsy, stoned on the fresh air that rippled in a light breeze through the night. The rear of the bright main house, where the residents were setting out the dishware on the porch, lit the slope of the field. There were about twenty visitors in attendance, maybe twenty residents, too, not counting Helen, and I wondered how she would fit all forty of us around two medium-sized tables. I dragged on the cigarette.

Two residents, a man and a woman, stopped setting the tables and peered inside the kitchen, seemingly to check whether anyone was paying attention to them. So, from my distance, finally, a plot, forming movie-like up the hill, with me its lone audience member about thirty feet away. The man, with sandy blond hair, leaned in to whisper to the woman, who stood across the table from him. Another woman came out and the man pulled back, though slowly, and the three stood together with rigid formality.

The new woman pointed into the kitchen, put her hand on the man's shoulder, and directed him back inside.

What was this? Everything about the project suggested two levels: the first the story Helen told us, and a second, the one that was truly taking place, organizing these elements—the residents, Helen, their collective politics, whatever those politics were—into actual, if cryptic, meaning. As a visitor, I couldn't quite see what was happening or what this place meant, either to Helen or to its residents, nor whether it did what it said it did. I had no reason to believe otherwise, Simon had nothing but good things to say about the project, and yet I couldn't shake the feeling that something was off, like I'd entered a room in which all the furniture had been moved just slightly, leaving behind a psychic imprint of the previous arrangement that suggested things were amiss. I had never been in this room before, but this was not the way it was supposed to look.

I dragged on the cigarette again, finishing it: a plot against what? The woman on the phone came back over with a sympathetic look, and retrieved two more cigarettes from her bag, one for herself and one for me. I took it and borrowed her lighter. Overhead, the stars constellated in bright hieroglyphics, caught in the clear white band of the Milky Way that fell faintly across the dome of the Earth like a sash. The house lights went out, as some of the residents were busy dropping mosquito nets around the porch, and the glow of the table candles set in. The thin sliver of a crescent moon hung in the sky like a tilted, archaic smile.

Inside the barn, the sound of clapping broke the mumble of the speaker. Claps. A pause. More claps. A definite "Thank you, thank you." Another round of claps, likely because Helen had come to the stage. I put out the second cigarette in the dirt and went back into the barn as the audience members were rising from their folding chairs to leave. Standing before the crowd, Helen tapped the mic, "Excuse me, excuse me." Everyone quieted or fell to a whisper and there was mostly silence, except for the mute shuffle of feet on hay as people quietly stretched, their attention strained with hunger. "So we're almost ready for dinner. If you want to make your way to the house, we'll be serving everyone on the porch. Please do not, and I'm very serious about this," she added, "do not sit with a friend."

Simon came over. "Guess we do it alone?"

"You have to sit with me," I said.

"No, it'll be more fun if we don't!" The crowd pushed us out of the barn. "I'll see you at the bonfire," he said.

I took a seat between the blond man whom I'd seen talking on the porch ("Hi, I'm Jeff," he said, taking my hand with both of his) and another woman named Cecilia, who had ignored Helen's plea and was sitting with her droopy-eyed husband, Ron, his face bloated and red from the sweaty lecture his wife had forced him to sit through. Across from me, the woman who had been whispering to Jeff introduced herself with her full name, Melissa Halpern, hi, and started: "So what brings everyone here?"

I didn't know what to say besides my name: "Hi, I'm Nick," and stopped myself there. I wanted the residents to set the tone for the evening given that this was their territory, their "story to tell," as Helen had put it. I swished my wine glass while Jeff introduced himself to Cecilia.

Taking my silence as her cue, Cecilia, frozen in a look of permanent disdain, recited her full CV, including curatorial work, editorial work, museum work, major-donor-liaison-whatever work, frequent travel to Europe for work, and so on. She told us that she went to Europe a lot, mostly France, where she "has an office in Paris" because she was very interested in the art scene there (she named names, dealers, artists, fairs, something about the board of the Palais de Tokyo), until it seemed she'd run out of work things to tell us about and, when I started to say that I occasionally wrote about art as a way of introducing myself to the conversation, abruptly turned to her slumbering husband and never looked back at the three of us again. "I'm a writer, that's what brings me here," I started again, though that wasn't, in fact, what had brought me to the project. Nevertheless, it gave me a role to play.

"What kind of writer are you?" Marissa asked.

"I'm a poet, but I write other things."

A poet, ahh, they said. They liked poetry, both read it often, though nothing very *new*, they assured me. Jeff liked Byron. Marissa said she enjoyed T.S. Eliot and Marianne Moore.

"Do you have a book?" Marissa asked. She was grave, a serious person who took other people seriously, with eyes that seemed to record rather than see, as though everything around her were being carefully cataloged for later reference. She pinched her glass at its stem and pushed it back and forth on the table.

"I'm working on it," I said. In fact, I didn't have a book, or even much of a manuscript. I had only begun to publish in the last year or so—a few poems, reviews for art magazines, an occasional essay, including one on Hurricane Sandy that I suspected could make for a longer project. Otherwise, the book I was about to describe to these strangers was nothing more than a half-formed idea, but one that might, in this instance, give my visit—and my role in the dinner conversation—some purpose. I was a writer, after all. Shouldn't I have a book?

"What's it about?" Jeff asked.

"It's about the weather?" I'd never said aloud what the subject of this nebulous, unfocused writing project was until then. It—if it could be said to be anything at all—hadn't taken shape yet, but

I supposed that was right, it was about the weather. Or rather, this tenuous idea ("It's about the weather?") presented itself before me and made immediate sense as my subject. My poems, essays, and short fictions, the things that I hadn't published but was grouping together in a single "Untitled book thing" folder on my computer, were about disaster, hurricanes, and storms. In these texts my sense of weather had enlarged to include the turbulent atmosphere of human events, the ways in which we face or avoid crisis, the ways we skid toward crisis, helplessly, together and alone. Crisis, the mom of us all. I didn't know if it was a book or not, but maybe now it was one, finally.

"Sounds interesting," she said. "Is it non-fiction?"

I wasn't sure. "I'm thinking it's a novel or something."

"Cool," Jeff said.

Residents carried out plates of risotto and large wooden bowls of spinach salad dressed with cherry tomatoes from the garden. At this, we dropped the subject of my work. Marissa and Jeff explained that they were both from New York. (Marissa was a journalist and essayist and Jeff was a painter.) They hadn't known one another before joining Helen's colony, but they'd become close almost immediately despite the project's insistence that people not develop "exceptional" friendships or "alliances" that might disrupt the whole, whatever the whole might be—neither answered with any clarity when I asked how friendship might disadvantage the group. We haven't disrupted anything, they said with a wink. Are you two together? I asked. Of course not, Marissa said. I couldn't tell if this was some coded language they were letting me in on, and so I attempted code myself and asked what the gossip was, miming scare quotes with my fingers as I said gossip. A potent energy zipped between them, like a toy racecar speeding up on a roundabout track, and whatever combustible desire existed between them was so obvious it was almost insulting to hear them openly deny it, even if I was a stranger.

"Gossip?" Jeff asked.

I thought, how stupid, yes, gossip. Like what's going on between everyone, who is sleeping with who, anyone leave suddenly in an unexplained rage? Or, more delicately: "Do people ever leave early, can't handle these particular rules?" I was drinking too much—and too fast.

Marissa shot me a suspicious look, so I pulled back and wished I hadn't finished my risotto so quickly, leaving me with nothing to do. Jeff distracted himself by opening another bottle of wine before saying, "Not really. Why?"

"Just curious." Hadn't they been the ones who'd almost confessed or at least hinted at some secret romance to a stranger? Had I taken my curiosity too far?

What had they been doing on the porch? Or what had they been saying? I wanted to ask, but I hesitated to confess that I had snuck out of the barn before the end of the third lecture.

"I'm interested because, like, I don't know much about this place."

"Why'd you come?" Marissa asked.

I considered this—whether we were all still playing a game that I was suddenly losing—and decided to excuse myself with the truth: "My friend Simon knows Helen and he thought I'd be interested in what she was doing up here."

"Are you thinking of applying for the residency?" Jeff asked. "You can't be a writer here," he joked.

"I don't know. Maybe. I could give up writing."

"Give up your book about the weather," Jeff said.

"The weather is so amazing here," Marissa insisted, her tone becoming friendlier. "You would have material for years."

Two other residents approached our table carrying dirty dishes. The dinner is wrapping up, they told us, can we take your plates? Marissa understood. She grabbed our empty risotto bowls, stacked them, picked up our silverware and left, adding flatly, "I'm on dessert duty." She followed the others into the open kitchen.

"Is she OK?" I asked.

"Oh yeah, she's got dessert tonight, which means she's on the cleaning shift, too. It's the worst part because you work while everyone gets drunk."

"Terrible!" I said. He laughed.

Simon sat at the opposite corner of the porch. He was in deep conversation with two nonresidents—an older gay couple who'd been on our tour—whom he'd said he thought were very attractive. They were. Fit and probably in their mid-fifties, both had wind-swept gray hair, commercially beautiful faces and looked like models for men's shampoo, though it was hot and the air was still, so their perfection was slightly askew in the aftermath of the sweaty afternoon. I was jealous, in a way, though I knew I had no reason to be. But this was why we struggled with one another, even at this early stage of the relationship, and I was largely to blame, since I was animated by both indifference and jealousy, a competition of awful feelings that trended in a narcissistic, downward spiral that moved me away from Simon. Work on that, he told me, when I once told him that I was upset that he had kissed someone else at a party. This was our trouble. Perhaps Simon would fuck or want to fuck these older men because we weren't boyfriends. What would I do in the mean time? They all laughed together and I turned back to Jeff, who was getting up to help out another resident struggling to clear the table. "Be right back," he said.

I pulled out my phone and scrolled through the *New York Times*, Facebook, Twitter, and Instagram apps until Helen sat down opposite me with a bottle of wine. "No phones," she said, refilling my glass. "That's our rule."

"Oh I'm sorry," I said. "I was just waiting for ..."

"This?" She handed me back my glass. I took it, raised it to hers.

"So you're a writer," she said. "Simon told me that you're working on a book?"

I nodded, "Yes, I guess so." I tried my new theme out on her: "It's about the weather."

"We've had so much difficulty with that. What kind of weather are you writing about? Good weather, I hope?"

"All kinds, maybe good. Mostly bad, for now. I just wrote something about Hurricane Sandy for a magazine. I think that's the start."

That, the storm, was already a year and a few months behind us, though it continued to stalk us with the frequent news that the city was not prepared for the next one, or any one for that matter.

Helen's cheeks were flushed a rosy, drunken pink. Tipsy, she coughed up a "hmm" as though she were preparing herself to make a speech. She topped off my already-full glass.

"George and I had had a home on the Rockaways before Sandy," she said. "Did you know that?" I shook my head no. I knew almost nothing about her life. OK, well, she said, let me tell you about my house on the Rockaways.

While she spent most of her time upstate with her residents at the project, Helen had two additional homes in New York, one on the Lower East Side and another in Belle Harbor. She was seldom at either, except in the summer when she would spend occasional weekends at the beach house with a few close friends, a dwindling group of artists who had once been force-labeled East Village Art and were subsequently dismissed by the critical establishment after they'd become passé and before any enterprising grad students could dig them up. They were George's friends, too, but he rarely—if ever—saw them. "George is never in New York anymore," Helen said. "He's famous now," with a faint pfft. Though they rarely spoke, she used to allow him to stay at either home whenever he was in town—unless she was there, of course.

What I knew of George, his bullying, difficult personality seemed his most distinct trait, and the one that had cost him the most friends—and institutional support. In the absence of much interest from the contemporary art world after the late nineties, he'd decamped to France to bum around their patron system. In Paris, he worked out of his apartment in the ninth arrondissement, where he kept a large studio on the ground floor of his building, making occasional work for his American and French galleries, though his exhibitions were less and less frequent on this side of the Atlantic. "He never goes out," Helen said, "which nobody minds because he's an asshole." She was ready to talk. He was a monk in an order of one. Few appreciated his pieties, though many admired his dense, research-heavy art and he remained a respected antique, someone whose death would likely prompt a major reevaluation of a body of work most had taken for granted or simply forgotten about. Being alive, puttering about western Europe, would provoke no such reconsideration. Still, George was smart, knew how to work obscurity to his quiet advantage, and his work conveyed this genius with an unapologetic charisma unique to male artists who have never been told a firm no.

"How *do* people get together?" Helen asked, tacking on a dramatic sigh to her odd rhetorical question. I considered my wine.

Despite their years of agreed-upon silence, Helen still loved him, sort of, she said, and she thought fondly of her time with him. But their relationship, beginning when he was her professor at

RISD, eventually "stopped making sense." George liked Paris. Helen New York. George did not want a regular rotation of residents at the project. Helen did. George preferred to summer in Sainte-Maxime, a French resort town. She preferred upstate. She hinted at infidelity. I guessed George liked to sleep with young girls, picking them up at the beach while they lounged topless on the white sand. A charming, befuddled man, I bet that he had a certain academic attitude that somehow construed itself into sex appeal, one that made it easy for him to find undergraduate girls to bring to the hotel room while Helen had whiskey on the resort veranda and practiced her French with sleepy locals.

Once, I imagined, on their final vacation together, she came back to the room and found him with two sixteen-year-olds. Refusing the invitation to a fight, this very last one, she packed her things without saying a word while George shouted at her because this was her fault, her stupid jealousy, very quaint, Helen, very quaint of you. She waved him off, idiot that he was, and left for a nearby hotel, a blue cube deposited in the green hills outside this town on the Med, and a tabernacle to the lost and dispossessed, where one goes when one is starring in a movie about the fuck-up of a lifetime. She did not want to cry but she did. She scolded herself in the room for coming with him to France when she had known their marriage was ending, for trying to restore whatever had been between them, for thinking that France would remedy anything. She hated France, really. But France is easy to hate. She was terrible at French, even after a year of private lessons. He didn't ask her to stay when she called the next morning to tell him she was going back to New York early.

She went over the course of these events in her head. On the veranda, a waiter had mentioned to her, cryptically, "Madame, I believe your husband has been upstairs for some time." What a very odd thing to say. She hadn't understood so she went up to her room on an impulse, what she later realized was the lizard part of her brain issuing its animal warning of betrayal in the den. Ah. How long had the waiter known, how many girls had he seen accompanying George to their room while she read *Middlemarch* in the open air, before he felt some vague moral responsibility to nudge her to face facts? I'll keep upstate, at least, she assured herself. She rubbed her eyes until her vision blurred, then stepped in the shower for forty-five minutes while the hot water ran cold.

George would never have the energy to maintain the nascent colony. In their divorce settlement, he argued for nothing, which was itself a painful gesture, since it conveyed to her that there was nothing from their life that he wanted to keep.

Years later, Helen told me, Sandy carried away the beach house and, with it, a substantial archive of her works, including many of the project's early written materials and some financial papers related to the deed on the project's land. She also lost her diaries from the second half of the nineties along with letters that detailed her early relationship with George. (Her eighties notebooks were safely upstate, in a box in the basement marked "Unpublished journals 1978–1989.") In many ways Sandy erased her—and ever since she'd felt like she was etching herself back into the picture. A month after the storm, an upstate newsletter ran an article about her loss. They published a photograph of Helen at the site of the ruins, taken by her neighbor a few days after the storm had passed, standing in a splintered pile of broken furniture. In the rubble, she recognized nothing of her past life. The fragmentary parts of what had been hers were foreign to her. In the image, gray clouds hang low over the blasted coast. She told the reporter she would not rebuild and she didn't.

"We were stupid not to think that would happen, to be honest," she said. She poured us both another glass. "I was here, freaking out, when I saw what was happening downstate."

Her eyes darted this way and that as she recalled the galloping fear she felt as she lay prostrate on her bedroom floor upstate. If she was lying or exaggerating about something, which she might have been since none of this had come up in my admittedly cursory research of her, her home and all that, her voice quivering at moments with a distinctly false note, did she mind its easy verifiability? Did it matter? Crisis gives us shape, the contours of sympathetic form, whether we call it forth or not, whether or not it happened to us as we claim—or remember—it did. I decided not to tell her about my own experience in the storm, which amounted to nothing more than that of a casual, removed observer, standing safely from afar, my face briefly lit in the white fire of the power-plant explosion. Was that even true—or had my mind added that detail later, to place myself among accountable things since I was otherwise left in the abstract space of someone else's apartment, just at the edge of disaster? I could have said anything about my past. It seemed, in any case, that one condition of the mediated present was not simply disaster itself and its immediate and obvious effect on a given reality, measurable in loss of life, loss of capital, loss of property, but the peripheral warp in the communications systems that had become central to our lives: stray tweets, hashtags, Facebook posts, news alerts, text messages, all of it evidence that something is happening, something often on the edge, in some close or far elsewhere, whether you are "in it" or not. A jittery, closed-circuit paranoia of an "event," where it remains unclear who's there, and whether it is even happening as it is said to be happening, given the diffuse authority of the speakers, the tellers of disaster. Helen was "in it" as I was "in it," even if our relationship to "in" differed so substantially, both between us and between others and us. I was "in" the storm, but in a luxury apartment. "In" being a function of privilege, one's "in" never quite resembles another's, and I did not trust Helen's description of hers—as I did not trust my own. She was elsewhere, as I was elsewhere, and this gave the lie to our shaky stories.

Whatever her politics, whatever her responsibility to her community, she seemed, to me, driven by untruths.

Last month, in June, she had spent two weeks at Sainte-Maxime against her better judgment to work on a memoir about her early years and the founding of the project. She told me it would be her story of this place. "There are many stories of this place, as there are for any place, but mine will concern *the land*, which I've been researching for years, including the Irish family that first purchased the property in the late 1870s." She hadn't told George she was going to France, but part of her expected she'd run into him on the beach. Never happened. While she was once again practicing French on the veranda at the hotel of her betrayal, he was in Bern, installing a show at the Kunsthalle there. He emailed her an invitation to the opening and the dinner with an offer to pay for her flight to Switzerland, but she didn't check her inbox until the day after the show opened. She would have gone.

"George is a sweet man and I love him dearly but I don't want to see him again." Around us, the candlelight rippled as the residents rushed to clear away the remaining dishes for bowls of homemade vanilla ice cream, coffee, and more bottles of wine.

"I hope you like ice cream," Helen said.

"I do."

"So tell me about your book. How far along are you?"

After her story, I couldn't imagine how I would explain what

I was writing since I had no idea what it was yet. "Not very. I have a few chapters," I lied.

"Are you enjoying it? It's hard writing a book, as I'm learning."

"It's OK." Marissa placed the ice cream in front of Helen and me, and lingered a few seconds, as if to eavesdrop on our conversation. There was nothing to hear. Helen wanted to know more but I told her I didn't have much, if anything, to report. "I'm far from done," I explained.

Simon came over and said hello to Helen as she rose to discuss the project's evening plans with Marissa. "I'll let you two catch up," she said. To me: "But let's talk at the bonfire. I want to hear more about this book of yours." She put her hand on Marissa's back and steered her into the kitchen, where together they waved everyone around them to organize the cleanup.

4

The bonfire was built midway between the house and the river, about a hundred feet from the nearest cabin, in a dugout cleared of grass. All the lights at the project had been put out, and the main house was swept into the country dark as the fire formed a lonely, bright point on the compound, outside of which the night seemed to revolve in a separate time from that of the penumbra that enfolded us.

After dinner, we made our way down from the house with folding chairs, bottles of wine, and a huge bottle of tequila that a guest had lugged up from the city. Helen's residents had set out logs around the fire for the guests to sit on, with trays of marshmallows, chocolate, and graham crackers arranged around the circle. (Simon: "I hate marshmallows.") About half the guests, none of whom I knew, were left. Marissa carried down a portable speaker from her cabin, to which a younger resident, a larger boy who had been wiped of any distinguishing features, hooked up his iPod and played pop music, beginning with Rihanna. The aging speaker crackled out her single "We Found Love" in a hiss of noisy, damaged sound, *we found love in a hopeless place*, she crooned, *shine a light through an open door*, but nobody seemed to mind the lo-fi disco our bonfire had become. With Rihanna playing, a few people began to dance together drunkenly, twirling and spinning at the edge of our small circle of strangers, where the fire's light tapered off.

The longer we drank the less anyone could sit still; or, rather, the crowd began to divide into those who'd become sluggish with the wine and those who wanted to do something with their newfound energy. A few residents and guests finally made the jump into night, where they stripped and ran down to the river to go swimming. Their laughter caught on the wind blowing up the hill, toward us, the lazy, drunken ones slouched against the logs. I collapsed on the ground next to Simon, who was fiddling with a flask of whiskey he'd brought from his place. We stared at the fire, arrested by its big, whooping flames as they struggled upward against the stars. He placed his hand on my leg, didn't say anything but squeezed my knee hello. "How are you?" I asked.

His eyes were glassy: "Oh, you know, I'm drunk."

"Me too." I kissed him and rubbed his back.

With Helen watching them in silence, a few residents stoked the fire with logs and sticks they'd harvested from the forest. Tiptoeing past us, careful not to interrupt anyone's conversation, they worked in silence. Jeff, who'd pulled off his shirt to reveal his impressive build, winked at me when he caught me staring at him. Some guests offered to help but Marissa, who seemed to be leading the night's efforts, shook her head no, they didn't need help. "We've got it." Eventually, two residents, including the younger boy who'd played music, went to fetch more wine from the main house while most of the other residents finally went to bed (many rise early in the morning, around dawn, to begin the field work). I wasn't sure what time it was, and like everyone else's, my phone was useless in the woods. Those of us who'd stayed drew closer to one another, though we sat together without saying a word between us. The radio killed itself by the tenth Rihanna song.

Marissa sat beside Simon and me, on one of the logs arranged around the bonfire. She'd rolled up her pant legs to her knees, revealing an extensive array of bruises spread across her ankles and shins that she rubbed absentmindedly while staring at the result of her work. Marissa, from what I could tell of her, did not seem like someone who enjoyed idleness, and she seemed to struggle with what to do even in relaxation, whether to say anything to us or the woman to her immediate right, who, in any case, appeared to be falling asleep upright.

"Hey," I whispered, eager not to break the calm.

"Hey again," she said.

"So you were a writer?" I asked.

"Am a writer," she corrected me.

"That's cool." I was drunk, probably too drunk to hold my end of a conversation. "Yeah," I added. Marissa paused, clearly debating whether she should talk to me or not, then: "I'm actually writing about Helen."

"Really."

"That's why I'm here."

"Wow," Simon said. "What are you writing about? I've known her for a while."

"I'm writing a book about different kinds of communities."

"That sounds really interesting," I said. "I didn't know you could write here."

"Yeah, you can't. But I got special permission from Helen. She's reasonable," she said.

"What, what got you started … on, on that?" Simon slurred.

Marissa: "Do you want some water?"

"No, no, I'm good."

"Well, actually, funny enough, it was because I was writing about cults for a magazine," Marissa said. She gave me a look, to let this sink in.

"Which magazine?" I asked.

"*Harper's.*"

"And you're writing about this residency?" Simon asked.

"Well, I was writing about cults. Not that I think this is a cult, actually. My book's changed. I'm writing about how 'alternative' communities form, like cults, residencies, even athletic teams. Some small, five-family towns out west, where there's, like, one post office and nobody has the internet."

I asked her what she'd written about so far and she told me she caught onto the idea when she wrote about the Dominion of Melchizedek for *Harper's*, which is an unrecognized country on a low-tide island in the Pacific that operates as an illegal haven for banking, securities, and passport fraud.

Her piece, "The Profit of Fraud," focused specifically on its elusive head of operations, a San Francisco-based woman currently known as Pearlasia Gamboa, but who has represented the Dominion under many pseudonyms. (Marissa's profile includes a full list of these aliases: "Gamboa has represented the Dominion as the Princess Bae Catiguman, Bae Katiguman, the Princess Bake Katigumen, Bae Cat, B. Cat, PBC, Rebekah Mesaleah, Elvira Katiguman, Elvira Catiguman, Bae Elvira Gamboa, Ming Zhu, Mingzhu, Pearlasia Korem, Pearlasia Julia Gamboa, Julia (Pearlasia Gamboa), E. Pearl Asian, Elvie G. Gamboa, Elvira G, Elvira Gamboa, Elvie Austin Gamboa, Elvira G. Austin, Maria Gamboa, Julia Gamboa, Julia Austin, Pearl Mayor, Perla Mayor RN, and Fei RN.") It launched Marissa's career, she explained to us. "And now I want to do a book on this."

"I see," I said.

In her article, Marissa writes:

Wrapped up in several legal squabbles in the California courts, Gamboa nevertheless maintains her innocence, and the innocence of her former husband, Mark Logan Pedley (alias Branch Vinedresser), insisting that they have never engaged in any illegal activities of any sort and have never taken anybody's money. They do in fact own an uninhabitable island off the Taongi Atoll, which is "around Fiji or something like that," and they also acknowledge that it disappears at high tide.

She describes herself as more of a religious woman than someone involved in business. In the early 2000s, for example, she claimed she died of a heart attack, but was resurrected by Jesus Christ. She declined to describe the afterlife to me, though she twice referred to that time in our phone conversation.

Per its website, the Dominion is an "Ecclesiastical Sovereign State" on the Taongi Atoll, the northernmost island of the Ratak Chain of the Marshall Islands. The government of the Republic of the Marshall Islands does not officially recognize the Dominion (formerly known as the Kingdom of EnenKio) and issued a statement against its territorial claims in 1998 that discouraged "all independent sovereign nations" from recognizing or establishing diplomatic relations with the unrecognized country.

At the bonfire, Marissa said she flew to San Francisco to meet with Pearlasia after she agreed to talk with her over email, following a long and difficult correspondence with the alleged scam artist. "She was confusing when we spoke on the phone, at first, and never wanted to confirm a time or location, which I should have taken as a bad sign," she said. Finally, they agreed to meet at a coffee shop in the Mission, near Dolores Park, but Pearlasia never showed up—nor did she answer any of Marissa's desperate emails until a week after she returned to New York, when a single sentence from Pearlasia appeared in her inbox explaining that she had briefly fallen ill and that she would be willing to meet in the future. Marissa took a swig of wine: "I sat there for an hour and a half, waiting on this woman. And she doesn't show."

"What did you do?" Simon asked.

"Wrote about her anyway."

The Dominion began, perhaps, as the Kingdom of EnenKio in 1987, when a man named Murjel Hermios alleged ownership of ten atolls of the Marshall Islands chain in a declaration that cited "2000 years of lineage preceding the ascendency of the Hermios Marshallese family to their rightful, recognized traditional post" as Monarch and Majesty King of EnenKio. By the early nineties, Hermios acted in coordination—and perhaps later as a mere front for—an American scam artist named Roger Moore, the "Minister Plenipotentiary" of the Kingdom of EnenKio Foreign Trade Mission.

Moore, a Hawaiian about whom almost nothing is known, Marissa writes, first assumed his role as spokesman in 1994 under mysterious circumstances when his contact information began to appear in newsletters, on EnenKio's websites, on message forums, and through various "rent invoices" he sent to "occupying forces," including the United States and the Marshall Islands. No one is quite sure where he came from. Neighboring states, the US, and the United Nations (to which EnenKio sent delegates seeking recognition) refused to acknowledge the Kingdom's sovereignty. The US, in several warnings to consumers against investing in the supposed state, argued that it existed "only in cyberspace" as a series of scams. EnenKio took particular umbrage over this charge in one of its late emails, which I found in my own research later:

Subject: EnenKio truth
Date: Tue, 1 May 2001 15:06:23 -1000 (HST)
From: enenkio@webtv.net
To: [Redacted]

—Present Status—

EnenKio is a sovereign state.

The government of the Kingdom of EnenKio was established in 1994 [sic] under authority and by direction of Head of State and the hereditary Iroijlaplap (Paramount Chief) of the Northern Ratak atolls of the Marshall Islands. The Constitution of EnenKio established and set forth the authority and responsibility of the government and established duties and succession protocol of the Monarch and Royal Family. EnenKio is a Limited Constitutional Monarchy. Representative citizens, acting as Founding Fathers, ratified the Constitution, recognized His Majesty King Murjel Hermios as Head of State, affirmed their resolve in the Declaration of Sovereignty and determined the boundaries of the new Kingdom of EnenKio.

Notice that EnenKio was a new sovereign state was sent to representatives of the Republic of the Marshall islands, United States, United Nations General Assembly, UN Security Council, South Pacific Commission, NATO, world media, Pacific Island nations and other nations. Legal action was then taken to set forth the claim against the foreign occupational forces of the United States, which failed to ever answer any actions and now stands in default with respect to demands for compensation and for illegally occupying of the king's ancestral lands. The effect of legal demands filed in U.S. federal court, unanswered complaints and failure to reply now have the force of law in commerce, under national and international laws and conventions. EnenKio is an "offshore haven for criminals and money launderers." Actually, the United States did reply—not directly to EnenKio, but with an insidious merciless campaign of disinformation broadly dispersed across the Internet and to its trading partners. One glaring example is a U.S. Department of State Report which compares EnenKio to the likes of Thailand, Colombia and Russia under the topic of "Money Laundering and Financial Crimes." This official report—International Narcotics Control Strategy, 1998—categorizes EnenKio as an Offshore Financial Center. This is a curious label as EnenKio has no bank, no financial center and no money to launder. It goes on to refer to another state and "Enenkio" (sic) as "...mere figments of fertile imaginations...," and as "...entirely fraudulent in intent and practice." The United States offers NO proof nor is it known to have ever found any. In fact, in February 2001, the Securities & Exchange Commission, together with other federal agencies of the United States, concluded an exhaustive investigation that failed to turn up even one shred (or hanging chad) of evidence of impropriety—in intent or practice.

EnenKio exists "only in cyberspace."

Such a claim might be made for Yahoo, Windows Magazine or any number of "dot.coms." Why, the United States itself claims over 25,000 web sites hosting millions of pages. Is this not a criteria for existence in cyberspace? EnenKio as a state has its roots in a 1987 document, but really, it is founded upon more than 2000 years of historical lineage preceding the ascendancy of the Hermios Marshallese family to their rightful, recognized traditional post. The EnenKio web site did not appear until 1998. It is a mystery how any reasonable person could examine the few dozens of posted documents, laws and letters—thousands of pages are not posted—and then say: EnenKio exists only in cyberspace.

"How long did it take you to research this?" I asked.

"Three months. Finally, Pearlasia seemed to want to talk to me, actually even promised something 'new,' but I was almost finished with the piece."

"What did you do?" I struggled with a twist-off bottle of wine. Simon took it from me and opened it easily, handing it back with a nudge of his shoulder.

"We spoke on the phone, but she denied everything or repeated what she'd told other journalists, like this guy at the *San Francisco Chronicle*, who had already done a piece on her. Nothing new. I hadn't believed her anyway."

"Your book is about this?" Simon said.

"No, my article was. This just prompted the book I'm working on now. I'm interested in … believers. Believers in false causes, I guess."

I nodded: so was I.

Between cyberspace and low-tide, the US alleged that the Kingdom engaged in elaborate financial fraud formulated and perpetuated by Moore through a network of websites that offered investment scams in the construction of a spaceport (this page is no longer active but remains available through the Internet Archive and offers a lengthy report on the economic investment value of the port, including a project summary, practical applications, benefits, and adverse impacts); an EnenKio stamps dealership (with a down payment of $2,850); and membership in an "economic citizenship" program (fees range from $500 to $10,000) for "individuals wishing to further the causes and development programs of the Kingdom by affiliation or involvement" and who are "overburdened by taxation" and experiencing "political instability in their country" that has made their "assets ... vulnerable to loss, attachment or litigation." This program offered a passport ($100) and a driver's license ($25). "None of the infrastructure described on the site, including a 200-suite floating hotel in a lagoon, ever existed," Marissa writes. "Nor did the billion dollars' worth of US gold bonds Moore claimed funded EnenKio."

By the early 2000s, Moore and the Kingdom began to disappear from inboxes, with the website finally expiring in 2009. Marissa writes: "It is difficult to pinpoint the exact time when the Kingdom of EnenKio ceded its territory to an interrelated scam, the Dominion of Melchizedek, but, sometime in the early 2000s, it did. On its website, the Dominion's 'historical background' page indicates that the Kingdom leased the Taongi Atoll to the Dominion in 1999 until 2049. Moore, who apparently directed the millennial transfer, was reportedly in his seventies at the time, and is likely deceased."

Founded over a decade earlier, in 1986, by Evan David Pedley and his son Mark Logan Pedley (who later changed his name to

Branch Vinedresser in reference to John 15: "My Father is the vinedresser. Every branch of mine that bears no fruit, he takes away ..."), the Dominion of Melchizedek is an "ecclesiastical society" and a "financial center" recognized by only a few third-world countries. Before acquiring their Pacific island through EnenKio, the Pedleys ran the Dominion out of their far less exotic suburban home on the Nevada side of Lake Tahoe in the late eighties. The Dominion first attracted major scrutiny when *Forbes* reported that Vinedresser had acquired Currentsea, a penny-stock company that he used to file an 8-K with the SEC and claim ten percent of the world's oceans even though the Dominion had a mere $386 in cash on hand. After *Forbes* published its report on the Dominion and Currentsea, the Washoe County Sheriff's Office launched its own investigation into Vinedresser's activities that led, ultimately, to his arrest for violation of parole.

In a follow-up article, *Forbes* reported that Vinedresser's arrest followed a long, troubled career of fraud and identity changes, beginning with a 1983 conviction for an interstate mail scheme, enabled by a California deputy attorney general (also convicted), that illegally sold land that neither man owned. In 1986, Vinedresser was convicted of fraud again, this time for running a Mexican peso conversion scam in the early eighties that had earned him $6 million. He was sentenced to eight years and a $25,000 fine. He was released in 1990 and joined his father, who was a crook with a career in fraud stretching back to the sixties, in setting up the Dominion before he was arrested once more, again on charges of fraud.

After a series of FBI investigations into the Dominion, Vinedresser settled an SEC lawsuit by agreeing to a permanent injunction that barred him from participating in penny-stock offerings, though by then the Dominion appeared to be run by his wife, Pearlasia. His father fled to Mexico and was not heard from again. A federal grand jury convicted Vinedresser on charges of securities fraud and conspiracy anyway and he was sent, in early 2011, to the Federal Detention Center in Miami until June 2012, when he was released per the US Bureau of Prisons website, though Marissa was unaware of his current whereabouts.

"So what happened to Pearlasia?" Simon asked.

"Like I said, she's living in California. Where all the nuts go."

"Just like that," I said.

"Just like that."

"So this article, it's a profile?" I asked.

Marissa nodded. "Yes, but since I didn't have much access to her—or to anyone, for that matter—it became more personal. It's about my search for her, for this place that doesn't exist, I guess."

"Wow," I said, though in fact I'd lost the thread long ago, both what Marissa was saying and what Simon's hand was doing on my lower back, his fingers tugging on the elastic band of my underwear. The fire had raged for hours and was dying out as the sky began to brighten with the coming morning. Most people were asleep, either on cots provided by the residency or in the cabins at the end of the field. Soon the early risers would be waking again to work the farm.

I stared at the fire while the names from Marissa's story bumped into one another in my head: Pedley, Pearlasia, the Pacific, EnenKio, Moore, Federal Detention, California. I couldn't keep them straight. All go to California eventually. To rip off others. To rip off yourself. To rip. I had gone out a few times, only to Los Angeles and San Francisco, but had been captivated by the blissy vastness of space that pushed in all directions, from wherever you stood. Hilly vistas, coyotes, and desert flora proliferating in dusty yards. The East Coast, where I was raised, did not match this vastness except in the long, spiked tail of its history, and so for more than a century the tottering armies of forward-marching hopefuls had fled, each seeking a community, or a scam, elsewhere, going west, toward the ocean, the end point, which wasn't so much an end as a necessary break. That was the story, or at least that was one way to tell it. Perhaps California would tell it differently. I would be there in a month, on my first major assignment for a magazine, to cover an artist's foundation in Silver Lake. It was the first time I had been asked to write about the state—and the first time I'd ever been paid to travel for work.

By the time Marissa was done speaking, Helen had retreated to her second-story room in the dark main house. I wanted to ask her more about her project, but I doubted she would have answered any of my questions—how does this really, really work, up here, and away from the world?—beyond the level of her usual talking points. If I had asked Marissa, I'm sure she wouldn't have known, at least not yet, though she seemed to be working on the answer.

"Let's go to bed," Simon said. "Yes," Marissa agreed. "I think we're out of sleeping bags ... I," she looked around to see if the residents had left any more behind, but found none. "Well, you two can have my room."

"Oh no, we couldn't," I said.

"No, it's fine. I'll go to Jeff's." She grinned, handing us her key. "It's the first door on the right in Cabin D, just over there. Bed's small but it'll do." She pointed to the cabin nearest to us on the hill.

"But what if we slept outside, would that be OK?" Simon asked.

Marissa shook her head. "No, you don't want to do that."

"Yeah, come on, Simon." I dusted off the grass from the back of my pants and lifted him up. "All right, let's go," I said, steering him toward D. "Thanks again, Marissa," I said.

"Yes, thanks," Simon called after her. The faint red of dawn was bleeding up into the sky, along the tree line. "God, we're up so late," I said. "You think that scam thing is real or did she just bullshit us? Like what was that about?"

"Absolutely no idea."

5

What would my book look like, the book I told the residents I was writing? It could be about cults, pick up where Marissa left off, or about fanatics who live alone on a hill, so terrified of their desire to make paintings that they give up their art to raise chickens.

In Cabin D, I dreamt of a large public garden divided by bushes that had been cut into various arches at different heights, with each arch opening into a smaller garden: one with an empty, unmade bed at its center, one with an alabaster fountain of an elephant, raised up on its haunches and urinating into a teacup, and one with a large Great Dane sitting on a bed of peonies. In the dream, we were in Madrid, the dog explained, and what do you make of this fine weather we're having? I sat with him in the soft grass beside Simon, who had been meditating for some time, long before I had arrived. Turning to me, he said, "We should have slept outside," before his body dissolved into an inky hole in the ground. I stood up in the garden in Madrid and said I'm sorry you're right we should have. The hole, widening before me, sucked in my apology, and then the next, and then the one I offered after that, until my voice was dragged down into it, leaving me speechless.

When you sleep outdoors, you don't think about the weather until it wakes you up. I've fallen asleep outside a few times, but only in summer, when the night is warm enough to cradle you in its seasonal comfort until dawn, when the morning heat burns off the dew and usually the first touch of sun rouses you into the shock that you have been left out in the open, unprotected, exposed. I've never camped, but I could write a book about sleeping outdoors. I've slept in a construction site on Fire Island. I've done it twice in a city, once in New Orleans' Audubon Park, another time in Maria Hernandez in Bushwick, near my first apartment, after I found myself locked out. I could do it more often, write about sleeping in parks.

In airy Cabin D, I wasn't outside, I was in Marissa's small bed, my legs wrapped around Simon's. I twisted awake, squeezed between Simon and the warm, wooden wall. My t-shirt was soaked through with sweat, and I felt feverish with the first tinge of a hangover. "Simon, wake up," I said, taking him by the shoulders. He sighed and pushed me away. "Let's go, c'mon. It's like eleven a.m.," according to her alarm clock.

He blinked. "Really?"

We made our way down the hill. Residents, sleeves rolled up and already sun-beat from hours working the fields, waved goodbye, and I felt like we were departing some other, still-unfamiliar country of vastly different customs for our own just over the border. Helen stood on the raised porch with an imperial aloofness, fearless leader of these happenstance farmers. She nodded when we passed under her. I waved.

Spears of morning light, each spoiled with dust motes and small galaxies of insects, cut through the upper canopy of the forest, down to the leaf-strewn floor. A breeze swept through the trees with the chilly premonition of a summer storm, the kind that rolls over the countryside from out of nowhere and breaks into several hours of thunderous calamity before slinking off into the oblivion of blue sky. "We should hurry. I think it's going to rain," I said.

"I think so, too." Simon walked quickly, about ten feet ahead, though his legs seemed to move independent of him. He stumbled a few times, over the knotted roots that rose out of the clay, until finally he hooked his foot on a dead branch stuck between two medium-sized rocks and tripped forward, smashing face first into the dirt. A cloud of red dust engulfed him.

"Are you OK?" I yelled. I leapt over to help him up.

"Yes, yes. Let's go. I'm so hungover."

"Meeeee toooooo." I lifted him off the ground. "You'll be OK. Almost there."

My book could be about the weather when you're hungover. Or when you're drunk. I could write only when I was drinking, in some perverse Oulipian conceptual experiment, walk out of the bar or my apartment after five shots of vodka during a summer shower or a hurricane or a blizzard or when there is no weather and force myself to make a description of what the air feels like, the rain, the snow, the sun, then and there. I didn't want to write that book, but I wanted to write about what the weather made people do—and the weather of what people did. Weather as politics, weather as history. Simon groaned as I guided him toward the base of the mountain.

In the car, he fumbled around in the glove compartment for a cord to plug in his phone. Like his legs, his hands seemed to move with a mind of their own, more certain of their search than his brain was, and he couldn't seem to grab hold of the AUX cord that writhed amid napkins and papers. In frustration, he started to throw everything onto the passenger-side floor of the car. "Hold on, hold on," I said and unthreaded it from an old map. Inspecting it: "Why do you have a map?"

"Let me have the cord. I'm sure Julia and Zachary are freaking out."

"Didn't you tell them we were staying over? I thought you said that."

"I can't remember." He looked at me. The color had begun to drain from his face. His cheeks were still blotchy and red, but his eyes were ringed with faint, ashen circles. "I think I'm going to throw up," he said, and then promptly vomited all over his clothes. Jets of mud-brown liquid shot onto the central console of the car, speckled with risotto rice. "Oh fuck," he rasped, "fuck, fuck," and let out another, more powerful burst of vomit, this time followed by a clear, greasy slick of saliva that clung to his cracked bottom lip. He wiped his mouth with the back of his hand. His eyes rolled into the back of his head. "Jesus."

The air in the car was suddenly cut by the sharp, vinegary smell of stomach acid, booze, and risotto that Simon had ejected. I started to gag and was afraid I might throw up myself.

"Out, out," I yelled, "out," between my own hacking coughs as the urge to vomit seized me, too. He opened the door and fell to his knees on the gravel parking lot before angling back to rest his head against the Jeep's wheel. He vomited again. I went around and crouched to wipe his mouth clean with a napkin I'd snatched from a pile he'd thrown on the dashboard. His head lulled drunkenly as I sopped up the mess dripping from his chin, onto his t-shirt. "Let's take this off," I said, raising his arms to remove it. I balled it up and threw it in the trunk. His pants, wet with a few splatters of vomit, were mostly clean. "I'm going to walk over to the gas station to grab something to wipe this up. Will you be all right sitting here?" I didn't want to leave him in the car with the smell.

"No, I want to lay down. In the car," he said.

I put my arm under his and raised him onto his feet. I'd never had to pick Simon up like this, when he was dead weight, and I was surprised by how heavy his body was. I could barely keep him standing as he helped me with the rear passenger door. Before I could clear away our bags, he flung himself onto the seat. "Wait, wait, Simon," I said. I turned him on his back, re-arranged the knot of his legs so that they'd hang out of the car more comfortably. The smell was unbearable, but he didn't seem to mind, or had simply lost any sense of the olfactory in the semi-consciousness of his hangover. "You'll feel better. I'll be right back."

"All right."

I struggled to the dumpy Stewart's gas station at the edge of the parking lot. My feet were heavy, as if weighed down by a different, stronger gravity, and I avoided eye contact with the few townspeople I passed on the street. The heat had already peaked in its exhausting campaign against the day. It bore down on me like a thumb pressed against a bug, though in the far distance there were storm clouds, as I'd expected, a hopeful respite from the hot warp of the early summer day. What was I doing upstate? Why had I decided to come up this way, for someone I'd only met recently? My head was swimming: we were a mess, or Simon was a mess and I was a mess and together we were an even larger mess. I wasn't sure how to get back to his place from here, and he certainly wouldn't be able to drive. I wasn't sure *I* could drive.

In the Stewart's, the dense smell of dirty laundry hung in the air, though I couldn't tell if this was just my nose, primed after Simon's vomit, and sensitive. I stared at the rows of canned soups, cereals, and rotating racks of flavored jerky. My stomach groaned in protest of whatever was churning inside me: an undissolved mash of risotto, salad, tequila, too much red wine, several gulps of whiskey. I went over to the refrigerators of mostly beer and soda and retrieved two large bottles of water and an orange juice. The cold air blasted my face as I pressed close to the fruit juices. Did I look wild to the attendant standing behind the counter, in front of a colorful arrangement of cigarette boxes and lottery tickets, or did he not mind?

I closed my eyes: Simon's whitened face, head tilted back against the car door, swam up in my head. I adored him, but I didn't want that adoration to cross its unguarded border into stronger feelings, chief among them the one I was unwilling to name or acknowledge to myself. That I liked him. A lot. I cringed at my cowardice, which, since last night when I had become jealous seeing him flirt with the other gay couple, had loomed larger in me, this incapable desire that I refused to address in myself—and accept. Lying in the backseat he was beautiful to me, but what could I do with that, with him.

I shut the refrigerator door and opened my eyes. Stewart's was bathed in a golden hue from the direct sunlight that spilled in from the windows, and all the cheap food that lined the shelves looked fine, maybe even pretty, in its plain, cheap packaging as I considered my options, though nothing seemed edible. I shuffled awkwardly around, between the aisles of cereals and road supplies, like I'd snatched someone else's body and was taking it out for a first spin. I paid for the water bottles, the juice, two rolls of paper towels, and a lemon-scented surface cleaner.

It took twenty minutes to sop up enough vomit for us to drive, and required both paper-towel rolls. "What's your address?" I asked.

"It's saved on Google."

I fiddled with the app, found it: 221 Archer Road.

Google directed me back to Simon's house, the flow of its voice stuttering when it announced the occasional names of the Dutch streets and non-English or complexly English place names in the area. Simon stayed in the back, his eyes buried in the crook of his elbow, groaning as we bumped along on the old back roads that led to the highway. "This is the worst I've ever felt," he said. "And I don't even really remember why we drank that much."

"It's OK. Everyone did."

"Did I do anything stupid?"

"Not at all. Everyone talked, then you dozed off on the field while Marissa was telling us about that woman, the scam artist from San Francisco."

"Oh right. Good, I guess."

"We'll be home soon."

We would not be home soon. I dialed Zachary on the car's dashboard. He picked up the phone and immediately began to shout about how worried they had been about us. He wanted to know where we had been, and I explained with undue calm despite my own raging hangover that we had slept at Helen's and were on our way back to the house, that we hadn't thought we would stay over but we were too drunk to drive. Whatever why didn't you call I can't believe you, you guys had us worried, Julia was going to call the police—all of it came out so fast his voice garbled with the bad signal. "Look, we'll be there soon," I said.

"OK," Zachary said. "How's Simon?"

"Noooooo," Simon shouted from the back.

"He's hungover. But let me get off the phone. I hate driving with this thing."

"Fine. See you soon." The car's stereo beeped, indicating that the call had been ended.

"When was the last time you were that drunk?" Simon asked.

"Not sure. In May, probably. On Fire Island?"

"Really?" He lifted himself up and stuck his head between the two front seats. "You never told me that. I didn't even know you went to Fire Island. I thought you said you didn't like it there."

We wound through a wash of canopied green that tunneled the road. Passing under the flickering shadows of the branches, the stroboscopic light worsened my own headache. I didn't want to talk about Fire Island. I didn't want to talk about the last time I was drunk. "It wasn't a big deal. You were with your parents that weekend, so I went to Fire Island. Anyway, I was at a party with people, then next thing I knew I came to a few hours later. I had to jump in the ocean and stay there for like an hour to feel better again."

"I wish we had the ocean right now." Simon fell back. "I hate this."

"Just lie down. Drink water."

"In twenty-five minutes you will have reached your destination," Google said, its map application rerouting itself wildly while its GPS function struggled to locate us between the mountains.

6

I came to at Pavilion, the nightclub on the ferry dock of Pines. Redesigned after a fire destroyed it a few years ago, it's a big cedar rectangle with a decorative cage of crisscrossing beams, more train station than disco. It's like a place one might only pass through, not stay at for very long, no need to because why club when you can take it to the beach or someone's house. I'd been to Fire Island a few times but had never gone inside the Pavilion until the jet-fuel of vodka and champagne propelled me there in the obfuscating fog of a blackout. I rose out of murkiness while dancing in my underwear in the center of the main room, surrounded by Speedo-clad men hopped up on coke or meth or steroids, all of them gripped in their desirous rage of muscles, cruising and dancing together, sloppily heaving themselves at strangers in a scramble to shore up the end of the night before last call. The crowd was already making its way out-side, back to their respective beach houses. Droves of men with sports bags slung over their shoulders, goodnight. I was dancing alone—why was I here? where had I been?—and didn't know any-one. My last memory, a hazy one, was of a hot tub, someone pouring me another glass of champagne, then another, and another, and then a man who I didn't know, speaking mostly in Portuguese, standing up over us, his speedo sliding down to his knees, his massive cock springing forth, the thick black tuft of pubic hair at its base, these boys I only half-knew moving toward it, slowly, rising out of the water to wrap themselves around him. Then: Pavilion, a vodka soda in hand, and a searing blankness where my memory had been. I'd been turned around, wound backwards, and my clock had stopped.

Without a phone, I wobbled between fleeing groups of strangers, unsure of what direction to take. I thought to borrow someone else's, but I couldn't remember any of my friends' numbers. And it was Fire Island—who had a phone with them anyway? You didn't need one here because you weren't required anywhere, with anyone, at any specific time. The tether of a phone held you back from whatever beachy moment you might otherwise dive headlong into, unwired, disconnected in a whirlpool of booze and gay boys. On Fire Island, you drifted, floated in a lazy river of other people's pheromones and bodily fluids, toward whatever house or cock or ass or what, whatever you wanted, that the current brought you to. I'd washed ashore of Pavilion.

I had no idea where the house I was staying at was or where my friends were. They had been at the party, perhaps had witnessed my downfall in the hot tub, or had joined me there, but I couldn't place them—or anyone—in the hash of details (face, hard-on, a hand here or there) I'd retained from earlier in the night. Or had they left by that point?

A flash of a face: "We're going back to the house? You'll be OK?"

"Yes, of course."

Why hadn't I gone with them? The community of Fire Island is such that you take your place in it for granted, trust that no matter what happens or who it happens with, you will find your way back. Without friends, in the presence of so many strangers, I couldn't find my way.

From the dock, I knew that facing the direction where the ocean lay beyond the patchwork of trees, I needed to turn left and head down a raised platform that ran parallel to a sandy road for about ten minutes before I turned right, onto the maze of elevated paths that threaded between the pitch pine. Rays of moonlight cut through the scraggly canopy of trees, falling in odd shapes across the otherwise dark path. Right. Then left. Walk awhile. Then maybe a left again, a quick right? Or keep going. I was on the sandy road again, in front of a trio of sympathetic deer and a naked man with a slack belly and a towel wrapped around his neck. He asked me what I was up to, was I looking for fun tonight. "Going home," I said after considering it. He came close enough to me to where I could touch him, grab his cock as he tried to grab hold of mine, and he smelled strongly of suntan lotion. "I have to go," I said.

"Where?"

"That's what I'm trying to figure out." Back on the path, wherever it might lead. I took a quick right without hesitation (seeing the vegetation I recognized it all), walked a few paces until, no, wrong again. Left right left, right or left? What time was it? The sky gave no indication as to when the sun might rise, but I guessed after four a.m., and so soon.

Right left right. The house, the one. I went up to the porch, unlocked the gate, a woman came out. Not a woman I knew. "Is this, do you know if?"

"You have the wrong house."

Back to the sandy path. Left, toward Pavilion. Pines was empty of its temporary cast of residents, illuminated in the fierce, endless swamp of moonlight unobstructed by the city sixty miles to our east. Overhead a dome of stars looked down with their grave, empyrean indifference: other worlds, perhaps one with a being lost on a beach like I was, looking up to its constellations, incapable of finding its way back home. Did it resemble ours?

I was so drunk I couldn't walk in a straight line. I slipped a few times off the walkway and into the thicket. Back to Pavilion.

Empty. Turned to face the direction of the ocean again. Maybe I'd had this wrong: turn right, go down sandy path, onto raised wooden platform toward Cherry Grove. No.

The editor of a queer film publication in London, Sam Ashby, once said that Fire Island is unique for its architectural communality: the dock where you land, the paths, and the houses are all built from the same wood. Sam didn't tell me that, a friend of his did. It's a seamless community-body, from boardwalk to bed and back again. At night, this was of no help to me. Going right was also of no help: none of the elaborately constructed homes were familiar to me. What am I going to do? I wondered. I went left again, path, right, house, not their house, not them, right, left, starlight, ocean. Since I was lost, I debated sleeping on the beach, then thought of Frank O'Hara ploughed over by a dune buggy on this very island (or was it technically Water Island?), asleep or not I couldn't remember the full story, the true story of dear Frank, hadn't it been more or less wrongly told for fifty years, he wasn't asleep, the headlights were off?, left right, had to take a shit, of course, this terribly large, snake-like turd that suddenly materialized in my lower abdomen, ready to slink its way into the world, left right left again, every house the same house, but where's their house, my bowels shifting in preparation for the inevitable release, until finally I had to squat in what passed for a clearing way off the path and out of sight of the last of the early-morning stragglers zigzagging drunkenly home. Did it, wiped my ass with a handful of prickly leaves, the only thing available there, from earth to ass and back again. A deer wandered over, only a fawn, and sniffed my hair, maybe even licked it, a deer, all these socialized deer and this one found me as I was defecating openly and with seemingly no end. Wiping my ass, where is this house?

The first threads of morning light scintillated at the ocean horizon, stitched between low-hanging gray clouds. I'm going to have to find somewhere to sleep, I thought, sleep outside, make the impossible possible. I would never find that house before morning, but near my provisional public toilet there was a construction site for a mansion on the beach, the getaway for someone who probably didn't deserve to get away.

I jumped the wooden railing that surrounded the front porch and slipped into the back of the house that faced a formidable view of the Atlantic. The lip of the sun had risen against the gathering array of clouds that drooped at the ocean's edge. A first, pale-blue light brimmed over the back porch like a tide rising at the beach, creeping sleepily over the wood, spilling into the empty pool, through the windows and into the house. It was built in an open style, two wooden rectangles stacked on top of one another with an improbable, pyramidal shape jutting toward the sea, with huge glass windows in the ocean-facing walls. It was very pretty in its fealty to the eccentric architectural tropes of the homes of the Pines, empty of its future residents, the men who would someday play in the pool and rub suntan lotion on one another's browned backs in thoughtful, circular motions, Mark, Travis, Juan, Juan's boyfriend David, James who goes by Jay, all these guys who will make knowing looks at people they already know and maybe really want to sleep-with-with-an-eye-on-dating or maybe just want to sleep-with-to-find-out-what-he's-working-with and then forget about as soon as the act that brings them together is done, the cum wiped from their stomachs or their backs or their faces with a stray towel or tongue, hey, we're just friends, and that's true, they are, friends who smile and flirt and fuck openly, even flagrantly beautifully adoringly under the middle-aged sun and for the obvious benefit of the neighbors who will also be poolside rubbing each other's backs as other men and maybe women though likely just men will splash in their pool, holding flutes of Veuve Clicquot above the waterline, shouting, hey, hey, careful, don't spill in the pool, I don't want to have to go back out to buy another bottle, don't waste it, their voices trailing off in the sea air suspended over the island.

I pushed open the door to a small pool house. Inside, there was a stack of moist deckchair cushions. I pressed down on them to test their weight, their comfort. What they lacked in the latter they made up for in the former. Whatever, I thought, climbing onto the pile of cushions. I couldn't get comfortable. The light grew brighter. Finally, I faced away from the doorway that looked out to the empty, circular pool and its pretty house before drifting off to an island bird's implacable song.

PART TWO

7

When Willa Rhodes got a toothache on Christmas Day in 1924, her mother consulted two oracles, May Otis Blackburn and her daughter Ruth Wieland Rickenbaugh Rizzio of Bunker Hill, Los Angeles. Inspecting the sickly child, Blackburn and Rizzio told Willa's parents that the girl had to ride out her rotted tooth, which had made her feverish by the time their advice was sought, for all of this was prophesied in the Book of Revelation and was to render her a miracle: the Tree of Life would soon sprout from Willa's chest. They needed only to wait, Blackburn and Rickenbaugh assured them. When the girl succumbed to the illness a few days later, the oracles and Willa's parents placed her body on ice in a cabin in the desert to wait for the Tree. Her parents remained firm in their belief that their daughter would resurrect, though her body never so much as twitched in their presence. Absent even a sapling for thirteen months, the oracles finally conceded that Willa was not the girl of their miracle after all, and so they buried her in the desert with seven puppies, one for each of the seven tones of the angel Gabriel's horn.

Studying Revelation in 1922, Blackburn and Rizzio became convinced that they were the prophets foretold in 11:3 ("And I will grant my two witnesses power to prophesy for one thousand two hundred and sixty days"), mandated personally by the angels Gabriel and Michael to free Angelinos from their lust for money through religion and sex. The angels ordered the mother and daughter to write a book called *The Great Sixth Seal* that would someday reveal the location of the world's oil and gold reserves, "the lost measurements," and to found a community of believers to wait for the end of the world. Blackburn met a wealthy Los Angeles investor who agreed to build their church in the Simi Valley, where they relocated with a small group of devotees, including Willa Rhodes's parents. Cecilia Rasmussen of the *Los Angeles Times* writes that the cult built a temple with "a massive gilded wood throne weighing 800 pounds, [which sat] upon four hand-carved paws and was adorned with a lion's head." The temple was not open to the public and was to remain closed until Christ's imminent return.

During the evenings, Blackburn, Rizzio, and their followers conducted obscure rituals that included the abandonment of cars outdoors to rust in honor of God, the sacrifice of mules, and nude dances under the moon. Blackburn and her daughter specialized in "cures," including one in which they baked a woman to death to end her "blood malady." By the late twenties, the Los Angeles Police Department became increasingly concerned about Blackburn's activities after rumors of orgies circulated in city tabloids. The LAPD was particularly interested in investments made by the cult's wealthy benefactors and took Blackburn and Rizzio in for questioning about their suspicious behavior, later charging them with fraud after several former believers came forward about missing savings. Blackburn posted bail, survived a court battle, lost the following that had been hers and her daughter's, and disappeared into the desert as the Depression wound west. The oil and gold promised to members of the cult were never revealed; believers went their own way. Willa did not resurrect.

In 1853, William Money, a mystic from New York who claimed Jesus had cornered him in a Manhattan alley and told him to cross the West for Los Angeles, arrived in Southern California to save the world. Like many he believed the East's spirit was spent, and that the new world could not be found there, buried under the centuries-long influence of Europe. A self-proclaimed healer and scientist, Money wrote many books about the medical and scientific fields that he claimed to be an expert in but knew virtually nothing about, including the first book about LA to be written in English. He made maps: "William Money's Discovery of the Ocean," which he completed at the end of his life, revealed that San Francisco—a city he deeply loathed after locals rejected his faith-healing practices and hauled him out of town—sat precariously on top of a secret ocean that would someday rupture the surface. He was an astronomer and a prophet of the weather. He founded the Reformed New Testament Church of the Faith of Jesus Christ and was nicknamed Bishop Money, Doctor Money, and Professor Money by his loyal followers. He healed thousands in the city before voluntarily retreating into the desert to found a spiritual commune of octagonal buildings called The Moneyan Institute, where he later died with an image of the Virgin over his head and a skeleton etched into his footboard. In dying he was said to have placed a curse on the city for refusing to publish his map of California's secret underground ocean, and predicted that Los Angeles would meet the same fate as San Francisco and fall into the sea beneath the state.

Neither prophecy has come to pass, but Money's deathbed wish sparked an imaginary of disaster that continues to destroy the city anyway: early-to-recent fiction, films, and videogames have all traded in on the suspicion that the city is cursed, sourcing LA's geological, climactic, and social precarity—and the anxiety it produces—for images of destruction and demolition in the visual discourse of the city's dystopian present and future.

In the early noir of the 1920s, Angelino writers revised LA as an amoral city and quickly scripted its destruction in their forecasts for its future, notably in Homer Lea's *Valor of Ignorance* (1909), a racist vision of a Japanese invasion of LA; and Myron Brinig's *Flutter of an Eyelid* (1933), a novel about Christian fanatics and an earthquake that destroys the city—apocalyptic tropes that were taken up and expanded in disaster films, including *War of the Worlds* (1953), *Earthquake* (1974), *Escape from LA* (1996), and *San Andreas* (2015), a film that imagines a spectacularly violent earthquake, "The Big One," that not only annihilates the West Coast, but much of the country. In it, The Rock, one of the stars of the film, circles the state trying to rescue his family while Los Angeles and San Francisco are destroyed around him, the concrete, wood, and steel dissolving into piles of dust before the viewers.

In a survey of fictional and filmic accounts of the annihilation of LA in the twentieth century, Mike Davis enumerates the modes of its demise: by nuclear weapons (49 times), earthquakes (28), hordes/invasions (10), monsters (10), pollution (7), gangs/terrorism (6), floods (6), plagues (6), comets/tsunamis (5), cults (3), volcanoes (2), firestorms (2), drought (1), blizzard (1), devil (1), freeway (1), riot (1), fog (1), slide (1), Bermuda grass (1), global warming (1), sandstorm (1), and everything (1). In destroying the city, Hollywood ups literature's speculative ante by additionally imagining the destruction of itself, presenting the epic as one of national tragedy—and cathartic fantasy (for the display of male bravery)—while covertly inviting us to imagine a world without the studio system that manufactured this work in the first place. If LA goes, Hollywood goes. Disaster films about LA (all great disaster films are about LA) are the entertainment that imagines a spectacular end to itself, a totalizing destruction not only of a place but of the medium, outsizing the US's doomsy anxiety about its future in the post-war to include one of its most popular industries.

In Brinig's *Flutter of an Eyelid*, one of the first novels to imagine the city's total obliteration, everything goes to hell when Angela Flower arrives in Los Angeles to found a church called the Ten Million Dollar Heavenly Temple. Instantly recognizable to most of Brinig's contemporary readers, Flower is a fictional stand-in for the Christian activist and mystic Aimee Semple McPherson, an evangelist and media personality who founded the Angelus Temple in Echo Park (its actual price tag was $1.5 million, not $10 million) in 1923 and who radioed to thousands her fiery and stupefying sermons. (Louis Adamic referred to her believers as "the undead.") In Brinig's novel, Angela finds and fucks a blond Jesus, later using his messianic powers to brainwash the city. With LA in thrall to her California messiah, Angela invites Jesus' true believers to Venice Beach to behold the miracle of him walking on water. He does so, impossibly, hovering briefly over the ocean for an audience of thousands of onlookers before a current takes him under (all of LA is structured as a series of disappearances), leading his shocked and now suicidal followers to fling themselves into the water after him, where they too drown when a massive earthquake destroys the city. (William Money's curse returns.)

In fact, McPherson staged her own kidnapping on Venice Beach and was later found to be hiding out in Arizona. She returned to LA under pressure from the local press and almost immediately regained the massive following she'd nearly lost. Angelinos greeted her as a hero with a parade that drew fifty thousand people, reportedly larger than the crowd for President Woodrow Wilson during his 1919 tour through the city. But the vice-minded Los Angeles courts weren't convinced of

McPherson's kidnapping claims and tried her for fraud after discrepancies emerged in her version of the events that had left so many Angelinos in a panic over their lost prophet. Intense negative coverage of the trial left her a laughing stock, though the case against her was ultimately dismissed.

Davis notes that Brinig founded a disaster literature that specified Los Angeles as a teetering platform for a city of fanatics, communalized and self-organized into delusional and profiteering cults. Coincidentally, when Brinig's novel went to print, an earthquake struck Long Beach and the southern parts of LA, actualizing the cheap novel's ending and seemingly assuring that Money's curse was real. Rumors of the city's destruction spread east; the disaster imaginary had entered national consciousness. By the thirties, suicide rates climbed to a rate much higher than the national average and stayed there. In his 1931 essay "The Jumping-Off Place," Edmund Wilson ascribed the trend to the region's communalized eccentricities. Angelinos

> stuff up the cracks of their doors and quietly turn on
> the gas; they go into their back sheds or back kitchens
> and eat ant-paste or swallow Lysol; they drive their cars
> into dark alleys, get into the back seat and shoot them-
> selves; they hang themselves in hotel bedrooms, take
> overdoses of sulphenol or barbital; they slip off to the
> municipal golf-links and there stab themselves with
> carving-knives; or they throw themselves into the bay,
> blue and placid, where gray battleships and cruisers
> guard the limits of their broad-belting nation ...

While the nineteenth century saw an increase in the number of small cults and eccentric Christian communities, like Blackburn and Rizzio's, the first large-scale cult of the atomic era appeared in Los Angeles in 1934, when Guy W. Ballard and Edna Ballard published *Unveiled Mysteries*, a doctrinal treatise on the Mighty I AM Presence. Hiking up Mount Shasta, Ballard was visited by the Ascended Master Saint Germain, who offered him a cup of "electronic essence" and a wafer of "concentrated energy." After eating both, Ballard was surrounded by "a White Flame which formed a circle about fifty feet in diameter." Within the circle, Ballard and the new god traveled through the stratosphere, where the mysteries of the Amazon, France, Karnak, Luxor, the Incas, the Royal Tetons, and Yellowstone National Park were revealed to Ballard. Everywhere, Saint Germain disclosed the spoils of the world and its great civilizations, which Ballard detailed in *Unveiled Mysteries*. On their heavenly sojourn, the Mighty I AM Presence described a mystical hierarchy of Ascended Masters who have lived multiple lives throughout history and ordered Ballard to found a religious system based on a direct, personal relationship between the believer and the Mighty I AM. Ballard claimed he was Richard the Lionheart and George Washington reincarnated, and anyone who believed in the Mighty I AM could discover their own historically important lives, too. The book was a commercial success. The Ballards started a radio program (like many other cults at the time), and the I AM spread east, with a recorded peak of three hundred and fifty thousand converts. In 1942, shortly after Ballard died, Ballard's son and wife were convicted of fraud, though the Supreme Court overturned the conviction in a landmark decision that held that the question as to whether they believed in their own teachings could not be submitted to the jury. Edna Ballard relocated the church to Santa Fe and its following dwindled.

Despite its obscurity, Ballard's organization remains active as the Saint Germain Foundation. The group still maintains an informational website—its graphic design strongly reminiscent of the early, GIF-laden web of the nineties—that includes instructional material on the nature of the True Self, the Electronic Body, and the Mighty I AM. The cult's most recent (and now deceased) prophet, Elizabeth Clare Prophet, a homely woman who was fond of flower-printed dresses and often appeared on late-night tv shows like *Larry King* and *Nightline*, filmed a lecture series with titles like *Your Sacred Labor*, *The Mystery of the I AM Presence of God in the Aquarian Age*, *The Sacred Name of God I AM THAT I AM*, *Mystery of the Universal Christ*, *Your I AM Presence Is God Within*, and *I AM Presence, Your Divine Self*. The videos are available on YouTube and on the Foundation's website. Resplendent in a white linen gown, Clare explains our relation to a revelatory, omnipresent deity who often emerges from purple fire, and through whom one locates the self in the god. Little is currently known about the church's numbers or activities.

Many of Los Angeles' early charismatic religious leaders were women. Following the Christian evangelical immigration to the West (and the mystical rhetoric of promise of Thomas Starr King, one of LA's earliest and most popular preachers), Theosophy emerged in Southern California in the early twentieth century as a dominant religious movement that boosted the region as a utopian promised land for a new Christendom. Theosophy originated in the nineteenth century with the teachings of Helena Petrovna Blavatsky, a Russian seamstress who came to New York in 1873. Two years later, she met the attorney Henry Steel Olcott and together they founded the Theosophical Society. It would become the leading organization for the group. Blavatsky believed that the human world intersects with the divine at the level of the natural world, and that God is not an anthropomorphic being, as the Bible teaches, but instead a karmic "universal spirit." Blavatsky collected her teachings in *Isis Unveiled* (1877) and *The Secret Doctrine* (1888) shortly before her death in 1891. The religion took hold on the East Coast and spread west.

In 1900, Kathleen Tingley, Southern California's first female prophet, arrived from New York and established the Point Loma Theosophical Community outside San Diego as a "practical illustration of the possibility of developing higher-type humanity." Known as the Purple Mother, the Veiled Mahatma, the Promise, and the Light of the Ledge, Tingley built a forty-building compound consisting of a mix of Egyptian and Moorish architectural styles where three hundred believers took up residence and practiced yoga, the discipline's introduction to California. Tingley was said to be a "witch" whose "spookery" hypnotized believers and she drew the consistent editorial ire of the *Los Angeles Times*, despite her popularity. Her death in a car accident in the twenties gave rise to another leading Theosophist, Annie Besant, who served as the leader of the Point Loma Theosophists until her own death a decade later. After the loss of their second leader, Besant's Theosophists sold Point Loma to a university, which demolished most of the complex. Few of the buildings from the original compound remain.

Tingley's primary doctrinal rival within Theosophy was Albert Powell Warrington, an attorney and banker who received a vision that encouraged him to shun Tingley's teachings and found a community of his own in Hollywood. Warrington purchased fifteen acres of land in the hills and built Krotona, a Theosophy-based colony that attracted some early movie stars, including Charlie Chaplin and Mary Astor. With an influx of converts, its Moorish complex sprawled in the hills. Warrington advocated for spiritual meditation and vowed that his strain of Theosophy would help his followers realize their true potential, an appealing promise for a city filled with those escaping old lives to start new. Warrington offered a belief system "somewhat on the lines of the sodality of Pythagoras," he wrote, "where people of all classes and ages can be taught how to put into daily practice the ideals which ... have advanced beyond high-sounding precepts, and so to demonstrate to the world the practical value of the higher life to the growth and life of a Great Nation." This higher life was focused on the "Third Object" of Theosophy: an "investigation into the latent powers of man," whatever those might be. Spanish palms swayed in the devil winds, the houses filled with cheery out-of-towners, and Hollywood transformed with the emerging film industry that surrounded Krotona.

The colony represents one of the first times Hollywood yoked itself to the occult. While Theosophy appealed primarily to progressive Angelinos interested in communal living, Krotona offered a kind of club exclusivity, one in which its members were not required to fully cede their off-screen lives while still enjoying the solitary perks of spiritual enlightenment. In 1926, a year before the first talkie, *The Jazz Singer*, Krotona sold off its territory, which was locally rumored to be "impregnated with occult and psychic influences," and moved to a hundred-and-fifteen-acre property in the Ojai Valley. The neighborhood became known as Beachwood Canyon.

In 1904, Satanist Aleister Crowley received a vision from the angel Aiwass in Cairo that inspired his *Book of the Law* and the occult philosophy of Thelema. Crowley based Thelema on a central precept—"Do what thou wilt"—that became a hallmark of his Satanism. Later, Crowley joined the Ordo Templi Orientis, an occult fraternity spread across Europe and the United States, and was tenured as the group's leader after its founder, Derik Kellner, voluntarily gave up his position. The OTO adopted Thelema under Crowley and began to expand until the Second World War, when nearly all the branches and their members were destroyed or pushed underground after the Nazis imprisoned Kellner. The only OTO branch to survive was the Los Angeles-based Agapé Lodge, which drew a wide range of believers and eccentrics, including the rocket engineer Jack Parsons, who joined in the early forties and who believed that rocketry could be used to realize Crowley's early writings, especially the law of "Do what thou wilt." Parsons was known to recite the Satanist "Hymn to Pan" during rocket testing for NASA's Jet Propulsion Lab.

Parsons eventually took over the Lodge and moved its operations to his own mansion in Pasadena, where he conducted elaborate séances with other wicked servants of the son of dawn, including the young science-fiction writer L. Ron Hubbard, whom Parsons personally educated in Crowley's teachings. Parsons and Hubbard conducted Babalon Working, a series of rituals intended to call back Thelema to the world. They failed in those efforts, and the spirit remained at its station in the underworld. Parsons continued to develop rockets under the belief they would someday serve (or be served by) Thelema, until he was expelled from the JPL for his "disreputable activities." Nearly broke, he founded a company to buy yachts to later sell at a profit with Hubbard and Hubbard's second wife, Sara Northrup, called Allied Enterprises. He invested everything he had—$20,970, his life savings—in the company after Hubbard suggested Parsons purchase three yachts from Miami and sail them through the Panama Canal back to the West Coast, where they could sell them off at a significantly higher price.

Parsons agreed to the plan, and arranged to have Hubbard fly to Miami to complete the purchase. In Florida, Hubbard took the money and ran. When word of Hubbard's deceit reached him, Parsons placed an injunction and a restraining order on Hubbard and Northrup and tracked them down to County Causeway in Florida, where they had already purchased the yachts. They fled by boat, but strong winds forced them back to port after Parsons recalled them through a lesser banishing ritual of the pentagram that contained a geomantic invocation of the spirit of Mars, Bartzabel. After the police detained Hubbard and Northrup, Allied Enterprises was ended. Northrup threatened to accuse Parsons of rape were he to sue them for theft, so Parsons let them go; Northrup and Hubbard returned to California to write *Dianetics*, the basis of Hubbard's new religion, Scientology. Foretell doom on someone else's body; begin the long history of taking others' bodies for purposes of control. "Because the fall of Because, that he is not there again," Crowley wrote. Each neighborhood begins to form under the influence of a culture of boosters who sell the East on LA's weather-therapy, "open-shop" economics, circulating outward. Or forward. Altar of glass flowers. Geological engineering, the redistribution of water. Irrigation, Chinatown, palms in the Hills. Hills haloed in orange. Krotona in the canyon. Drought-resistant: gates of Paradise, white fire, Pasadena. Walking through Silver Lake with Richard, passing the dirt yards where the grass was allowed to die to conserve water. Cacti. Strawberry ice cream. The Laurel and Hardy staircase. Sunset. "Abrogate all rituals, all ordeals, all words and signs." Abrogate all words and signs, desert flowers, their leaves rotated in purple to a geometric point, pentagram for Mars. Alegria, on Sunset, in hot sauce. Watermelon juice. Rocky road at the Ben & Jerry's. Up the stairs because the fall of Because.

8

Over dinner at Alegria on Santa Monica Boulevard, the painter Richard Hawkins told me about the Brand Bookshop in Glendale, which was once famous for its occult section of local religious pamphlets, tracts, maps, and books written by Southern Californian cultists, Theosophists, Christian fanatics, the evangelical right-wing, and Scientologists. I'd come to LA to write about the Tom of Finland Foundation, where Richard once worked, and decided, at the same time, that I wanted to know about what drew people to California in the first place. "Want dinner?" he wrote to me over email, when I told him I was coming out to write about his old job. "Yes." The restaurant, cast in a dim yellow light, was mostly empty, and the single Latina waitress working the dinner shift circled the tables dreamily, refilling napkin containers and greeting the few diners in a whisper as though she were conducting them to bed. Richard wanted to talk about his LA, the LA of, say, the eighties to now, the LA that had changed, the things that had become history, private history. That time, the time that was, lingers in the unresolved present. I sipped watermelon juice and played with my burrito, a habit—playing with my food—I often fall back on when I'm nervous, until the tortilla split and rice and chicken spewed onto the plate. He talked about the artist Larry Johnson, who was somewhere in the city but who seldom came out anymore, at least not to any event related to the nebulous, scrappy LA art world. Then others: Mike Kelley, Tom (of Finland), lovers, friends. When I said I

09

had been thinking a lot about weather and place, and what about LA appeals to alternative communities, he mentioned the Brand. There was a connection between things that I was struggling to make. He saw that.

"I'll have another watermelon juice," I told the waitress. She nodded sure. Richard cut through his enchiladas with his plastic knife with care. "Check it out," he said about the bookshop, "it's an important place for your research." He forked some food into his mouth. "It's this—or maybe it's gone—at least it *was* this great resource for anything you want to know about freaks around here."

Richard's an artist and writer from Texas. He speaks softly, though with a sharpness in tone skewed by an occasional, drawly uptick for emphasis, the remnant of a twang he lost sometime in the decades since he's lived in LA. He smokes Capris, the tooth-pick-sized cigarettes of pure affect, and makes paintings—often of gay men, or at least gay things—that collage found material and, sometimes, his own writing. It's a bit exclusive, all these gay male bodies, but I like it. He worked for the Tom of Finland Foundation in the nineties, which was (and still is) run by a tight-knit motorcy-cle gang that knew the artist when he lived in the city in the seven-ties and eighties. This experience was definitive in the way that only Tom of Finland can be. My editor had said that his readers were interested in what I had to say about "these particular fetish-ists," though it was not clear to me that they were fetishists, or what, if anything, made them particular. From the distance of my research they seemed like true art lovers, perhaps the truest. Richard told me they're "great guys."

The magazine put me up at the Highland Gardens in Hollywood, formerly the Landmark Motor Inn, a glassy throwback motel from the mid-century. In the late sixties and seventies, it was a drop-in center for drugged-out rock stars stalled out in LA. Janis

Joplin OD'd in the room across from mine. Photos of the stars who had once-upon-a-time slept at the hotel lined the wall behind the reception desk in the retro lobby, their black-and-white faces arranged into a grid of some previous era's passing glamor. Simon came, too, since he hadn't been to LA in years. It was our first vacation together.

When Richard and I first met earlier that week, at a dinner for a gallery at a Hollywood hotel, I thought he didn't like me. He kept me at a distance when we spoke, eyed me with suspicion when the table got into a roundabout discussion about bad art, as though he were waiting to see if I'd reveal any immediate and damning flaws in my character through my defense or dismissal of some artist or artwork. I felt stupid around him every time I talked because my catalog of experiences in the world tallied up to nearly nil and I wasn't at all like him: none of my close friends were accomplished or dead (Richard lived through the AIDS crisis, lost many, and his work is often about—or maybe the mawkish phrase is *shaped by*—this loss), I hadn't produced anything of note except for a few poems, short stories, and some essays. I was an occasional contributor to some magazines, a few of which he read (though mostly not). At that dinner, I told him I was probably writing a book. "About what?"

"Not sure. I keep saying the weather but I'm not sure that makes sense."

"It probably doesn't." Richard had just published his own book, an autobiographical novel about his childhood in Texas called *Fragile Flowers*. Had it been hard to write? Sort of.

At the hotel, we were seated next to one another at the end of the table near an artist who had recently opened a show in the city. "I didn't know you were an artist," Richard said to him. "I just thought you went to art fairs." I buried my smile in my napkin. The restaurant was at the top of a luxury hotel and opened to a wide view of the city that it must have thought compensated for the middling quality of the food, and I watched the marine layer drift toward us in the middle distance, a faint and cloudy blue that slowly covered the white roofs of the houses below still visible through the waning sunlight. The artist laughed and shrugged his shoulders. "Oh well," he said and excused himself to go to the bathroom. Richard smiled at me. So we got along.

In his art and writing, Richard is interested in the mechanics of sexuality, like how sex becomes a machine, a discursive machine of language and symbols—a device through which we desire and become desired. Over dinner at Alegria, we discussed the speculative technology Antonin Artaud drew while he was in the asylum, robots of the libido, big cocks and vaginas swirling on the page that Richard later showed me examples of in old French art catalogs he'd collected. He talked about what the philosopher Sylvère Lotringer talks about regarding Artaud—a rehearsal of a lecture Lotringer probably gave years ago—and I listened and said, "Uh huh" a lot because it was great, what he said, but I didn't want to interrupt. Richard wanted to make something out of these drawings, though he wasn't quite sure what then. Later, he would approximate these robots and symbols in ceramic paintings, the figures twisting off the wall and out of their frames. Art is like that: it borrows one thing to make it another.

"Uh huh" Richard knew about LA because he'd been in the city forever. I sensed these disappearances in his history, lovers, places, and the frayed structure they provided in the narrative he'd written for himself, like pages torn from a book one cannot put down but, in its incomplete state, can no longer fully understand. I didn't ask much about his past. I thought I should, but the questions got stuck in my throat, clung to the roof of my mouth when I tried to spit them out. In the early nineties, he co-curated *Against Nature*—a controversial exhibition of gay art that featured images of unprotected sex—with the novelist Dennis Cooper at Los Angeles Contemporary Exhibitions (LACE) and they both took quite a bit of flak for it, the fury and rage some gay men felt at the inclusion of this art in a time of plague, among other things. The activist and art historian Douglas Crimp criticized it publicly because it jeopardized the good work AIDS activists were doing at the time. Dennis Cooper called Douglas Crimp a Stalinist. Richard is against, slanted, leaning.

"I guess I'm just trying to understand something about this place..."

"What about this place?" Richard asked.

"Why people come here to realize these utopian fantasies, to get together like at Krotona, the people I was telling you about, the I AM."

"You think this matters for your Tom of Finland thing?"

"No, not necessarily. I'm trying to give myself a context."

"Oh, you won't find that out," he said.

"Yes, but I'm still interested in it."

The issue at hand was my own inarticulate desire to know a place I didn't live in, the intimacy I wanted to produce out of visiting it, specifically in writing. Beyond the Tom of Finland Foundation, I understood that this trip would somehow find its way into my book, even though it was still without a name or shape: an essay? a poem? a novel? Or, I wondered, would it simply not work out, and Los Angeles prove unknowable to me? I knew so few people in the city, had seen so few places within it, and it seemed plausible that I would never understand it. Richard sympathized in part, at least the part about working on a project meant to fail. A desiring machine that breaks down. Expectation that I'd figure it out kept me going, as did my sense that I'd eventually know what was going on in Southern California (who related to what), and yet the more I tried to see the city the more it obscured itself from me. The same question kept bouncing around in my head: what would the book I was writing look like? All I could find were palm trees, strip malls, hills in the dry, plain weather of the desert when Simon and I drifted about in our rental. California: watermelon juice in a dimly lit restaurant. Clouds. Lists of things. I made mental notes about the three as though they categorically represented life in Southern California. Of course they didn't. Strike that.

Richard set down his fork and knife. He folded his hands and leaned forward like he was finally ready to explain things, all things, facts I should have already had in mind in the first place, the Brand Bookshop, for example, what has gone and what remains. This was the point in our conversation where he would identify and communicate all that was wrong with the way I thought about his world. He paused, then decided against it and sat back, his chair creaking as he briefly looked up at the ceiling. He cut through his enchilada, then:

"Well, you'll figure it out. How long are you staying here?"

I wasn't quite sure. Simon would return to New York at the end of the weekend, but I had decided to stay for a few days longer.

"You should stay awhile and write."

"Maybe," I said.

Richard laughed. "All right."

California is the end of an arc constructed over the dead who resisted it: all dreams, especially the terrible promise of an American one, seek a port, a jumping-off place, palms, ocean, a final stop. Do you fall back in earnest on the pop adage that anything is possible here? Come, and disappear. For Richard, every version of the city results from a disappearance.

"Good luck then."

Later in the evening when we cabbed to Akbar to meet Simon, who had spent the day with a friend in Griffith Park, we passed a donut shop where, in the early nineties, Richard told me he used to hang out at night. Once, he was standing outside smoking a cigarette when Felix Gonzalez-Torres stopped at the light. Felix was a friend of his, but wouldn't get out of his car to say hello after Richard waved to him because Kaposi's sarcoma had destroyed Felix's face and Felix didn't want anyone to see what had happened to him, even though it was happening to so many men and women then. Felix, who would die a few months later, waved back but shouted to Richard not to come any closer because he couldn't stand the idea of his face being his face and it being the face everyone would see. Richard relayed this to me flatly, almost like he thought I'd already heard this story of Felix before. He said that when the light changed the car lingered a second, then the artist drove off and they never saw one another again. Walk over, chat, turn back, depart.

I cabbed out to Glendale the next afternoon to find the Brand. Richard wasn't sure if it was still around anymore, and although Yelp indicated that it had recently closed I had decided to go out to see if I could find any of it left. The long streets led to rows of small houses, all of them blotched out in the sunlight. They looked the same everywhere, strip malls and pre-fab apartments and houses, seemingly uninhabited, the yards yellowed with drought. Curtains drawn, the homes were animated by a shadow life, and I imagined they concealed other, darker truths behind their repeated facades, all in solemn service to purposes other than the routinely domestic. Figures occasionally appeared in the windows to peek out from behind the white shades.

Jerome Joseph ran the Brand for twenty-nine years before he fell and badly injured himself, and had to close the shop. In articles about the store, patrons mourned the Brand and the effect its absence would have on the city's culture. Their neighborhood, where national chains had risen to crowd out smaller stores, family-owned restaurants, and local markets, had lost yet another local institution to the gentrification of LA. The *Glendale News-Press* reported that the Brand once had between twelve hundred and fifteen hundred categories of books, with the "occult as the most sought after topic." I was seeking that topic and it was gone.

I got out of the car near the intersection I remembered the store being at, though I wasn't quite sure because my phone died almost as soon as the cab driver issued the fare. (Later it turned out I was off by about a mile and a half since I'd put in the wrong address.) In the heat the air sapped me of energy, leaving me stranded under the huge eye of the desert sun. I walked a few blocks in the glare of light but there was no sign of the former bookstore among the various bodegas and cellphone shops, and the only person outside was an older woman in a stained t-shirt and short-shorts standing under an umbrella, shouting into her phone in Spanish.

"Do you know where the Brand Bookshop is?"

"No, I don't think so," she said before returning to her call. I kept walking.

I imagined the end of the world would begin in Glendale, likely at a McDonald's where I stopped for water because it was the cheapest place I could find that sold food and had air conditioning. Inside, I waited behind an incongruous man in a suit who ordered two Big Macs (both with a large fries), a large soda, and a microwaved apple pie served in a paper box. The bleachy, sterile smell of the restaurant was briefly broken by the sweet aroma of the pie that wafted past me as he carried his tray to a table. I ordered one large fries and a bottle of water and took a seat in the back of the restaurant, near a window facing the road, and checked my phone to see if I could bring it back to life: nothing. The man ate his Big Macs a few tables away. I got sleepy watching the cars go by, and wondered if it was possible to get a cab back to Silver Lake for under $20, the only cash I had in my pocket. Cue end of world: dissolve into sunlight, the golden arches melting down, my body blown back as the glass shatters under the force of the bomb. I left.

Outside McDonald's, a sustained, mercifully cool wind broke the heat among a wavering row of palms planted along the sidewalk. I sat between them to finish my fries, watching the suited man sitting in the front window finish his second hamburger. His thrill for the Big Mac was something I'd never known for McDonald's before but I was envious that he'd found something he liked in Glendale.

The sun beat a path to the concrete, heat waves wobbling over the road as cars shot onward, into the mess of afternoon traffic forming across the city. The wind ceased. In a moment of private drama, I wondered if I might faint.

Simon was back at the hotel with our rental car, probably swimming. With my phone dead, I wasn't sure how to reach him. I wanted to throw it in the road. I had no idea how to get back and felt stupid for getting lost, all ways to the hotel seeming impossibly distant, obscured by the vastness of urban space, bus, cab, what passed for a subway, phone charger. I leaned against a palm and dug through my bag for coins for a pay phone should I come by one. Get up. Go find a phone. I walked a few blocks, passed some of the same streets as before, but saw none. In any case, how would I call Simon or the hotel when I didn't know their numbers? Three different gas station attendants refused to let me use their cellphones, high-school boys whose faces were each marked by aggressive bouts of acne. Disappear into the west.

Two women, one walking her dog, passed me as they talked about the movies. The woman with a dog loved the movies. Would you like to go see something, Sarah? she asked. Sarah hesitated, checked her phone, and said, yeah, I have time.

I circled back to a convenience store I'd passed at the intersection the cab had let me off at and purchased an iPhone charger. Back at the McDonald's, I plugged it into a grimy outlet near the bathroom and called Simon to pick me up. "I told you to bring your charger," he said. I bought a Diet Coke while he lectured me on the phone. Are you coming? "All right," he said, "I'm coming."

9

Doctor Money once claimed he was born with "four teeth and 'the likeness of a rainbow in the eye'" (Carey McWilliams).

10

The Tom of Finland Foundation is located at the top of a palm-lined hill in Echo Park. Parallel parking nearby, I didn't realize how close I was to the curb until the rental car's passenger side grinded into the high sidewalk, shaving off much of the paint of the lower part of the Toyota Corolla. "Oh shit," Simon said. He got out to eye the damage. "It's pretty bad." I got out to look at it, too. The passenger door was bent into a grimacing face that stared up at us. Oh shit's right. "Well," Simon said, running his hand over the dent, "there's nothing we can do now." I emailed myself a photo of the damage. Standing in the shadows of the curbside hedgerows, I looked at the car in dismay. How'd I wreck while parking? I was sure they'd charge me a small fortune—probably my entire magazine fee—to buffer it out, meaning the trip would be a net loss. The smug face in the paint knew it, that I'd pay, but Simon was right, there was nothing we could do now, outside the Foundation. "Let's just go to the house," I said, and locked the doors.

Durk Dehner and S.R. Sharp were both members of the Dehner Boys biker gang when they befriended (and modeled for) the erotic artist Tom of Finland in the seventies. In 1979, Durk and Tom founded the Tom of Finland Foundation as a merchandise company to promote Tom's work before they changed its tax status in 1984 to that of a nonprofit foundation that they housed in Tom's former home and where Dehner and Sharp now live. In addition to Tom's estate, they manage an extensive collection of erotic art and a yearly erotic art competition that awards each year's winner with a prepatory Tom of Finland drawing. Simon and I met my friend Jakob there, who'd arrived early and was sitting on the couch next to Sharp when we pushed through the gate. Jakob is a poet from Berlin, mostly a poet of the art world (his one-word poems often appear on walls in galleries, is what that means), with an antsy nervousness about him. Gawky in manner and speech, he tends to throw the people who meet him with his flat, if droll, and near-adolescent humor that he punctuates with uncomfortable silences and makeshift one-liners. He wears horn-rimmed glasses, Brioni suits, and, at the Foundation, his hair was dyed red.

"The, the … princesses have arrived," he said. We found him sitting with his hands stuffed between his thighs. This awkwardness—honed with years of practice among the art world's rich—is a distancing technique, one he deploys to remake any given social space on his terms. With Jakob you find a workaround. "Hiiiiiiii," he said, waving to us without getting up. Europe's dark winter hadn't quite left him yet, and his skin seemed untouched by the California sun, though I knew he'd already been in the city for three weeks, his first time in Los Angeles.

Sharp, who had been sharing what seemed like a lengthy, uncomfortable silence with Jakob over Jakob's Gauloises cigarettes, got up to greet us. He shook my hand and asked if we'd like coffee. I said yes. He wore a Tom of Finland t-shirt and fatigue shorts that extended just past his knees, like capris. His legs were also pale, dimpled with the first blooms of age spots. Sharp was steeped in a world of his own making, whose taste and lifestyle runs counter to most, a sexual eccentric. He'd strung his share of boys up in a dungeon or he himself had been strung up by those same boys: whichever. Jerked off in the half-dark, his balls tightened in a grip and patted with a whip. Or so I imagined. He put out a cigarette in an ash-stained porcelain dish and brushed back his long gray hair before disappearing into the house to fetch the coffee, which he served to us in Tom of Finland-branded mugs.

It was hot outside (still), a woozy desert heat that seemed to distort the air, but under a fan in the shade the dry summer obtained a coolness that one could relax in, doze off while staring at the bushes while Sharp passed around a milk carton for the coffee. Each of us lit up one of Jakob's cigarettes as we began the usual pleasantries, most of which had been covered in an email chain that Richard had initiated on our behalf. With coffees in hand, we told Sharp who we were when he asked our story. Richard hadn't said much about what we did or where we were coming from, only that we wanted to pilgrimage to the house. This left Sharp curious about our interest in Tom of Finland. (None of us had a particularly good answer, though Jakob's— "Um, we like gays"—was the closest to true for all of us.) Simon said he came along with me and Sharp took this in with a knowing, distracted smile.

At my turn, I explained that I was a writer. "I'm actually writing about the Foundation. We've been in touch?" He nodded absent-mindedly. I was happy he didn't want to talk about my piece. Most subjects want to shape your view of them, of course. Perhaps not Sharp, though in his pause after my introduction he did twinkle a bit at the idea of a writer being present, and I wondered if, strangely enough, he had forgotten that I was coming to do something about his work. He smiled sure thing, whatever you say, you're a friend of Richard so it's cool. I stole a glance at Jakob, who'd wrapped his hands around his mug as though he were trying to hide it from someone. His head lolled on his shoulders as he took in the cluttered porch. Sharp began to tell us the history of the Foundation: "So, let me start by welcoming you to the Tom of Finland house. This house ..."

Durk—a gaunt, thin man in blue jeans and a tucked-in white t-shirt—came out and we all went instinctively silent. Sharp scooched over to get a look at who was behind him: "Oh, Durk! This is ..." he started.

"We don't have, we don't have guests on Sunday," Durk spat out. He looked like he'd been practicing this line for an hour, but at the long-awaited cue had forgotten the exact order of the words he wanted to use. "Excuse me," he added, quivering: "We have one day off and it's *Sunday*. Seeing as it's *Sunday* today we haven't had the chance to clean up but of course you're welcome here, welcome to see our home, however, I'd ask you, I'd ask that you, that you try not to make too much noise as today is our day *of rest*." He bowed and left. Sharp turned back around to us and smiled.

I asked if we should go, if we were imposing on them. "I'm here all week, I can come back." Shaking his head, Sharp mouthed no. "That's Durk, our founder. You'll meet him later. He's just tired."

"OK," Jakob said.

"Touko Laaksonen gave us a vision," Sharp started over, using Tom's given name, "a utopia, where you could pursue your desires unafraid of what everyone thought." I nodded—I liked Tom of Finland, but I'd never thought of his work as utopian, as being part of any utopia I'd wanted to live in, though our differences were plotted so far apart on the timeline that bound us that I conceded that post-Stonewall, post-AIDS-crisis, my position was rather cushy and I could do whatever I wanted and no one cared, it was already on tv and the internet anyway. Not so for Touko. "Tom gave us this world where you could just fuck ... in the park, in a public park, and no one is ashamed. You see it in the drawings. For us," the Dehner Boys, but he meant gay men everywhere, "it was good to see sex without shame, especially during the eighties." I passed my empty mug between my hands. One of

Tom's beefy, leather-clad bikers stood grinning in Superman pose on it.

Sharp and Durk are not only the stewards of Tom's legacy, they are firm believers in its power to change the world, and they carry within themselves a dream for men liberated of sexual and social constraints imposed by the straight world off the porch. Together, they are caretakers devoted to a single body of work (one, as it turns out, in which their younger selves are represented), though as Sharp spoke it became clear that any distinction they might have once made between their job and their lives, that is, any life outside Tom's world, had long ago ceased to be meaningful and the Foundation had rather become something else—a calling, from their lost lover, that they could not resist. Their relative freedom from the outside seemed exceptional, even enviable. Together, they were the Church of Tom of Finland, in eternal deference to the corporeal god they knew. "Do you want to see the house?" Sharp asked.

"Yes, please," Simon said.

In addition to Tom's work, the Foundation has amassed an enormous collection of erotic art—much of it sent to them voluntarily by fans of Tom of Finland—that they have archived throughout the years, both in the salon-style rooms of the house and in large storage units in the yard. Much of it isn't any good, even what is on display, what I assumed was the best of the best. (Later Richard said the best is hidden, for whatever reason.) Many of the works fall into two loose categories: stylized depictions of the male figure and scenes of group sex and/or cruising. Tom's work often blends these categories, collapsing images of the voyeuristic and the participatory into overlapping fields of sensuality. Men peer out from behind trees to watch other men fuck, their expressions coy or filled with knowing satisfaction. Both the voyeurs and the participants are given equal attention in the foreground because everyone has their dick out and that's the point. Backgrounds—the spaces where men usually aren't—tend to be vaguer, often simple parks or non-places (in my favorite Tom drawings, the backgrounds are usually blank spaces with, at most, a few trees floating in the white). Pointing to one drawing of an orgy in an Edenic park that hung on the wall of the dining room, Sharp explained that this work illustrated Tom's utopian project, which held that men ought to behave sexually in public unashamed of their bodies or their desire. We got closer. It was a drawing of five men sucking one another off, but Jan Brueghel's *Adam and Eve in the Garden of Eden* (1615) came to mind—a work in which the artist presents an exotic array of animals (peacocks, leopards, monkeys) in the foreground while those he was less personally familiar with are relegated to a less-defined background (elephants, giraffes). Tom seems to have not known much about the world outside of men: references to those categories that define the shape of things external to the erotic scope of the work—cops, sailors, bikers, even Nazis—are non-specific types, the politics of the uniform fetishized or side-lined for a reality Tom does not include except as costume, as drag. Inverse to Tom's vivid men, Brueghel included the only humans in his painting, Adam and Eve, in the background.

Sharp showed us through the mess of the rooms, where he pointed out collection highlights on display. On the second floor, one piece, painted on the ceiling, shows a man, seen from below, standing over a broken floorboard, revealing his fat, hairy balls and drooping cock. We looked up as Sharp explained that the commission came about after the ceiling was damaged. "We thought, let's not just paint it when we can have someone do something with it!" Across the hallway, a door was opened a crack to a room where a boy sat motionless in front of a tv with a blinking error screen. I peeked in. He didn't turn around to say hello. It was like he'd been paused.

There were men everywhere. Nearly every inch of wall space was dedicated to a Tom of Finland piece or a work of erotic art acquired intentionally or by accident, sent in the post by anonymous artists, artists who worked under—and because of—the assumption of erotic genius, forgotten artists, works Sharp glanced at, pointed to with a bony finger, nodded politely to on his tour, occasionally pausing in his grand monologue to throw out the artist's name, the highlights of their career, all of it so brief I either forgot their name immediately or wrote it down wrong, misattributing pieces in my notes. The images ranged in size and content, from small portraits of naked men done by an unknown Japanese man who, for years, sent them his postcard-sized works until he abruptly stopped, to large paintings from semi-known gay artists. We passed a painting of a cruisy, pre-Stonewall bar of cartoonish patrons, all of them arrayed at various outdoor tables in a tableau of libidinal heat. The moony, grinning faces of the men represented in the work were contorted in repressed expressions of desire, their sexuality submerged in narcissistic masculinity: fat businessmen eying one another and a few discreet boys, perhaps sex workers, carousing for their benefit. Sharp explained something about something, but I glazed over the scene as he spoke, not quite hearing him, and followed the zigzag gazes of the various figures at the bar. The painting seemed to nod to Paul Cadmus's *Bar Italia* (1953–55), with its big, flamboyant queens out for the night. I kept thinking a utopia of men is no utopia, and as we followed Sharp's tour I internalized a chant: *a utopia of men is no utopia, a utopia of men is no utopia.*

Sharp led us into a room where the Foundation organizes its archive of erotic books and magazines. Much of the material was piled up on a large table in the middle of the room. "We'll never finish," he said. He held up a few examples of recently acquired material that the Foundation still needed to file in its cabinets: jerk-off zines, issues of *Straight to Hell*, a few postcards of vintage porn, one anachronistic glossy with a sailor undressing on the cover, his fat hard-on visible through his white pants. That their work is seemingly endless is less of a challenge than a point of pride. Each room of the Foundation is tasked with some project that will never be finished, whether it's rearranging paintings and sculpture, finding a spot for a newly received drawing from some anonymous artist in Missouri or Taiwan, or managing the competition. It's work that will always go on, and when Sharp stressed there was still more to do he smiled and paused for the effect: all of this, all you see, will never end, and while we'll eventually die, fade out, Tom and the art accrued by his foundation will not, someone will always be there to collect and organize things for more visitors, for more writers and artists to see.

I looked at Simon and Jakob. They both nodded whenever Sharp finished a sentence. "So, let's see some of his photos."

We climbed a staircase to a room where the Foundation kept its framed photographs of some of Tom's models, many of which were presented next to his drawings for side-by-side comparison. He pointed to one: "The thing you notice is how faithful he was to the people he drew. He accentuates features, of course, but they look like ... themselves." Like him, like Durk.

I leaned in, "Uh huh," surprised to find that Sharp was right. The men in the photographs looked like each of Tom's drawing of them on paper, more so than I would have expected after seeing so many of his generic-looking hunks. He straightened the jawlines, beefed the boys up a bit, significantly enlarged their cocks, but to a far lesser degree than I had imagined he would have. (Except the elephantine dicks.) The drawings were realistic, it occurred to me.

We went through more photo and drawing comparisons. In each case, the men looked more like Tom's version of them than not. We stepped back. It was obvious here, in these comparisons, that the works resulted from love, not utopia. He loved these men, adored them, wanted to set them on the page to immortalize them, make them stay put, exempt from human weakness, like aging and death and disease. The drawings are a declaration of friendship—or of more than friendship, of transcendent adoration for those whose company he kept. Simon nodded and took a photo of them with his iPhone. I stared for a long time in silence. I understood it.

Durk never came back but I wondered where he went. I passed over several photos of him, the accompanying drawings hung beside them. He modeled for Tom for years and was his long-time lover. In an interview I later found online, Durk said that he had first come across Tom's work at twenty-six, when he was living in New York. At a Manhattan leather bar, he "recognized" himself in a Tom of Finland drawing someone had tacked to the bathroom wall. For him, the drawing represented who he was—or who he wanted to be—in a way no other art ever had before. Who finds things like this in a bathroom, only for it to change their lives? He kept the reproduction and showed it to a friend, who told him that it was by Tom of Finland. Nobody he'd heard of before. Durk wrote Tom a fan letter, which Touko responded to graciously and invited him out to LA for a visit. With this invitation in hand Durk went west to become someone else, Touko's chimerical muse and confidante, leather-clad and newly re-christened a Dehner after he joined a biker gang, the Dehner Boys.

Bruce Weber photographed Durk in the seventies. In Weber's portrait of him, Durk's face is smooth and muscular, his shirtless torso slim and chiseled, though not as much as those in the drawings Tom made using him as a model, but still the resemblance is uncanny, Tom's cop and Bruce's Durk, establishing a feedback loop where it's difficult to tell whether he transformed himself into a work by Tom of Finland or Tom of Finland transformed his men into Durk. In other photos that I found online, Durk wears the police uniforms that Tom liked to draw: tight leather, the breeches protruding in the fascist style. He'd become the art he cherished, remaking himself into a flat type in the photographs, a cop without the law, deputized by sexual immanence.

I had heard there was a dungeon in the basement of the house but that it was under renovation and unavailable to see on public tours. I didn't ask Sharp about it, but as we walked around the house I pictured a cavern of ropes and equipment below, all the boys and men who'd been tied up or hung upon a St. Andrew's Cross, edged, their balls squeezed tight, wax dripped across their pecs, down to their stomachs: the agonies of pleasure that had consumed the martyrs of that underground world. Perhaps Durk was down there meditating or working out as we toured his home, away from us, the public. Who was the public in this instance? My heart jumped at the thought that it was me, or that I was not the public, that I didn't even know what the public was, and a sharp pang hit my stomach as I realized that I was either hungry or sick or the two were combining into a panic attack. In the face of all the cocks, I was overwhelmed and in desperate need of air or space.

"Where's the bathroom?" I asked. Dizzied, I leaned against the wall. I wasn't sure if I'd gotten the words right or if I'd rearranged my three-word question into nonsense. Simon and Jakob looked at me with some concern. "The bathroom," I started again, "is it, um, where..."

"Just down the stairs, across the hall," Sharp said. "Want me to show ..."

"No, I've got it."

Inside, I paced. I opened the window to get some air. My chest constricted (a sign in my own somatic lingo that I might be having a panic attack, triggered, as always, by some random external event, like seeing photos of Touko's models). I took a seat on the toilet and buried my face in my hands. Do I need more coffee? Am I hungover? Am I having a panic attack? Am I a desiring machine? The bathroom was cold. Behind the toilet, a sculpture of a penis urinated into a bowl after you flushed. Too much cock. I got up to splash water on my face. In the mirror, I looked like myself, my eyes were still green, my complexion a bit red from the sun (not quite tan) but nevertheless mine: I had hoped I would find myself recognizable, that I'd look different from the person I was when I'd entered the house, changed in the blip of a panicky moment in the face of this curious utopia. I needed out. Earlier in the day, we had gone to an exhibition of Tom's early drawings, mostly from the forties, at David Kordansky Gallery. It was the first time I'd seen real works by Tom and not reproductions. They were beautiful: portraits of idealized men sucking one another off, cuddling. Some of the drawings, mostly his earliest works, were more like sketches than finished works, and were so lightly done they nearly disappeared into the paper. When I looked at Tom of Finland I didn't feel like Durk in the leather bar, I didn't see myself, I didn't see the people I knew, I didn't see Simon or Jakob, I didn't even see Sharp or Durk, both of whom see themselves in the work (and who are there); instead I saw bodies sealed within a realm of ideals I was otherwise meant to dream of, hope to realize at the gym, but never would, though of course that isn't the point at all and yes, I am a desiring machine, a robot assembling and disassembling itself at the whim of others, but I couldn't shake that this didn't suit me, this wasn't me. Of course, then, who was I? Nick who? We went to the gallery with a friend who is trans and she said fuck Tom of Finland. I disagreed but maybe not. There are moments, brief but nevertheless powerful, where art carries me off from myself, from my body, temporarily relegating me to an alien subject position in the back of the room, a place from where I might observe, or at least begin to observe, a representation that seems impossibly far from my experience of the world and yet one that I nevertheless find myself contained within: the drawing (a blond man in the throes of some romantic passion with a boyfriend, say), but also the relations the drawing establishes within the room, between it and me, the others milling about, the security guard if there is a security guard present, and each object—camera, spotlight, frame, press release, whatever—that confers upon that drawing its status as art, and therefore my status as viewer, the super-charge of those conditions that reaches a low, if intolerable, vibration of histories that ultimately repels us farther away as it recedes in time. I enjoy that feeling but I wasn't sure I enjoyed it when I looked at a Tom of Finland drawing. Am I a prude? it occurred to me. I looked in the mirror again. No. Richard worked here in his early twenties, collecting and organizing and figuring himself out through the process of doing so, honing the collagist's sensibility of the possible relations between unlike things or things only tenuously related to one another, related because of how hot or how cool or how cute or how good they look when they are brought together for the first time, cleaved from one context to energize another, combined and recombined into tiny machines. I wasn't him, no. I'd never be him—and I'd never be a Californian either, despite how much I wanted to set that place down in words that would enable me to work out both an art and an argument.

To take a place and arrange it in language: not as a representation or a surrogate, but as an equal in words that approximates how history feels when it reaches down through experience to grab you by the shoulder and shove you forward. I tripped. I could not do it, could I. Melissa Halpern's face flashed in my memory: our conversation down by the bonfire, where she talked about her book. "It's taking me forever, but I'm getting there," she said, finishing another glass of wine. "Poetry and fiction are easy," she said. "I'm not so sure," I said. "No, because what do you owe the world? It's just imagination," she retorted. I needed a subject, or a subject needed me, though perhaps this was it, the unifying pursuit of a subject: Tom of Finland, Helen Hunley Wright: this desire, found in outsiders, to remake the world on private terms isolated from the larger, fluctuating and unruly vocabulary of contemporary life that refuses to be made private, refuses to bend to individual use. Tom of Finland wanted to bend it, to isolate a part of that vocabulary, and in doing so—as Helen's project did—to freeze it in time and out of the world, much in the way that a drawing or a novel or a poem draws itself into an object, fixed and permanent. A faint breeze passed through the open window. Go out, I told myself. I stalled. Go out. I wiped my face with a towel. Go. Out. And went back to the magazine room. Simon looked at me. Are you OK? he mouthed. I nodded, Yes.

Sensing that something wasn't right or that he was slowly losing our attention, Sharp said, "Almost done."

He led us back downstairs to a room filled with Tom of Finland memorabilia, most of it behind glass. Much of Sharp's job is dedicated to raising awareness of Tom's work in the artist's home country of Finland. Ignored for most of his life by the bashful Finnish cultural authorities (whoever they may be—Sharp was never very clear about who in Finland should be recognizing him), Tom had recently received some renewed attention there for his work. The country issued a popular Tom of Finland stamp, for instance. A towel and clothing line featuring Tom's work was also a bestseller, at least in Finland: "You could see stores with it in the windows all over Helsinki," Sharp said handing me one. It was so soft. I handed it over to Jakob, who rubbed his cheek on it. The

Foundation still prints facsimiles of his zines, t-shirts, most of it for sale at the gift shop though he didn't ask us if we wanted to buy anything off the Foundation. Other items, rare or discontinued, were kept in cabinets. Sharp held up the Finnish stamp like a rare coin. "Slowly," he told us, "Finland is recognizing its favorite son."

Outside the house, Sharp led us around to the driveway adjacent the storage facilities, where the Foundation's rusted black El Camino sat in the sun. They'd once covered it in decals of Tom of Finland drawings for a gay-pride parade years ago, but most of the stickers had since faded or were scraped off and only the faint outline of a few of the drawings remained. "Maybe one day we'll get it done permanently," Sharp said.

"I think I like it this way," I offered, the residual outlines of the drawings making for necessary ghosts. Jakob agreed. Simon stood there quietly. He ran his hand across the back of the car, where a few stickers were still mostly visible. "You could get this done in vinyl," he said. "It'd be more permanent."

"That's what we want to do," Sharp said.

I tried to imagine the parade in which Durk and Sharp drove this car. I wanted to place it in the nineties, but it probably happened more recently, early to mid-2000s, during the first days of relief that the plague might finally subside. Sharp said everyone cheered when they passed through the crowd at the slow clip of the procession. Tom is famous in LA, where older men still remember knowing him personally, seeing him at bars, and so they must have lined the street in the sun to cheer as the Foundation's car passed them, Durk and Sharp sitting in the back like a president and first lady in their motorcade, waving back to the crowd with men dressed in leather and sailor outfits smiling around them. The parade is huge and, in the end, held mostly for Tom, Tom's the star, or at least the idea of him is, and everyone in Los Angeles is celebrating that idea, which they equate with a kind of freedom, his sempiternal triumph over death through his drawings, the man they knew. The El Camino advances slowly in the city where there is no plague, or there is plague but there is no plague stigmatized by theirs or any other community, community sounding kind of dumb to everyone as they drunkenly scream Tom's name because who? what? why? where?, it's Tom, that's all, Tom, Tom, Tom, they cheer, Tom, they cannot holler his name enough, their shouts growing louder as the car follows its path under the sun.

11

Headed from the Foundation to LACMA with Simon and Jakob, I confessed I'm a terrible driver, and lack both adequate experience behind the wheel and the normal motorist's desire to master the road. This admission didn't endear me to them, but we went with it as a conversation piece anyway. "Maybe I should drive?" Simon said. I said no. I wanted to try, at least. Growing up in North Carolina, I took the bus to school and never owned a car. In New York, I take the train. In addition to the traffic, LA's crisscrossed with construction, accidents, and often confusing side roads, all of it marked by signs and lights I couldn't interpret in the time needed to follow Google Maps' instructions. When we hit Echo Park (I mistook it for MacArthur Park, telling Simon and Jakob that Donna Summer has a song about it, my favorite song, in fact), my iPhone directed me to turn right on Echo Park Avenue, onto Bellevue Avenue, then left onto Glendale. I fucked up, distracted myself while changing the song to "MacArthur Park," Simon said let me do it, and I missed the right turn onto Glendale as I resisted his help. "You went the wrong way," he said. "Come on."

"I know." Frustrated, I went down Glendale, turned left onto a small street and circled back on Park Avenue to reconnect with the iPhone's suggested route, screwed up once again on a turn by taking a right (instead of a left) onto Montrose.

Simon sighed. Jakob was silent in the back, and generally didn't seem to mind the prolonged detour or what I was doing behind the wheel. I rolled down the windows to let in the warm air, neutralizing any icky feeling except that happiness compliant with the sunshine, the feeling of not-being-back-east, not being in New York, not being in Berlin, and our attendant moods slackened into indifference to my navigation, sort of. "Just fucking stop. Let me drive," Simon said.

"Let me try one more time. Next screw-up, I'll get out." I did it all over again, circled the park, then ramped off the right way onto Glendale, and headed to LACMA, "ha," where the Pierre Huyghe retrospective promised the French poetry of the last decade, glassed apart in the artist's famous aquaria.

We arrived, parked the car in the underground garage, and headed up to the open campus of the museum. I bought everyone's tickets as mea culpa for the drive. "Thanks," Jakob said. "You're just the, the sweetest."

In the first room of the exhibition, an aquarium held a hermit crab with a Brancusi sculpture for its shell. I watched it inch cautiously up a steep coral ravine in the mauve light that bathed the scene. Occasionally, the cube darkened to obscure its contents and my face swam up in the dark, reflective glass, a shadow image of myself, until the lights flipped on again and the sight of the crab in its lowly world returned. The bronze replica of Brancusi's *Sleeping Muse* hid the animal within it, though its long, spindly orange legs occasionally extended to drag itself up a rock, its shell—perhaps based, in part, on the face of the Baroness Renée Irana Franchon, an early supporter of the sculptor—glinting in the light like the broken-off, diminutive parts of classical statues adrift on the seafloor off the Greek and Italian coasts. The crab tells us we are rubble, composed of rubble, decomposing into rubble, too. Huyghe's subject is our drift off the map. I was with the subject. Where had Jakob and Simon gone?

The retrospective had traveled for the last year and was at its final stop in LA. Huyghe had recently added the film *Human Mask* (2014), his lyrical portrait of the fallout of radioactive Fukushima, to the LACMA edition of the show. In it, a monkey in a dress with a girl's porcelain mask and wig scours an empty home for human and usable things, most of which it doesn't seem to understand. Or it understands that some of these things, like the body, that give an object its use-value, its purpose, are gone. The monkey scuttles about the house in its search for life in the house's rooms, overturned bottles, and cupboards, but it finds only its reflection among what remains, the last human a mere mask. In the film, the apocalypse is blue, cold, and lonely, a glassy surface upon which things—household goods and household gods—skid off the board, vanish. Watching the film on the wide screen in the main foyer of the exhibition, where I found Jakob and Simon, I thought about the hypothermal, almost psychedelic images of the veins of the Fukushima reactor fluid draining into the Pacific that were circulating online as warnings of a doomed ocean. These images, while not in the film, haunted *Human Mask* for me. And while it doesn't show any direct evidence of Fukushima's destroyed power plant, the film presents the muteness of the town surrounding it as evidence of an environmental cataclysm of expanding, almost unknowable dimensions moving across the face of the world. Everything is cast in blue or gray shadows. In this half-dark, objects sit motionless, missing those who would use them—to pour tea, to make food, to lie upon. The monkey, whom Huyghe hired from a man who forces it to play a human child on the streets, moves its hands through its hair, contemplating its wig.

It was cold in the museum, but the three of us watched the film twice, sprawled out on the floor before the large screen. When it stopped the second time, the interactive exhibition space brightened and the ceiling transformed into a game of Pong for museumgoers to play. This felt like a too-sly choice to me—and when a few kids began to take up the game, Jakob laughed. I was already exhausted by the experience of art and wanted to leave. "No," Simon said, "We just got here."

The art world is an unregulated economy that borrows from other economies—theory, poetry, and scientific research, in this case—to continually update its relationship to the world and, in acting as a conduit for other (and all) disciplines, strives to become the clearest image of the world in which we may better see ourselves. By this I mean art tries to be everything for everyone at once, all of it contained within salable products that can be exchanged between artists, galleries, individuals, and institutions, across media, in a "conversation" about what now means, and what that now once meant and will someday come to mean. This isn't necessarily cynical, though much of the art world is cynical, it just means that it reaches out, with many hands, to grab what it can and mash it into its ever-widening category. Everyone wants to be an artist because everyone wants to speak about the now.

Huyghe adds to this discourse the notion of the ongoing catastrophe of the world, the catastrophe of representation, the catastrophe of any effort to speak of the catastrophe itself: literally, an overturning of the world as its climate and attendant civilizational norms begin to crack, break at their points of stress. In the face of this are we silenced. Like silt sifting across a sea floor, or sand banks deposited where one body of water meets another, history piles upon itself.

I thought sure.

I stepped out to buy chips at a stand near the museum's restaurant after Jakob and Simon split off for more Huyghe. When I stepped back in, the retrospective had gone quiet; the various screening rooms were empty of any visitors, so I took it in alone. In another film of Huyghe's, a forest teems with insects, each gnawing through their environment, destroying it to make it new. The thought of disaster, from Sandy to here, tugged at me, and I was reminded—for the first time in a while—of the anxiety I had felt in the days after the storm, when the lights were still out on Lower Manhattan and before I went to Miami. I sat on a bench in the museum and closed my eyes. One night, probably the third in the week after the hurricane, I decided to walk across the Williamsburg Bridge, into Chinatown, just to see the city as I hadn't seen it before: empty and dark, a stranger to itself. After the storm, the city across the water was a gray, shapeless mesh of buildings, jutting upwards in the moonlight and in the light pollution of the other parts of Manhattan that had power, but once inside the neighborhoods, it was incredibly black, a kind of bumbling darkness that enclosed within it unfamiliar figures and objects, all moving in mutual confusion. Most restaurants were closed, though a few bars were open, illuminated only by candles.

Is this the future.

I circled a few blocks before stopping for a drink at a bar on some street (in the night I lost track of where I was, probably for the first time since I'd moved to New York). The bartender said this is the worst but at least it's pretty. Someone else said this will happen again.

Huyghe's monkey says it's happening now. It being disaster, the disarray that continues to push and define present conditions, always beginning elsewhere—in the far north, in the far south, at sea—and landing at your doorstep. At the bar, surrounded by others like me who were bored or curious or lonely or, in their way, a little frightened, I contemplated my mask, which was also my hopelessness. Or not my hopelessness so much as my future, which was also my hopelessness, my "present extremity." Over a whiskey I resolved to make something of it, a writing that would attempt to describe— and account for— the state of things, the state being disaster, that would in turn look like a writing that would become a book, one that organizes the anxiety of that extremity into a fiction or an essay or a poetry or a thing that reads like all three. Winds, oceans, landmasses, cracks, fissures, floods, stress points, breakage. Wigs of weather we wear to convince ourselves that we are something that we are not; springs like summer, falls like summer, winters like summer—the planet of summer, and its eternal present.

While I sat at LACMA before a slab of ice near the exhibition's rear, a dog with a pink leg passed by, as did a man with a mask made of lights. Both were works of art. Clouds, palm trees. I went to look for Simon and Jakob, but couldn't find them anywhere— nor could I find anyone else and I wondered if the museum had closed (it was the late afternoon, and nearing the end of museum hours, but certainly it couldn't have done so with me still in it). The back of the exhibition led outdoors, to Huyghe's *Untilled (Liegender Frauenakt)* (2012), a statue of a woman with a beehive for a head that had first premiered at dOCUMENTA 13 as part of a larger installation that included, according to David Joselit in his essay "Against Representation" (I wasn't there), "an array of plant, mineral, animal, and human elements in a forlorn composting area of Karlsaue Park in Kassel ... [as well as] a man, two dogs (one a white Podenco with a foreleg painted bright pink), a pile of concrete slabs, and various other components all amidst a muddy profusion of plant life." Alone in the courtyard, bees—are there bees in Southern California? in Los Angeles? certainly, though I'd never seen them before—swarmed their hive behind a sign warning those who were allergic to keep back. They buzzed in the sunshine with Michael Heizer's *Levitated Mass* (2012) floating in the distance behind them.

In his essay, Joselit argues that this work "instantiates a kind of ecology":

> With this aesthetico-cultural compost [of Huyghe's larger dOCUMENTA commission] stood the sculpture of a reclining nude, a giant swarm of bees in place of her head. At the heart of *Untilled*, then, was a hive mind whose constituent beings dispatched themselves to various plants in the neighborhood, helping to establish an integrated ecology. What emerged from this moldering compost of objects were images: Not just one image, but as many as there were impressions conceived by spectators. And while every artwork functions in this way—as a device for receiving and transmitting images—*Untilled* resisted its own smooth functioning, producing a theater of meaning's ruin; its collapse into compost.

Went down with it. I texted Simon, "Where are you?" but didn't get a response. The ruined theater of meaning mesmerized me. What a broad refusal of the salvage effort. Considering their widespread die-out, *Untilled* struck me as a perverse gesture at that integrated ecology, one in which the primary aspect of its spectacle—the hive of bees—was unsustainable in its LACMA location and beyond, broadly speaking. In the news at the time the bee die-out became a frequent reminder that the basic ecological tenents of our world, like pollination, were increasingly in jeopardy. Whether or not the bees hummed off to pollinate various flowers in the concrete-surrounded gardens of the museum, the colony could not exist where it was (unlike in Germany, perhaps), and so the institution compensated by stage-managing its collapse over the course of the exhibition: and isn't that the oddness of LA, the ways the city must devise itself out of nothing, out of dry earth and air, the illusory but spectacular ecologies that define it. Warning sign.

Simon came out. "There you are. Let's go," he said and we headed out.

Leaving the museum, we listened to "MacArthur Park" in the car without talking. "Can I drop you off somewhere, Jakob?" I asked. I looked in the rearview mirror: he seemed to be asleep though his eyes were open. "Jakob?"

Simon shook him awake. "Jakob," he said, "where should we drop you off?"

He looked at us, puzzled. "Oh anywhere. Where are we?"

"We're in Hollywood—are you in Silver Lake?"

"I'll just get out here."

"Are you sure?"

"Yes, I want to walk around." At the intersection of Hollywood and La Brea he exited the car, calling back goodbye.

Later at the Highland Gardens, I wrote the lyrics to "MacArthur Park" in my notebook after listening to it again on my iPhone while Simon went for a swim. It was an exercise in poetry that I did every so often to keep myself attentive to certain kinds of language, specifically the language of pop. I'd wait a few minutes after hearing the song before trying to see how the words would change when I tried to recall them, but I couldn't get very far from

> Spring was never waiting
> For us dear

It's fled
Into the depths
MacArthur Park is melting
In the rain
I don't think that I can take it

This wasn't right. Can't take what? She can't stand to lose
the cake, or the recipe she's already misplaced, and it's the cake,
the final cake, that's melted in the rain, not the park, its instanti-
ated ecology. Or the park has melted—into the depths that suggest
the rain, the implied storm clouds that roll through (it seldom rains
in Los Angeles, so when is the "time" of the song?), but the cake
has dissolved with it, too.

Crossing out the lines I tried to remember how the cake fit into
the narrative Donna was trying to tell, how her song led into "I'll
never have that recipe again," when she queers the whole thing—a
cover of Richard Harris's somber, self-serious ballad (once named
among the worst songs ever written)—into long-form camp, like this
camp where the everyday suddenly takes on its own voice of coded
in-knowledge, like you're hearing something for the first time and it's
saying one thing that almost anybody can understand on one level,
but which you understand to mean another thing all together, a gay
thing, a wink toward those nights when you go out dancing and, in a
fit of energy, you rail line after line of coke off the toilet seat in the
club and then get fucked in the backroom surrounded by other men
who watch while disco blares in the old speakers. Someone even
hums along while stroking his cock. That's disco. I don't think that I
can take it. What kind of cake could it have been and

I don't think that I can bake it
I don't think that I can take it again

With that I agree that I don't think that I can take it, the claustrophobic metaphor that presents the cake as something more than it otherwise would appear to you were it to form the basis of an event, my birthday, your birthday, the prism of cake that absorbs the objects not designated cake in the room because sugar is beautiful and necessary and pulls you toward it. I'll never have that recipe again, of course. And this makes it matter even more, losing the recipe or the cake or the afternoon to the rain, what is an otherwise welcome respite from ubiquitous California drought, so I wrote happy birthday a few times in my notebook,

> Happy birthday, Donna Summer
> Happy birthday, California
> Happy birthday to me

Are lyrics of any kind recoverable? I can't hear anything when the music is that loud, especially dance music. In the ride back from LACMA (Simon drove) we had turned the speaker all the way up.

I closed my notebook. A friend used to play "MacArthur Park" in high school every time we drove at night to a nearby lake, as we often did in the summer. We would typically leave my house in the suburbs around two a.m., just after my parents had gone to sleep. Amanda would pick me up, signaling she'd arrived with a quick beep of her car's horn from across the street, and we'd put in a CD for the hour-long drive, almost always a disco and house mix that began with "MacArthur Park" and concluded with Diana Ross's "The Boss." Disco is like driving. It is a system that distends information, prolonging—often via the remix of the longer, club version of the song—sounds, lyrics, and vocals into a flattened field wherein the point is not a specific message, as in a topical song or a three-minute pop ode to teen love, I guess, but rather to participate in it as a medium, as an experience, as a fluid space into which emotions flow under the somatic-romantic regime of drugs and dance and sex. You keep going. Disco continues and continues, repeating itself to sustain an event—the night, less a period of time (the clock lurches forward or winds itself back) than a space within the interior of the club—and perpetuate the circulation of its faithful, who attend to its mass for hours, often until eight or nine a.m. Often later. Don't stop. You can't stop. Is it all over my face? Is it all over yours?

I go for hours. We drove in the long, hot night with the windows rolled down since Amanda's A/C was broken and sang along to Donna Summer, sometimes playing "MacArthur Park" several times in a row to keep up the dizzying levity we felt whenever her voice smashed through the speakers and into the car's cabin. Whatever that was: we couldn't define it for ourselves, but every repeat play only made us want it even more. We didn't watch the road. We rode the song.

In "Disco as Operating System," the poet Tan Lin writes that disco places you elsewhere:

> Disco exposes even as it camouflages desire as programmable function. Or to put it more simply, in disco, noise is reprocessed against a background of minimal information or exclusions. This is understood by the general vacuity of disco lyrics. And so the social world of language production and meaningful utterances is rendered obsolete and automated. Social realism is antithetical to melodrama and its subspecies funk and should be the first category of the social to be dismantled, along with an unbroken social scene:

marriage, straight sex, the recession, suburbia, a drug-free world, blue jeans, liquid modes of intoxication, clear vision. In its place: the all-night disco with lit up dance floors, tight trousers, mirror balls, polyester, faded industrial infrastructure, inner-city blight, an hour hand that throbs, and amyl nitrate.

I don't think lyrics are vacuous, but an essential component of that liquid mode. Disco lyrics are one of several important access points into the song: repeated, they become a chant, one that lulls the dancer who sings them, who whispers them to herself as she moves, into the dreamy meditative state the music solicits. Via disco, Summer plays the song's seriousness against itself, cribbing a strings arrangement from part of Harris' original to set up a sentimental expectation that she halts when she screams and the beat jumps up. Jump with it. This gesture is so gay, really. She opens, "Spring was never waiting for us, dear. It ran one step ahead as we followed in the depths," whereas the depths lead to somewhere you can dance, far from wherever Richard Harris thought they led. I have never been to the real MacArthur Park, though I've driven past it many times, and each time it's seemed so open and bright under the California sun. Her depths must be somewhere else.

Amanda pulled the car over and we sat in a parking lot overlooking the lake. There were no clouds overhead, the scene not quite Southern gothic but close enough to evoke for us a filmic sense of this tired, rural place's post-reconstruction heritage, with a lake folded into a tree-framed landscape, the moss clinging to the low branches and trailing down toward the onion-grass below. No dented trailers, wrapped up in fields or squatting in the dirt, in the distance. Rather the lake was a lake. Garbage piled up in the parking lot, probably two weeks' worth, and in July the stink hung low over much of the area.

The air smelled of rotted apples and fast food. Old meat. The moon, clinging to a patchwork of stars far above us, seemed smaller than usual, and there wasn't as much light on the water. Amanda turned the car off. "What should we do?"

"We could go swimming. It's so hot out." It was humid, and my clothes were soaked through with sweat. I got out of the car, pulled off my shirt, and walked down to the water's edge. I didn't like swimming in lakes all that much, how the bottom muck (and the rot of its sharp, eggy smell) tends to cling to you even after you've wiped it off. Amanda sat on the hood of the car.

"You coming?" I asked.

"Why don't you go first."

"Do you have a towel or anything?"

"Yeah, in the trunk."

I unbuttoned my shorts and stripped naked. She pulled out her camera and took a photo of me. We were at the end of high school, when both of us had decided—and committed to one another—to become artists (or, in my case, a writer), a pact that required us to take as many photos together as possible for an undoubtedly fascinated and curious posterity. I turned to avoid her when the flash went off, but I was too late. "Stop," I shouted. I hated my body: despite how skinny I was, I never seemed to develop the proper muscles I'd noticed in other boys my age, no matter how little I ate or how much I worked out, and I had become deeply self-conscious about the oddness of my lanky, but not clearly defined figure, especially when I compared it to the hormonal, densely muscular lacrosse players, soccer players, swimmers, and runners who dominated the school's hallways. I tended to wear a lot of clothes to hide my body from others, and from myself. Amanda knew what I was doing: "Oh stop," she said. "You look fine."

I waded in, slowly, sinking my feet into the lukewarm mud until I couldn't stand its touch anymore and I dove in, pushing my head through the water and the plants that gutted the lake near its shore. Out in the center I dove down to see if I could touch the bottom, but couldn't; when I opened my eyes, it was pitch black, and instead of emptiness I felt I'd stumbled into something's lair, an obscene consciousness that gathered force in the water. I rose to the surface and turned back. Amanda took another photo and the flash went off.

"Stop!" I yelled. "Are you sure you don't want to come in? I hate swimming alone."

"Nope! How is it?"

"Warm," I said. "But creepy. Can you play music?" She went into her car and turned on her CD player and upped the volume. Frankie Knuckles' "Your Love" blared out from the car. The song's spare synthesizer clicked through its opening arpeggio: "I can't let go," he sang in a clubby whisper that gave me, and still gives me, chills, "I can't let go." I paddled about the lake while Amanda reclined on the hood of her car. In high school, we read southern novels and those novelists described this kind of place in terms of its religious character and the spectacularity of its violent insistence on conformity to a twangy, unwritten social code, mostly enforced by social conservatives, tucked away in profligate kudzu. The southern novel does not prefer disco, and I knew then that I'd never write one, though at that time I had badly hoped I would someday be responsible for some classic in the regional lit. "Well, I need your love," Frankie sings. "Don't make me wait too long." I understood this, but at seventeen I couldn't say how as I had never been to Chicago or New York, nor had I ever left the south, really, and didn't have any plans to do so. Disco performed travel for me. With "Your Love" and "MacArthur Park," I left wherever I was, the lake or my bedroom or even my body, a powerful if somewhat silly feeling of liftoff that nevertheless sustained me behind my locked bedroom door. I floated on my back. Amanda turned the music louder. "I can't let go," Frankie repeated.

Strike this out, too. The lake is melting / I don't think that I can take it. Strike this again. Garbage collects. Time is fleeting! Donna Summer sings. This is not true: we are fleeting; time remains the same. In the Highland Gardens, I kept trying to write out the song but couldn't find the words as they had come to me in my earphones, I don't think that I can bake it or take it, MacArthur Park is melting and I can't remember anything at all, back with Amanda at the lake, or any time for that matter. The lyrics otherwise dissolved into sentences that structured this period: Spring was never waiting for us, dear, its time has passed, of course, and likely never existed except in the studio production of the drama of its loss, loss not even being very convincing in the end. Once recorded can it go? Of course, like bees in Southern California, or everywhere else for that matter. Float on the surface, the surface as it breaks. I'll never have that recipe or the time that produced the day that brought about the cake in the first place again. The cake is a cube that spins on the plate she's placed on the picnic table. As soft architecture, it isn't built to last, rain comes through; the party forgets it as they head for shelter, and so it begins to break apart in the storm. Slices fall off in clumps of vanilla debris while the chocolate cream disintegrates and flows onto the grass, the entire structure lost to dirt. The cake is a theory for cake that proves cake doesn't last.

12

Notebook, continued:

> A couple is drinking near the bean-shaped pool behind
> our room at the hotel (how much longer am I in this
> hotel?), their feet kicking the water in some removed
> pocket of romantic time. (Not my time but close to it.)
> They knock their bottles against one another in a
> cheers darling. How to describe the smell of this after-
> noon: eucalyptus, tinged with the burnt air of traffic,
> the severe lemon fragrance of the hotel room wafting
> out of the open sliding glass doors. No breeze. No
> smell, really, just words on the page. Simon put on
> Janis Joplin in memory of her death across the hall.
> He's in the shower while I'm writing about Donna
> Summer.

The hotel's backyard didn't smell of eucalyptus, but certainly
the description was lovely. I watched the couple from our porch
and smoked a cigarette, one of Jakob's that I'd bummed from him
outside LACMA. It was the start of early evening, with the last bit
of the day's sky still visible through the palms around the patio of
the Highland Gardens, a fine pink bleeding sherbet orange to red.
Primordial blast of sunset that's "so LA," the cool air motionless
while Simon sang in the shower.

"What are you doing?" he called out from the bathroom.

"Smoking a cigarette."

"Are you going swimming?"

"No," I said.

Joplin: *But until that morning, honey, nothing's going to harm you. No, no, no, no, no ...*

She died across the hall in Room 105 of a heroin overdose. Her producer found her after she failed to show up at Sunset Records for a recording session for her second (and last) album *Pearl*, most famous for "Me and Bobby McGee," which piped into the room after "Summertime" finished on Simon's laptop, and "Mercedes Benz," which she recorded the day before she died. Perhaps she had practiced the song across the hallway, her windows open to evening air, a halo of cigarette smoke hovering over her in the yellow lamplight.

I went back to my notebook:

Saw Huyghe exhibit this afternoon with Jakob and Simon. They connected with it (together) while I felt very third-wheel, though there's nothing between them, of course, since they'd never met before ... I just lost my bearings after the Tom of Finland Foundation. Not sure, in fact, how I'll write about that place, and probably need to go back to see more since the first round was overwhelming: so much stuff, so little of it organized.

Richard texted me to say he'd go with me if I wanted to get a better tour since he knows the place so well (maybe even better than Sharp, whose taste is skewed by love for everything Tom and therefore lacks any filter).

Decided to stay another few days to write—return to Foundation, see more museums. Simon goes back tonight. Julia recommended that I go to San Luis Obispo to see the Madonna Inn, if "you want to understand how fake California can be." That's not what I'm looking for but after Googling the hotel— chintz & glitz of pastel pink and theme rooms à la fifties—I thought I might get something out of a visit.

Simon, wrapped in a towel too small for him, joined me on the porch. He pinched the cigarette out of my mouth and took a long drag. We suddenly passed for the couple we were not, like the one drinking beers by the pool. I resented it and felt betrayed by my own romantic complacence. We were boyfriends and who cared. We had dated or not-dated for just over a year. The trip had gone perfectly well, without a single fight, something that I hadn't anticipated. In New York, we fought often, usually while drunk and after we'd returned to his or my place from a party, *No, you go to the bodega for water. I'm too tired to go out.* The point of this was what.

"I could live here," Simon said. He finished the cigarette and stomped it out on the concrete.

"I don't know if I could."

"I'm moving to LA" had become the dullest, most predictable refrain from anyone with more than three drinks in them and dim job prospects, with the city assuming a central position in the collective fantasy of club kids and anyone under thirty as social, romantic, and artistic salvation, a release from New York's brutal parade of humiliating and public trials of the spirit. Life between the coasts had become a predictable circuit of desperation, with fewer and fewer opportunities as various "markets" contracted, and each day offered a slightly harder battle for cash. LA offered elsewhere, the promise of the jump-off.

"Try," on the computer: *Well, I'm going to try a little bit harder.*

"What time should we leave for the airport?" Simon asked.

"Soon, I guess. I'm sorry you're going."

We finished the cigarette and went back inside. Simon let his towel drop. I pushed him onto the bed, falling on top of him. We kissed, but went no further. He hesitated when I went to grab his cock, and I pulled back. We hadn't fucked in two weeks, and neither of us seemed to be sure of what to do about it. It had begun to seem easier to do nothing, for us to satisfy ourselves separately—and alone. We were slowly sliding apart from one another, even if neither of us wanted to admit it, but I decided not to pursue that thread. None of this seemed to bother Simon very much, though, of course, it must have. The situation left me uneasy about us at first, but I'd already become more comfortable with the arrangement, the easiness of our slow drift into friendship.

"I'm going to get dressed," he said.

"OK."

I watched him pull on jeans without his underwear on, then a white t-shirt, and pack his things, clothes first, then laptop, and finally a James Baldwin novel that he'd brought along. When he finished, he looked at me with a straight, if sorrowful face, his brow knit with an undisguised sadness that I recognized from earlier moments of disappointment. "Ready?" he asked. I nodded. He was disappointed to be leaving, likely, but probably also in us. This trip, like much of our relationship, had revolved around me, and so I had mostly ignored him during this supposed vacation. I would make it up to him in New York.

"Let's go."

We went out to the hotel garage to retrieve the Corolla. Simon rubbed his hand over the dent. "I bet you could get this buffered out for cheaper than the rental place would charge," he offered. I nodded.

I'll consider it, I said.

We pulled out onto Franklin Avenue and headed down toward LAX into unbridled sunlight, past Hollywood, new and old malls, the differing aspects of crumbling LA and resurgent LA and no LA at all bumping into one another as space narrowed and widened with apartments, stores, long imperial rows of palms, taco trucks, traffic. Simon talked about how much lonelier he would be if he lived here because he'd never see anyone if he had to drive everywhere. I agreed.

I would never understand LA as I had hoped when I'd had dinner with Richard, though this was entirely beside the point. I didn't understand New York, nor had I understood any place that I'd lived in. Wherever it is, a city occludes itself in order to continue its propulsion forward, to widen and contract its social spheres, which overlap in communities and places and moods and weather in an essentially unknowable movement of this system of civic bodies, all tumbling in a cluttered revolution of the stuff of the city, the overturning of some places in favor of others, loss, gain, entangled languages, the revolving, if speculative, forms of the future competing for their stakes in the present. So Los Angeles fled before me, into the afternoon.

13

I tried to check into the Madonna Inn under the name Rocco Ciccone, fully expecting the attendant at the front desk to get the joke or at least pause and ask me if I was actually Madonna's son, but of course the Inn had nothing to do with the queen of pop, and the joke was lost on her because she either didn't catch the reference or didn't care and because, in any case, it wasn't a joke at all, just some dumb idea I'd come up with while I was finishing a joint in the hotel parking lot. My name on my Visa and driver's license was Nicholas. "I just go by Rocco," I said after realizing immediately how all-too-elaborate the prank (it wasn't much of a prank) had become. "But," she started, inspecting my ID. She turned it over, as if to check whether it was a fake. I shook my head. I wanted to stop explaining why I had said I was Rocco Ciccone when "your state ID gives your name as Nicholas Fowler." So, I was Rocco, Rocco Ciccone, a nickname, but legally Nicholas Matthew Fowler, and headed from Santa Barbara to Los Angeles on a "business trip" that delayed me in San Luis Obispo for a night.

I paid for Room 143, "The Rock Bottom," a subterrane-an-themed novelty "pad" that the glitzy lobby's brochure praised for its "mystical charm." It was available after a last-minute cancellation. ("You're very lucky we have this room for the evening, sir, it's *never* available." All right, I said. I was lucky.) The room seemed so very un-California in its offering of a pretend life in an underground, "primitive rock basin" with its "sculptured waterfall shower" while outside, the city, crowned with palms, beamed witlessly on the central coast in endless sunshine. The Madonna is a grand cliché of the Golden State, a temple to twentieth-century fantasy where I hoped I might find what Richard said I was looking for, that thing, the thing that was the place that I might set in words. Not quite a cult, it was cult-like, or cultish in its following. Perhaps this would be where I would encounter California.

"The room isn't quite ready yet, Mr. Fowler," the woman at the front desk said. It was noon; check-in was at two p.m. "But may I recommend you visit our restaurant for lunch?"

"No problem," I said. "Can I leave my bag with you—and I'll … I'd love some lunch."

"Our Copper Café is just down the hall, adjacent to our steak house, which I also highly recommend for dinner this evening."

"Yes, of course," I said, adopting her flat manner, "I think I'd love that." She took my bag and pointed me in the direction of the Café through the main restaurant. That room, which wasn't open until the evening, as she said, is an enlarged, impossibly hideous chrysalis of marzipan pink and dusty, faded gold paneling (like much of the rest of the inn), organized around an absurd chandelier sprouting from a tree trunk at the room's center that spreads upward into a canopy of thick vines chained to gold Christmas lights threaded with an additional patchwork of big lightbulbs and electric candles glimmering among bunches of fake pine needles. Below the tree, Pepto-Bismol-pink booths link in rows around tables, curving in S-shapes over chintzy carpet patterned with roses and blueberries. I continued to the half-circle bar at the Café that's set back under an ornate wooden alcove carved with leaf and berry-bunch motifs, the phrase *Let's eat and be happy* engraved in Gothic script over the alcove.

A few elderly and middle-aged iPhone-distracted couples sat at the bar and at a scattering of small tables set back near the windows that viewed, distantly, the Inn's tennis courts, while a cheery waitress named Margaret puttered between the kitchen and her diners with plates of cold sandwiches and sides of steak fries. She handed me a salmon-colored menu and a "famous goblet" of water with a howdy, welcome to the Copper Café. "What can I start you off with to drink?"

"I'll have an orange juice, please." Her face mechanically arranged itself into a smile and she nodded, sure thing, hon, and slipped off to the bar.

I called Simon. "Hi," he said, picking up after the first ring. "Hey," I said, explaining that I'd made it to the Madonna, finally. (I decided not to tell him I was stoned.) "How are you?"

The same. "I saw Julia last night for dinner," he started. "We talked about you going to the Madonna Inn. She said it never fails to deliver."

"So far, yes. How is she?"

"Well, funny, she told me she's been thinking about applying to Helen's thing upstate for next summer, so we talked mostly about that. She wants to get out of New York. I told her I'm not sure that's the way, but she seems to think so."

I pictured Simon lying on his back on his bed, his feet extended up along the wall—his typical pose when he talks on the phone.

"God, really?" I said, half-distracted by Margaret, who'd returned with my orange juice and to ask me if I was ready to place my order. Nodding yes, I pulled the phone away from my ear and pointed to the tuna salad sandwich. Sorry, I mouthed to her, for my rudeness. She shrugged this off with a whispered, "No problem."

"Are you there?" Simon asked.

"Yes. I just ordered lunch. I can't check in yet, so I'm sitting in this ridiculous café. Do you want a souvenir," I started, reading from an advertisement in the center of the menu, "'Treat someone to a gift or take a Madonna Inn memento from any one of our specialty stores. Start your own collection of our famous Madonna Inn water and wine goblets.' Do you want a wine goblet?"

"Duh."

We talked about New York: Julia's application to Helen's; his shitty, crowded flight; the woman next to him who ate greasy chicken out of a plastic bag; how bad traffic was from JFK to his place in Bushwick; what else he and Julia discussed at dinner last night (Zachary's developing but always inevitable coke habit, our trip to LA). Julia was lost, though he didn't use the word lost but instead "searching," "She was still searching for herself," he said, rather melodramatically, but this came as no surprise. For months, she had been complaining about her job at a café in Williamsburg, about her writing, and about a fidgety older man she was seeing, but whom she felt was sleeping with someone else. (He lived in Philadelphia, came to New York twice a month, and Simon and I suspected he was married.) None of these things amounted to any real crisis of identity, but for whatever reason she felt she lacked direction (to where? I asked Simon, but he didn't know, though now she seemed to be pointed, inexplicably, toward Helen's) and she was frequently threatening "to just go," though she had no idea as to where. She was twenty-seven, and was fast approaching her Saturn Return, which she was currently obsessed with, and this cosmological reorientation of the planet to her birth year produced in her an awful, restless malaise that she never stopped talking about. I assumed she'd stay in the city, like everyone else does when they hit New York's occasional social turbulence, but Simon disagreed. "No, I think she's serious now."

We were each serious in our own crisis. Julia, who wanted to leave the city, couldn't find any way to get out, and so her complaints had become increasingly circuitous: too broke to cling to her pricey apartment, too broke to leave. I understood—and was likewise caught in the financial slipstream of New York—but I refused to give in just yet: I would not go, no matter how hard it had become to cobble together freelance and art-writing gigs. Zachary had resolved his crisis of ambition—what to do, when to do it—through the distraction of nightlife. It had left him spinning and narrowly focused on himself, his only subject, and on his plans for the night, the only thing he ever bothered to talk about anymore, the "literal spiral" of Friday, Saturday, Sunday, with an occasional break on Monday, then some regular party on Tuesday, possible break on Wednesday, then out again on Thursday until Sunday morning, when he'd finally make his way into his (or someone else's) bed. Simon, whose crisis was us, focused and refocused his efforts on these friendships, but I had become tired of the distended, regressive conversation about aimless ambition, the tweaked logic of finding oneself trapped when one wasn't. Julia would do something, I was certain of it, because she was smart; it was only her attention that seemed misplaced, distracted by her deep insecurity about her writing. Whenever we spoke I told her to just sit down and do it, just *write*, and not to be too concerned with its final shape until she had something to work with. She'd shake her head you're right. Zachary, on the other hand, was a more hopeless case, and this had made him into an encompassing recuperative project for Simon. Zachary could be saved from himself, Simon insisted. I wasn't so sure.

"I just don't know about Zachary. Like what to do," Simon said. Zachary sometimes threatened to leave too, this time for his parent's place in New Hampshire, and then possibly Chicago, where he had friends. I didn't know either.

I nodded along as he spoke about them, idly tracing the flower-and-vine illustrations that decorated the menu with my finger. I shouldn't have called him: I didn't want to be brought back to our New York life quite yet, but here he was, retelling stories I'd heard many versions of before. Simon himself was in a paralysis. Luckily he received a weekly allowance from his parents in addition to his intermittent styling gigs, and could afford to spend time negotiating with Zachary to drop this or that bad habit or shitty boyfriend. You shouldn't go out for, what, the fifth night in a row. You're wearing yourself out. I can't lend you money. What did you do with the money I gave you last week?

"Yeah," I said a few times into the phone. "I agree. You should. Yes. For sure."

The waitress set the tuna sandwich in front of me as Simon was telling me about what he had planned for the evening (a warehouse party in Bushwick with a friend from out of town and Zachary). "Sounds fun," I said. "But I should go. My food's here."

"Oh OK. Bye," a pause, "miss you."

"Miss you, too."

The sandwich, a soggy heap of tuna on white bread, frowned on its white porcelain plate. I took a bite then set it down. I opened my notebook to the first few long-form notes I'd made about the Tom of Finland Foundation, from which I anticipated extrapolating a larger argument about this specifically Californian notion of community; not only cults, religious sects, and the like, but how the landscape—and, in particular, the way in which the landscape is described—makes it uniquely suitable for outsider communities. How, for example, the use of Spanish to describe geological and ecological phenomena differed from the English, which does not have the words—and therefore the concepts—to describe such a place. An *arroyo*, for example. This I had cribbed from Mike Davis. I wanted to make wide use of as many references as I could assemble. Place names: history of the Salton Sea, from resort to dead land; history of irrigation, the Los Angeles River. Scenes from films: all the warning signs, for example, in Gregg Araki's *Doom Generation* ("Shoplifters will be executed," "Prepare for the apocalypse"). The views of the LA skyline from Sarah Conner's hospital ward in *Terminator 2*.

I wrote at the top of the page: "How to fit these into a narrative about place, and the representation of place by the people who inhabit it? Why write about this?" This being the communal ethos that had shaped Los Angeles and San Francisco, from Krotona to Hollywood, Satanism to Scientology. In art about Los Angeles, and California in general, the city and state play an outsized role, even in absentia, as in *The Doom Generation*, where LA is never seen (except at night) and yet the film remains "so LA." What is that *so*. I felt it everywhere.

This was difficult writing. The itemized list of places that I had wanted to visit or research while I was in Los Angeles—Point Loma, Krotona, Tom of Finland Foundation, Agape Lodge, Brand Bookshop—ceased to mean anything to me the longer I stared at them, the longer I tried to understand the narrative they fit into. This, of course, was not how to approach writing about California; it would lead me nowhere.

Where in California is California. And what was its weather?

I had written down a list of places, groups, cults that I had researched before I came to Los Angeles: Annie Besant, the Mighty I AM, the OTO, Theosophy, which had led me down a still-stranger path into the origins of that movement, including one of its best-known advocates, Eliphas Levi—the French occultist who believed in "transcendental magic," Jewish mysticism, and who had pioneered astral travel in the early to mid-nineteenth century, something I had never heard of until my visit to Helen's, when she mentioned it to me in passing. Levi never visited California but the meditation he practiced belonged in the long list of spiritual practices that had shaped the kooky religious sects that had gone west to group suicide in Nike tracksuits and build their desert compounds.

"Have you ever heard of astral projection?" Helen had asked me, apropos of nothing, when we were talking by the bonfire a few months ago, her residents circling with kindling while the visitors, including Simon, picked at marshmallows.

"No, what is that?"

She stared ahead, her hands resting on her hips. "It's a form of meditation. You go deep inside yourself and, ultimately, leave your body to travel—really travel, apparently—to other planets, other times. We had a group of them here a few weeks ago," she said, adding that her project sometimes hosted visitors for a night or two.

"I've never done it."

"Nor have I," she said flatly. "But they sat out here, actually around this pit, for hours and hours with their eyes closed, sometimes shaking, muttering to themselves. It was the strangest thing, but now I can't shake the image of them every time I'm out here. Just about ten of them, all in a circle."

"You didn't try it?"

"No, it doesn't work that way. They sat there for about fifteen or so hours until slowly, one by one, they woke up. One woman though, she was sitting there," she pointed to the log where Jeff stood talking with another boy from the project, "she was a little slow to rouse, and when they tried to wake her she shook like she was having a seizure, real violently. And then she started screaming at the top of her lungs, apparently because she couldn't get back to her body. This kind of thing happens where they get stuck on some planet or whatever. All of them kept trying to get her up, but she was convulsing, yelling, and so we all ran down from the house to help. I brought a bucket of cold water and threw it on her and that worked. She sat up, breathing heavily. Couldn't stop shaking, but she was all right."

"Jesus," I said.

"It was something to see. I asked the woman who led the session, an old friend of mine from Marin County, if she was OK and she was, of course. All she said was, 'There's always a screamer.'"

I looked at Helen. She didn't take her eyes off the fire as she spoke, absorbed by the work her residents were doing around her. Later, I wrote down "astral travel" in my notebook to look up when I had my computer again.

"I wanted to know where she went," Helen said, "where she 'projected' herself, but she wouldn't say."

I wrote down a few observations about the Madonna Inn—the smell of the dining room, different names for the color of the décor (light pink, orchid, Pepto-Bismol, pigskin) in my notebook, then closed it, finished the sandwich, and slid the plate away.

Margaret, the waitress, brought the bill: "Whenever you're ready." I pulled out my wallet and handed her my credit card. Since I still had an hour until I could get into my room, I decided to skip a tour of the grounds—I'd seen enough already—and to go into town instead, where Google suggested a new age shop for those interested in meditation and the future.

I, Rocco Ciccone, the eldest son of Madonna Louise Ciccone, squatted naked in the middle of the Rock Bottom, surrounded by an alternating circle of black and white candles with one very expensive crystal at its center that I'd purchased from a new age shop near Chinatown, my laptop open before me to the Wikipedia entry on astral projection. I was certain I wouldn't be able to achieve this kind of travel but the remote possibility of something, anything happening felt, at the Madonna Inn, strangely plausible. It was ridiculous but I had become ridiculous and why not.

Rob, the new ageist who sold me these meditative instruments, was a thin, lemon-scented man with a mop of gray hair he kept in a ratty ponytail, what had once probably been dreadlocks or some attempt at dreadlocks, and he twinkled peevishly when I asked him if it were possible to communicate with worlds outside this one using these very crystals. Dude totally. I held up one that I'd picked at random off the shelf. It was about the size and shape of a large dildo. "Is that what you're looking to do?" he asked. It isn't that I necessarily thought I could, or would, communicate with the stars, only that meditation might allow me to project myself elsewhere, might release me—if briefly—from my increasingly limited thinking in writing. So for Rob's purposes I said, sure, I wanted to speak to the stars. Yes, this one. He nodded and said that that one was suitable for the transference of various energies between its user and the world, this one or another. He'd done it himself, plenty of times, was, you could say, "conversant" with the spheres. "Rocco, man, you could reach the end of the universe if you want," Rob said. "Who you trying to talk to?"

"I don't know. I've just had a feeling, is all."

Rob had used crystals for just about everything, even the treatment of a tumor on his right ankle. He said he knew exactly the kind of rocks I would need. While he collected the appropriate quartzes from the display shelves, he told me about life on other planets. "I've been reading about this system, Kepler-186, you know it? Heard they discovered life there, or they think they heard signals from the stars in Kepler, a message, something like that."

"Wow," I said. "Yeah, I don't know anything about it."

"You gotta read up on this, seriously. Kepler-186. Write it down." I didn't move, unsure of whether Rob actually wanted me to make a note of the address for these aliens. "No seriously. Write this down. You got paper?"

"I have my phone." I opened up the notes app on the screen's main page, beginning a new one—"How do you spell that?" "K-E-P," he paused to think, "L-E-R-1-8-6"—and I added, "Alien life found there." "Thanks so much for this," I said.

"How much for, like, six crystals?" I asked. "You think that would be enough?"

"That'd be plenty, man, but those will be about $120 a pop."

I set down the one I was holding. "Oh, wow," I said, "well, do you have anything cheaper, maybe just one?"

Hmm, let me check.

I left Rob's with one $40 crystal and some sage, incense, and about six small candles. I wasn't sure I could even light them at the Rock Bottom, but Rob insisted that it would improve the chances that the crystal I could afford would lull me into a deeper meditation since incense has a calming effect on the nerves.

"You let me know if you have any luck," Rob said, waving me off.

In the Rock Bottom, I smoked a joint, the last of the weed I'd picked up from a dealer at Akbar after I dropped Simon off at LAX, and sat in the dark to maximize the effect of the high and, hopefully, my meditation, even though I still hadn't taken very seriously—or at least I didn't anticipate—intergalactic travel without practice (astral projection requiring years of it, apparently). I closed my eyes, began a series of breathing exercises that I'd invented for myself, tried to concentrate on some internal vista of total blankness, the slate wiped clean of any thinking, but could not, in my high, clear my head of the droopy, sluggish feeling that anchored my body to the floor and the proliferating thoughts that accompanied this rather heady weed.

They flickered through my mind like a broken slideshow, first general shots of New York's skyline, then the pristine and beautiful faces of Simon and Julia, perfected in memory, followed by views of my old apartment, the look of the juniper plant that Simon kept on his windowsill, a man I hooked up with, no, sucked off, after we met in the Union Square Barnes & Noble bathroom, the face of Janis Joplin, driving up the Taconic Parkway, New York Harbor in rain. Childhood followed suit in clipped flashes of an adolescent world: my sister, running into a prickly berry bush that scraped her face, the lines of blood that marked her cheeks when she extracted herself from its nest of thorns, my mother and father standing in the yard with a new puppy they presented to us one Christmas, boys and girls I had known, the time I pulled out my penis for one boy slightly older than me, his curious delight as he massaged its tip until I ejaculated for the first time, the shudder after that first orgasm, which subsequently produced an elated but otherwise unknown pleasure that trailed off into a cold fear that I'd committed some crime against a nature I'd never really understood but was crucially contained within, a circle I'd been crossed out of, into a self-exile that would mark me an outcast.

Not *that*. My breathing quickened. I opened my eyes: my meditation had reversed from calm to an anxious excitement, a thinky, almost overwhelming drumbeat of thoughts I wanted to shake. I was dizzied. So this would require practice, and probably sobriety.

I stood up and brought my computer over to the desk near the bed to distract myself with my email, Facebook, Twitter. I felt as far from New York as possible, the endless scroll of updates and notifications about this or that event, a photo Simon posted to Instagram of himself at dinner with the friend I didn't know, a boy who was his type. They felt as distant as whatever was in Kepler-186, beaming incoherently to us. I wasn't sure if I believed in the possibility of alien visitations, but I accepted the mathematical certainty of extraterrestrial life, so it followed, sort of, that one *might* be able to communicate with them if the conditions were right. Likewise, it seemed that that communication would take an organic, rather than mechanical form, since our communications technologies would likely be incompatible with theirs. This was my line of thinking about five long hits into the joint. Wetware—the word was wonderful—that is, our bodies, might offer a real chance to say hi. I scrolled on, grew bored of the feed with its unending offering of selfies and baby animals, and searched ufo-hunters.com for their list of recent sightings in the area around Los Angeles, found none that interested me until I came across a few pages of a message board about San Luis Obispo. One: Thursday, June 13, 2013—only a year or so ago.

"A patterned flying object hovers until I completely pass by," the person who reported the sighting to the National Unidentified Flying Object Reporting Center wrote. "I was driving with my parents on the highway 101, when my eye caught sight of a huge saucer about 50 ft long, backing into the clouds. I could see a pattern of curved lines. After about 10 sec it was gone. The lines had a pattern similar to some sort of ancient vase."

What vase? Curvy, horizontal or vertical lines, like in ancient Greek vases I remembered from studying art history in college? I started to Google. (I could recall very little about the history of vases, Greek or otherwise, so I wasn't even sure where to begin.) Was it a language, one that described the craft's origins? I wished the author of the post had made a drawing of what he had seen. I continued to Google different vases, but there were so many types to choose from, it could have been any pattern. My sense of how to search the web for anything art-historical was also crude, so many of my search terms and combinations—"vase lines," "Greek markings," "ancient vases," "famous ancient vases"—offered no visual information that might give me a sense of these markings.

I typed San Luis Obispo in Project Blue Book's website and read pages NARA-PBB1-128, 158, 160, 395, 598, 386, 429, and 450:

DATE	LOCATION	OBSERVER	EVALUATION
June 5, 1955	San Luis Obispo	Redacted	Insufficient data
December 2, 1956	San Luis Obispo	Newsclipping	
November 1, 1957	San Luis Obispo	Redacted	Aircraft
August 2, 1966	San Luis Obispo	Multiple	Aircraft
August 28, 1966	San Luis Obispo	Lampman/ Drake	Balloon
July 7, 1967	San Luis Obispo	Redacted (Photos)	Sighting: Insufficient Photos: Insufficient
April 8, 1968	San Luis Obispo	Redacted	Aircraft

July 7, 1967, Blue Book Case #11864: a photograph of a silver disc, tilted slightly over a rocky hill beside a deep, black blotch of what must have been palms or some trees in the middle distance, a sliver of cloud in the far-right corner, just at the landscape's horizon.

I took another long hit of the joint. The hot air threw me into a coughing fit. When I recovered, my heart rate picked up—why was I looking up UFO sightings? In San Luis Obispo? For what? To write? I stared at myself in the large mirror that back-ended the desk, my face lit in a faint blue by my computer screen. I practiced breathing again, allowing the exercise to steady me. I shuddered with renewed calm. I went back to the mat with the candles still lit in a circle around it, held my lighter to sage and wafted it over the crystal in the center of the meditation ring. This was not me, but some approximate version of myself, sitting at the Madonna Inn, doing something I wouldn't normally do, and so, in the room, I entered the third person, and viewed myself from above.

What did you do, Rocco?

Squatted in the dark of the room, stared into the candles, picked up the rose quartz nearest me, brought it to my lips, kissed it, what else does one do, spoke into its pointed tip, *hi*. The room did not seem, at first sight, like the place where one would convene with aliens on some crystal-communicator, but why not—and where else? I knew I wasn't going to make first contact in a novelty hotel room in California or anywhere, for that matter, but, high as I was, I let my disbelief slough off, as many others had before me, and again considered the possibility: of contact, astral travel, whatever. Floor to ceiling in stone, with cow-skin sofas and a leopard-print king-size bed, it made no visual sense, either as a rustic getaway or as a fancy, if eccentric, hotel room. Instead, it more closely resembled some mindless, unchanging diorama at Disneyland, one that a viewer might pass in a plastic boat while traveling by underwater track through a piratical exhibit of mid-century fantasies of another, ahistorical time. Despite its impracticality as a space for communion with the stars (the few windows, mostly stained glass, offered no direct view to the night sky), I appreciated this chintzy man-cave for its otherworldly privacy, like I was alone in a theme park after hours.

Hi, I thought again, into the cloudy pink stone I held in my hand. Not so much an actual, audible *hi*, but the idea of *hi*, the idea of the friendliest, most welcoming *hi* I could muster in my head and likewise could concentrate into a signal that could be projected from the center of my forehead to the general vicinity of Kepler-186, wherever that was, I wasn't quite sure and relied instead on my gut. My eyes closed, I willed myself again into mental blankness, this time with some success: I slackened, and eased into calm. At this, a great lightness lifted in me, like butterflies in the stomach, though these butterflies were more like moths, night creatures nibbling at me from within, and while I continued to squat on the mat I felt a dizzying nervousness at the thought that this might work, might bring me into contact—or at least a closeness—with beings from space.

What I didn't know was whether I should remain concentrated on Kepler-186, as Rob had suggested, or if this kind of projection, like the one Helen described and some Theosophists had apparently believed in, required that one lose sight of some object or place and rather remain passive, allow the mind to take the traveler where it wanted to go. I was mixed up in my aims. Neither felt like they would work, so instead I tried to mix astral projection with Rob's crystals, pictured the communicating planet in the Kepler system as a verdant orb with two moons, suspended in the vacuum of space near a small sun, and overlaid this image onto the hotel room that would grow weaker as the orb grew stronger, essentially teleporting me to that world, projecting me closer and closer, into its hive-like cities, where small, deer-sized creatures stood upon various cliffs, watching me. To their faces, haloed in mauve light, with six small, black eyes set equidistant on their triangular faces, *hi*. Surprisingly, this exercise in the imagination set me at ease (the weed certainly helped), even energized me a little, and I felt prepared for it, for the *hi* in return. In my head, these vivid deer creatures stared intensely at me—or so I imagined: their eyes meeting mine. And *hi*.

The door slammed. I fell out of my trance, out of the ridiculous image of hooved aliens I'd dreamt up, and onto the carpet. I opened my eyes to the bright lights of the room. The manager, or someone acting as the manager, had flipped on before rushing over to see if I was OK. "Sir," this person repeated. "Are you OK?" I blinked. "You've been out, or just sitting here … And I'm not sure …"

Before the sight of me lying naked on a mat, surrounded by candles and a crystal in the Rock Bottom, he seemed stunned, more stunned than I was, and unsure of what he was looking at except that, whatever it was I was doing, hotel policy forbade it. Or I assumed hotel policy forbade it. "You can't have candles in your room. We received a complaint about a burning smell ..."

I looked up at him. He turned his head in deference to my nudity and handed me a towel he'd retrieved from the bathroom. "I am very sorry, I didn't ..." I stammered out but he raised his hand:

"Look, I don't know what you're up to here, but our policy is clear about candles or fires in your room ... and if you violate it ..."

"Like I said, I'm so sorry. I didn't mean ..." I tried to act as bewildered by the situation as he was. In fact, all that preparation for first contact left me thinking that perhaps it was he whom I was supposed to meet. He stood there, nervous and fidgety. I wondered if I should lie about what I was doing, tell him I was conducting a private religious service. Which? "I was just, I don't know, having a moment. I shouldn't have. I'm really sorry about all this. I don't want to be a problem."

The manager stared at me without saying a word; his soft and sympathetic eyes took in the scene as he processed this odd clutter of candles and incense at the Rock Bottom. The crystal cock lay provocatively beside my thigh. Naked and sprawled out on the floor, I must have seemed crazy. He asked me if I was OK and if I intended to do myself any harm. No, I said. He asked me if I would please *really* stop and I said yes. This probably wasn't the strangest thing he'd seen at the Madonna Inn, I imagined, but it clearly made him uneasy to see a guest ... performing ... a ritual of this kind in the hotel. It was close to the strangest thing I had done. "Good," he said, putting his hands in his pockets nervously. "Not another candle. If you need to light a candle, you can talk to the woman at the front desk and she can show you to a small chapel we make available to guests."

I nodded. "Not another. Thank you."

Headed back to LA, I rolled down the windows to let the big whooping air of the California coast fill the rental. The radio was tuned to the news, but I could barely hear what the monotonous commentator was saying about basketball, the mid-term elections, the other problems that seemed to persist outside the world of Rocco Ciccone over the wind. Names, place names, movements, scores, hostilities, reconciliation. When I woke that morning, I was shaken, and my mind wasn't quite right; it spun in my head like a top, detached from the rest of my body, a whir of mixed-up think-ing. I couldn't shake the feeling after I left. Perhaps it was the weed. Brainless, my body did what it did best: steered me back to LA, toward the Highland Gardens, where I would stay one last night.

The woman at the front desk of the Madonna had given me a deeply suspicious look when I checked out of the room. Someone, probably the manager who'd interrupted me in the middle of the night and broken my connection, a connection that I found I could not make again later after he left, must have let slip that I had been up to mischief in my room. With the crystal and incense in my backpack, I'd paid and walked away with a smile that I hoped would disarm her, though her opinion of me didn't matter, thanks for the lovely stay, it's a wonderful hotel. Should I tell her that the world was not the same anymore after I'd spent a night at the Madonna Inn, that I might have found California or some version of it? Was that true, had it changed? I thought better of it. The world seldom changes.

14

In his audition for *Saturday Night Live*, the comedian Andy Kaufman improvised a rendition of "MacArthur Park." The lyrics came to him as he sang for the camera, glazed-over while he twittered out his own Donna Summer, disco being both a ridiculous thing to him (and so a thing worthy of his attention) and a peculiar access point for Kaufman's peculiar comedy. Andy gets it:

> S-s-s-spring was never waiting for us, girl,
> It ran one step ahead as we followed in the dance,
> Between the parted pages and repressed in love's hot
> fevered iron like a striped—stripéd—pair of pants,
> MacArthur's Park is melting in the dark,
> All the sweet cream icing flowing down—
> Someone left the cake out in the rain,
> I don't think that I can take it
> 'Cause it took so long to bake it
> And I'll never have that recipe again ...

PART THREE

15

In a fit of anger in mid-August, Zachary, who was leaning increasingly on his drug dealers to get out of bed at night after having spent the whole day asleep and hungover, decided he would no longer speak to Simon, Julia, and me. He resented Simon for our relationship. I felt this attitude was unworthy of a response on my part.

"It's really weird of you to let this get between us, between you and your friends," Simon yelled at him. It had seemed that their friendship was devolving into a forced cordiality and, for Zachary at least, this was largely my fault. They were in Simon's kitchen while I sat on his bed on the other side of his closed bedroom door. It was thin so I could still hear them even when they dropped to a whisper, regardless of how quiet they tried to be at points in their argument. Zachary lowered his voice to say, "But he's such a jerk." I was him.

"He isn't a jerk. You just don't like him, and you never gave him a chance."

I thought about getting up to defend myself to Zachary, but I decided to concentrate on the book I was reading instead, a collection of poems by Eileen Myles called *School of Fish* that I'd bought at the Strand. Reading her poetry with Simon and Zachary's voices in the background my eyes glazed at the words, though scraps of lines from "Twilight Train" flashed in my head as I scanned the page:

... To count
them one by one
as the wires slip
by. It's the sultriness,
the smokey approach
of the loss of
light that I love. The
homosexual lilac
comes & it's ours
& everyone like us. The
bright compartment
of white lights &
gleaming flip top &
yawns rage
on ...

I underlined "homosexual lilac." "Listen to me, Zachary. Listennnnnnnn."

      ... A clear
      swipe to night. Everyone
      in my compartment
      is tearing now ...

"No, no, you need to listen to me. The problem is you never listen to me. That's your problem. You don't listen, Simon."
    "That isn't true—and it isn't fair to say ..."
    "It is fair. It's ..."

      ... & boats are sitting
      on purple sand
      the mountains

are bland & blue
a woman's sigh …

"No, see …"

… I think "time."
Then "cargo."

Cargo time: packed away in Simon's room, their voices rose and fell as Zachary tried to shape his anger into a knife he might use to finally dispatch Simon. It was true that he had never given me much of a chance since the night we had met, at the Spectrum, and I had gone home with Simon. The three of us had never discussed what had happened between us because Simon mostly deflected my questions about his past with Zachary as not relevant to now, the "now" of our "thing," though he later admitted that he had slept with Zachary out of boredom a few times before we met, and only when they were "totally wasted" and no one else was around for him to choose. In any case, he regretted it, of course. Well that sounds smart, I told him. And Zachary doesn't mind? "Not at all," Simon said. I thought there was more to them, but Simon waved this off as my own jealousy.

"I did give him a chance, Simon," Zachary yelled back.

"You're being so dramatic. And stupid: you're turning this into something it doesn't have to be. I don't even know what it is that you're so mad about, what I'm defending here. What do you want me to say to you? Like what can I even say?"

"I just don't know if we can … hang out. I just don't know."

In the approach to fall after we returned from Los Angeles, planning for weekend trips upstate and for Labor Day—still a few weeks off—had produced unspoken but obvious tensions among

Simon, Zachary, and Julia, as each of them struggled to finalize their respective schedules for the holiday, which had never seemed to me to be a very important one but had, in the long run-up to Zachary's unfocused rage, become a flashpoint for the three of them. Labor Day was no longer the reason for a three-day weekend at the beach, but a last stand in their axial friendship that would decide whether or not their bond would hold. For his part, Simon wanted to stay in New York, with me, but I had already decided to fly down to my parents' place in North Carolina since my grandmother had become ill. Considering my absence, Julia suggested that the three of them go upstate to Simon's, but Zachary said he wouldn't go, for whatever reason, and that upstate was "stupid." This offended Simon, of course, and he complained to me about it often in the two weeks after the "stupid comment," as it became known between us, though he refused to engage Zachary in any argument about the "stupid comment" because he felt it would get him nowhere (true) and that it was too soon to care about this long weekend anyway (true, though their threesome's obsession with it suggested otherwise).

Seeing that Simon had no intention to fight back against Zachary's petulance, Zachary decided to take a more direct approach in his confrontation with his former best friend and past lover and showed up to Simon's apartment unannounced, ready for a long fight with a pre-determined conclusion. In the middle of their argument in the kitchen Zachary played his final card and announced that he was going back home to New Hampshire, and that he wouldn't come back, he was over New York.

Aren't we all.

"What?" Simon said.

They exchanged a few more accusations that the other didn't listen enough, Simon didn't love Zachary, Zachary didn't care about Simon's interests anymore, Simon was too focused on me, Zachary was too focused on himself. Perhaps they did love each other, and perhaps I was this sticking point between them that prevented them from being friends or more. And perhaps we weren't, as Julia had once told me drunkenly over dinner, "very good for each other." I asked her why, though I knew why, or I understood that our frequent public fights laid bare so many fissures in our love for one another that it was obvious to anyone who found him or herself an observer of our screaming matches that we were not always good for one another. In truth, I had thought these were mostly private but Julia snorted at the suggestion. "Are you kidding me?"

We skidded between emotional disasters in public, blatantly mean and careless with one another's emotions. But that was not why she thought we needed to split: "You're the way Simon avoids having to think about Zachary," whom he knows, she said, he could never date and yet finds himself attracted to …

So I had found myself with no good choices, is all, I snapped back. She didn't mean to hurt my feelings, she explained, and I understood that. Then she quoted a line she'd read in Christopher Isherwood: "He who travels alone travels further." I thought this was in bad taste, to throw a handy line from an author I was reading at the time back in my face. Auden had praised Isherwood for the weather of his characters' lives. Our lives were stormy, unpleasant. More wine.

"What do you mean you're going to New Hampshire?" He was incredulous, as though Zachary were moving to India and not a few states over.

Zachary left the apartment in a rage, probably crying, sobbing even. Simon followed him out, slamming the door behind him, but returned within a few minutes, apparently unable to chase him down.

"…"

"I know he's a jerk," Simon said to me, closing the door behind him, "and I know he hasn't made any effort with you, but I wish you could be nicer." He was sweating and red-faced, and probably had been crying too.

I got up to hug him but he didn't want to be touched. "I am nice to Zachary," I said. "We hang out all the time."

"That isn't really true."

By September, Zachary did keep his promise—perhaps for the first time—and left for his parents' place. Julia shrugged her shoulders when he emailed her a rather curt goodbye, the only person to whom he offered any sort of farewell. He would be back seeking forgiveness in no time, Julia told Simon, who had fallen into a low-grade but persistent depression at the thought that he had lost his best friend. I agreed with her. It wasn't worth going out to see him in Portsmouth, where his parents lived, as Simon had wanted to do, and he needed to give Zachary time. Later, this became evidence to Simon that I had in fact acted as a saboteur in their friendship.

When that charge arose, I told him, "Do what you want then." This only made him angrier with me. Zachary was right, he argued back.

"Yeah, he's right."

By early November, I was annoyed at Simon's continued worry over Zachary, and moreover at what I felt was the unspoken blame he placed on me for Zachary's coke-fueled departure for Portsmouth, where he made himself thoroughly unreachable. He deactivated his social media accounts and refused to answer the phone. Simon raged. Things, the things that had bound us together, sex, friendships, boredom, seemed to be moving against us, like we were standing on a floe that had begun to heave and split under us, leaving us apart and adrift on separate but doomed islands of ice.

We were convoluted in our time together, unclear about what we wanted from one another and from ourselves in the late autumnal fog that prefigured winter and had wrapped around New York. It was especially cold, even for fall. On one particularly clear evening before Thanksgiving, I went over to Simon's and sat him down on his bed. "Look," I started, but he understood what I was going to say and had already decided upon the same thing himself. "I think we should take some time off."

"I agree," he said. He put his hand on my knee. "I really love you but I think I need to be alone."

"Yes."

Then Simon met another boy, Frederic, in late February of the following year, an Austrian DJ who went back to Vienna in early March. And Simon, whose French citizenship permitted him the right to live anywhere on the continent, went with him, out of New York.

16

New York, suspended in the crystal of a snowstorm: through the flurried white, the stoplights flashed across the snow- and freezing rain-stricken windshield as I cabbed up Lorimer Street, a forbidding red, the red of any season, but in a snowy March, a glowering red like an eye, or a chain of eyes strung over the street, wobbling at the blurred limits of the wintery mix. We waited. At green, the car lurched forward, sliding another six blocks. I paid the driver when he let me off at the curb a block short of Metropolitan Bar, and exited into the foul weather.

My friend Stewart, who had invited me out that evening, stood smoking a cigarette near the bar's entrance. He nodded at me: "Hey." Born to two Korean immigrants in Northern California, he was handsome, if somewhat aloof, with a gray and black mop of dreads that framed his sharp features. When we'd met at a party in Bushwick a year ago, he had intimidated me with his default indifference to strangers, but later I found that he was quite warm and funny, with a tumbling, phrase-y humor based on wry observation for peculiar detail (about someone we knew: "He's a fifty-year-old radical fairy hen that lives in this squalid apartment on University Place with all his fairy minions"; a doctor we both happen to see was "a grasshopper"; someone he sat next to at a movie theater: "He was picking his nose, picking and licking, your typical basic nerd-hipster who likes to clear his nose all the time and lick his fingers in a very involved way"; it went on). If you recalled a story that didn't follow his wordy lead, or didn't start with how someone was dressed, their tone, whether they reminded you of something or someone we knew, what else had gone right or wrong that day (for you, for them, whoever), he'd grow impatient and interrupt: "You're telling me nothing." It became easy to lose yourself in these interruptions. Let me start again.

"You're looking good," he said.

"Thanks. You, too," I said, and bummed a cigarette off him.

Stewart makes photographs and sculptures. I first became aware of his work when he began to show *No Sex No City*, a series of junk-stuffed mannequins, each impaled upon an industrial pole that juts from the floor or wall that he styles after women of the HBO show *Sex and the City*. I reviewed them for a magazine. Stewart burns each of the girls, shreds their clothes, and mangles their jewelry until they obtain the diminished look of the undead survivors of some stormy end-days: Carrie, Samantha, Charlotte, Miranda, horse-women of a galloping apocalypse. Or something like that. He threads their charred bodies with phone chargers, costume jewelry, and barbed wire. They first showed at a small gallery on Canal Street, and then at the Whitney in a dual presentation with the painter Jana Euler called *Outside Inside Sensibility*.

Earlier in the year he'd been invited to do his first show in Germany, where he exhibited window grills with knobby joints of synthetic flesh and colored hair, creaturely security devices that lay prostrate on the gallery floor or were drilled into the wall. Alongside those he showed photographs he took of various artists and performers in a wintery future, posed in the snow with strange guns or against shadowy warehouses. The mood of these works is hard to read. Funny, but darkly serious, they don't quite seem to belong to "the" future so much as "a" future, the possibility of another timeline whipped out of some alternate present. The photographer Wolfgang

Tillmans liked the show and befriended Stewart after his debut in Germany. He told Stewart he wanted to hang out the next time he was in New York. Earlier this afternoon Stewart had texted me: "Want to meet at Metro then go to Spectrum? Wolfgang is in town."

In the moody pink light Stewart and I found Wolfgang—tall, with a teddy bear's face and a slightly crooked mouth that made him somehow more handsome than he would have been other-wise—near the pool table at the musty end of the front of Metropolitan. He was famous enough for some of the men at the bar to recognize him (or at least to make curious, lazily knowing eyes in our direction when we joined him), including a short, burly professor of art history at Princeton, who couldn't believe his luck when he sidled up to see if Wolfgang was Wolfgang.

They were talking when I walked up with my tequila soda. Wolfgang and I had never met before but the professor completely occupied him. "It's nice to meet you," Wolfgang said to the profes-sor, who had just unspooled a long justification for why he'd come over to say hi. The professor rubbed his bald, shapely head, an inscrutable smile forming under his thick black mustache. Wolfgang, for his part, seemed unsure of what to do. Or he knew exactly what to do, and appearing to not know how to address the situation was a pretense to avoid sliding further into the tedium of a conversation with a stranger whose everything—the whole force of his being anywhere at all and talking to anyone, especially an art-ist like Wolfgang, whom he'd probably never expected to meet—seemed to be anchored by the fact that he was a tenured professor at an Ivy League university. Why this mattered I wasn't sure but it must have carried some special valence among the twinks he caroused with at Metropolitan (which at the moment was over-whelmed by a strong gassy smell of unknown origin), probably because his position could be plotted somewhere on the power–money axis in the charitable vision of drunk boys, professors being these figures vaguely redolent of sexual (read: worldly) authority, and probably because daddy intelligence has a real sway with a certain kind of twenty-three-year-old badly missing his rowdier college years. He pressed us into the corner, chatty with approbation for all these things, exhibitions, photographs, whatever. He talked into Wolfgang like he was a live microphone, while Stewart and I stood quietly, waiting to see how it'd play out. He ignored us. In the end what he wanted was for Wolfgang to visit his class.

"I'm just over at the Princeton. That's in New Jersey," he offered, now for the second time, letting the Garden State's name hang in the air. Wolfgang knew where Princeton was. We stood in the corner of the bar behind the pool table, where butch, indifferent fags struck balls back and forth in feigned indifference to the soup of hormones that pooled around them. Guys, skinnier, less macho, looked on in restrained longing, almost blue-faced with this boozy desire. Stewart rolled his eyes for my benefit.

Wolfgang smiled and excused himself: "I'm only here for a few days. I'm not sure I could," then pivoted back to us. Stewart introduced me and Wolfgang's expression immediately changed, happy that I'd arrived and we could make our way down to the Spectrum rather than stay longer at Metropolitan.

"Should we go?" he asked. It was twelve forty-five, still early for the Spectrum, but if we walked (the snow seemed to have let up somewhat) it'd put us there just after one a.m.—an OK, if not ideal, time to show up.

The professor said maybe he'd see us later.

"Sure, let's go," Stewart said.

We wound down through South Williamsburg, toward Broadway, while the flurry dwindled to a light, speckled dusting that clung to our hair and coats. Wolfgang explained that he had come to town to do a site visit at a gallery in Chelsea, his first exhibition with them. I was quiet while Stewart and he talked. I wasn't sure what to say exactly, since I couldn't imagine that I'd have anything interesting to offer to the conversation. I had begun to write much more frequently, and with better pay, for more and more art magazines, but to mention that—that I "write about art" and am "working on a book," one that was possibly "about the weather"—seemed painfully unrelated to what Wolfgang wanted to talk about, which was anything unrelated to anyone's career, really. He asked me if I had any shows that I would recommend when Stewart explained that I wrote reviews. "Go see Greer Lankton," I said. A small retrospective exhibition had just recently opened at Participant on Houston. "Right," he said. "Of course."

In the on-and-off-again snowstorm, Brooklyn hung on its icy air, and except for a few cabs that scudded along the side streets, the borough was shuttered and unusually quiet for a Saturday night. You could never tell if the Spectrum would be busy or not on winter nights, though often the evenings (or early mornings) when nobody showed up were the best since this allowed you to seize most of the space that would otherwise be devoted to some overwhelming, pushy crowd. Wolfgang was curious whether the Spectrum had changed since Gage had expanded the backroom. "It's so much better. All the boogery tweens from NYU stay in the front now," Stewart said. I agreed. Wolfgang laughed.

A small group stood outside the Spectrum waiting to get in. They were in a ruckus in their drunken, unfurling winter spirit, and even though I didn't know them, they all waved to us when we walked up to the entrance, probably excited that the club wouldn't be empty that night after all, despite the weather. "Hey, Stewart!" one girl said. They hugged while Wolfgang and I stood quietly by their side. We were early, but a line had already formed inside the house and we would have to wait to get in. The bouncer, a woman who sometimes covered for the club when the police showed up by explaining away the noise as her own stereo system, told us we needed to wait around the block a few minutes while the line inside cleared up.

"Come back in five."

We circled the block of housing projects across the street twice, Wolfgang said I wonder if we'll see the professor, we laughed at this, and I thought what if he does come and what would his portrait by Wolfgang look like since, in my opinion, that's what the professor was gaming for all along, it was what everyone wanted from Wolfgang, but I didn't ask Wolfgang if he'd ever take his photo (or how Wolfgang decided whose photo to take), returned, and went into the Spectrum just as the snow started to pick up once more, queued near the stairwell while Stephen, a poet who sometimes doubled as the bartender, let us in for free with a small X he marked on our wrists with a sharpie.

The hallway from the entrance to the dance floor bridged waking life to the dream world of sweat and smoke—what together formed a "wallet of feeling" (that's from Eileen's "Twilight Train") that infused the room with ludicrous energy, the libidinal slide of sweat-slick limbs against limbs—that jostled together up against the mirrored walls, still smudged, forever smudged with the paw marks of hands that had been pressed, repeatedly, against the glass. Winter sloughed off. I'd come here hundreds of times, and it somehow never got old to me: the same beers and cheap liquor, the same DJs, the same friends. We crossed the main dance floor—already in full tilt in its dank citadel of body heat—and made our way to the noisy backroom. Opposite the bar a row of couches lined the wall near the new, functional bathrooms, a welcome change from the earlier days, when to shit was to depart for the evening.

A big group occupied a silver couch in the corner. Some were taking selfies in a mirror leaned against the wall next to them. They couldn't look away from themselves. We were in a glassy, self-reflective age, overstuffed with verbose blogposts about the value of the selfie, since that's what everyone was doing all the time, distributing the self across media platforms. I hated taking photos of myself and hoped to avoid these iPhone-equipped boys and girls. In any case, everyone not in front of a mirror had already lost themselves to whatever they were on at the moment, alcohol, drugs, one another, or merely the delirious heat that distended and abstracted the social logic of the room into a pudding of hungry faces, each hoping to be photographed without flash. I wanted to lose myself with them.

"I'm going to have a look around," Wolfgang said. He had his camera out.

"I wonder if people will recognize him," I said to Stewart, who distracted himself with his coat. "Like that guy did at Metro."

"Probably ... Can you ..." I helped him with his jacket. He shrugged his shoulders. "I don't know."

They did. Within the hour the backroom filled, and many of the boys who poured in seemed to recognize him, locked their eyes on Wolfgang as he circulated the crowd with his camera. He took photos, but so discreetly that it was like he wasn't doing anything at all, though increasingly whispers of a famous photographer rose around him. How everyone recognized his face I didn't know. Before that night, I had never thought about what he looked like, but many apparently had. "Is that?" Yes. Finally, the rumor of his presence at the Spectrum was confirmed and the famous photographer was declared, among the knowing, to be the real Wolfgang Tillmans. More and more boys shuffled into the back, from the dance floor, at the news. This was a topic we all shared an opinion about, a swimming admiration for Wolfgang wow, can't believe he's here, but is that him, yes, he's taking pictures. "Is that?" someone asked me.

"Did you come with him?"

"Yeah."

"Do you know him?"

"Not really."

If fame, even art fame, had transfigured him into some lofty and indifferent figure, there were no signs of it despite everyone else's gawky enthusiasm for his presence. Instead, Wolfgang dug in, made himself one among many and one of the same, a body in circulation with others rather than someone whose face the art world had minted as valued currency. Wolfgang clicked. In the corners of the room boys made themselves into pictures—or what they thought a Wolfgang picture looked like. Without trademark athletic wear on hand for the typical Wolfgang *track suits nudes abstract wave flowers trees a cock your cock balls caught from behind a few stray hairs ass static a sign a boy a girl*, they aped his lean European subjects with their own slim New York bodies, sucked in their cheeks to elongate their already-slender faces and pulled off their shirts to show off their smooth, lightly toned torsos, each spritzed with sweat, the ripple of abs that began at the Calvin Klein waistband up to their hairless chests.

They let their best angles get caught in the best light, the light they assumed his camera would need to best capture them, cool and level-headed expressions of feigned disinterest that they must have practiced in the mirror for exactly these moments, the moments when someone with a camera (someone famous, especially) might be present, and which they held tightly for as long as they could in the heat of the Spectrum: for Wolfgang, but more so for the object in his hand that transcended its mechanical representational role to become some kind of envious totem, a sign of elsewhere that drew those present before it closer, enchanted by the Good Eye that wards off time, an eye that sees beyond itself, beyond Wolfgang, beyond the Spectrum to the time of the photograph, the time not-here but which might take hold of here and make it last forever: a history, partially made up of queer boys and girls, in a room in Brooklyn in what would become the venue's final year, the year of Wolfgang, the year of heat, the year of pictures.

I watched them and did not, not once, allow myself slip into their time, into their year, rather felt it define the space around me: picture-time, the time that takes up all other time, that eats through the room, that ate through those potential subjects.

Wolfgang smiled, chatted, raised the camera up and clicked. He clicked around the room, taking photos of the boys and girls and of the Spectrum, its exposed ceiling, the bar, the ripped-up fabrics that dangled from the roof, walls covered in reflective wallpaper or not covered at all, the crowd that shoved itself back and forth, from one room to the next. In the various lights that lit the Spectrum they flickered against the dark, their faces waiting to be identified by the camera. He followed them as they spilled out onto the front dance floor then back to the bar, like fish pursued by a dolphin, corralling them, clicked when they fell on the old couches, dirtied from all the bare asses dragged across their surfaces, clicked when they kissed, clicked when they did what they did, it was whatever, it was them, the year of them in the year of my watching Wolfgang watch them. The girls who'd occupied the silver couch were gone. I took a seat on it next to Stewart, who was sitting with a group of our friends.

"I didn't realize he was so recognizable," I said to Stewart, interrupting his conversation.

"This crowd? Yes," Stewart said. "Where'd he go?"

"Over there." I nodded to the far end of the bar near the makeshift coat check, manned by some frantic woman knee-deep in winter wear, where a silver mannequin sat on the countertop. It leaned back, propped up by both arms, with its right leg raised at an acute angle while the left extended forward. Human-sized, but faceless, I had never noticed it before until I watched Wolfgang stand before it and click. He slipped back into the crowd.

I stood up on the silver couch to get a better view of the mannequin he'd just photographed. It wobbled in its object life, halfway between living and never having lived, a street busker reversed into its statue or some superman whose ambiguous powers resulted in an awesome, silvery stillness, an X-man, or rather an X-woman, an X-no one, its flesh freakishly unmoving yet wavy as it reflected everyone around it. Its face had no eyes or mouth, only a slight bump that suggested a nose. Why had I never noticed that face, the face that sucked in the light, the purple and pink and yellow light that rose from the bar's filtered bulbs and eddied in its face, its face staring ahead like an alien god who leans forward to touch its cold nose to yours and grant its select wisdom of the unknown on those suppliant believers kneeling before it.

"To count / them one by one / as the wires slip / by." I stared amid the throng that gathered on the couches, in the corners, near the bar, and they pushed me back against the wall as more and more people entered the backroom, naked and half-naked, in chains and S/M gear and homemade clothes of mesh and neon fabric and whatever else they chose to wear, all of them cheering and laughing and spilling their cheap drinks of bottom-shelf booze, felt myself snag on that wire and drag with it, drag into their pool that widened and widened, drag through the rippling heat and the odor of bare flesh, the intoxicating pungency of people in heat, those who rarely shower, those who never shower, allowed it to pull me in, and drag me under.

I was their subject, or their subject was me: hooked on their wire, I wanted to continue along, into the density of figures cajoling in the tight area of the Spectrum, enter their center to make an image, maybe in writing, of them myself. If I had chased an idea of community in California and found nothing, or nothing that resembled me, in the Spectrum, in New York, I stumbled on what I was looking for, what I had always known was already there. Contact, as it were.

Stephen had taken over bar duties and stood behind the mannequin, sliding vodka soda after vodka soda to the impatient crowd with their fistfuls of money extended outward. Its body reflected theirs, his too, and swallowed them into it. I sat back down on the couch. Stewart was gone.

Zachary—sallow-faced, his eyes bobbing in his skull, nearly unrecognizable with his gray, sunken cheeks—dropped down on the couch beside me, like he was cast out from a dream into real life. "Hey, Nick," he said, slowly, as if he'd forgotten my name. Stunned, I stared at him, our eyes not quite making contact, but rather looking past one another, as if into some past trailing behind our heads since the present wasn't believable, wasn't fixed enough to allow us to stand before one another. If the crowd was a text, it felt as though I had just improvised Zachary's appearance in it. He seemed to think so, too, and his expression was vacant, even as he tried to conjure up a smile. Nothing, but everything, had changed.

"Hey," I said. "I didn't know you were in the city."

"I'm not," he said. He was visiting, getting a few things he'd left behind at Julia's apartment, then was headed back to New Hampshire, briefly. Afterwards he would head to LA. I hadn't expected him to be the one to make any serious migration west, but he said he needed the change LA would supply. He'd already found a place in Mount Washington, up on a huge hill.

"That's all great," I said. He nodded along, yeah, yeah. "When do you leave?"

"Next week. But," he said, his eyes finally coming into focus, his voice drawing into seriousness rather than the small-talky tone he'd adopted with me, "I want to say I'm sorry for how shitty we were to one another, back when I was living here and you were with Simon."

I hadn't remembered being the one responsible for how we were to one another, but sure, I said, I understand, it's good to see you, Zachary. I stood up to leave. Zachary, shaped by loss, could keep it; I didn't want to see him again, hadn't wanted to talk about the past, his or mine or ours together, since already that time—the time of Simon had taken on a bitter contour in my memory, especially after his sudden departure for Europe—was not one I wanted to return to, at least not then. New York hurls back private history endlessly, in faces and relics. Zachary tugged at me a little: wait. How are you? I was OK. We talked about Wolfgang, who had apparently taken his photo. We talked about Julia, who was doing well. This went on, until finally I decided to get up: "Anyway, I'll see you around."

He stopped me again: "I was wondering, though, if you've talked to Simon lately?" I looked at him. Had he not?

"A little, actually. He's in Vienna. You don't speak?"

"We do and we don't."

I put my hand on his shoulder. "You should call him or something. Tell him you're going to LA." I wanted to ask, for the second time: Are you OK? but the question seemed immediately ridiculous, even cruel. Of course he wasn't. He was skinny, almost sickly, and he looked like he hadn't eaten in a week. Then, finally: "Are you all right?" My tone was graver than I'd meant.

"Yeah," he said. "Totally."

I got up. For sure.

17

The Spectrum paused around four a.m., when three performers
took over the rear of the front room, near the DJ booth, and put on
a show, something between a drag pageant and an absurd attempt
at performance art, broadly speaking, though it wasn't quite either,
and the visual and aesthetic coordinates of the event shifted as the
performers began to move along to music, approximating both a
vogue ball and a cotillion, or neither. Two female performers, both
of whom I knew, mimed along to the voice of a singer whose song
I didn't recognize, and rubbed their hands up and down their bodies in slow seduction of the audience that had suspended its own
movement to watch them, while behind the two women the lights
began to flicker and a third performer, a boy, rose up in a dress
stitched together with a variety of colorful, floppy fabrics into a
kind of goofy human flower, its stigma his beautiful, smiling black
face dabbed with blue paint. They were like a chamber opera, the
central drama of which seemed to be that there was no drama
among them, only a limitless and motivating sexual agency that
propelled them and their audience forward. None of this was very
good. In fact, it bordered on awful, and cheesy, but I stood and
watched regardless, captivated by its self-serious logic. I wondered
if Wolfgang was watching them. The boy on stage motioned his
arms in such a way that he seemed to be gathering those of us
around him closer, into whatever cabal the three had formed on the
makeshift stage in the relentless, exhaustive heat of the Spectrum.

We came closer in a forward march. I wiped my face with my white t-shirt. It was soaked. I took it off and wrapped it around my neck like a scarf. A racket of music continued to blare from the speakers in the corners of the room, and the performers moved faster, linking arms before raising the boy in the dress up above us in what seemed to approach a climax. On the far end of the stage, I saw Zachary watching the performance pensively, his expression unchanging as he attempted to understand what was happening. I texted Simon, though service was bad in the Spectrum: "just saw zachary. looks sick. hope ur well."

I recognized many of the faces that surrounded the stage, many that I knew through other parties, or galleries, or readings, or performances, or hook-ups, or as people "from the internet," in the neighborhood. At this point I had known these faces for years, even if we had never exchanged a word. Some I had danced with on occasion. Others I didn't know, and likely wouldn't ever. We were each entries in some larger text, though the meaning of its plot was more or less unknown to any of us, unknown to me, though I felt that we—this underbelly of the last years of the moneyed Bloomberg mayoralty, not so long after the occupations of Lower Manhattan that protested his and all efforts at privatizing, and thereby destroying, the commons—formed a demon world within the city, an anterior, but stronger commons within that larger commons that had been growing weaker every day under the persistence of the city's cops and rich, whose tandem-alliance continued to deprive us of space to do what the Spectrum allowed us to do, slippery with sweat.

In a few years, the Spectrum would close, and then reopen after a year in a new, larger space in Ridgewood called the Dreamhouse. The second iteration contained the same and also different energies and in this it was neither a continuation nor an improvement but something else, a place unlike the previous one that the name "Spectrum" did not apply to. It was of its own order, as was the Spectrum on Montrose. But despite its eventual recovery, the closure of the old one enacted an at-first imperceptible shift in nightlife, one that became more and more felt—or at least I felt it more and more—as its absence was prolonged and the people who had composed that place diffused into other events, other places. It occupies no romantic position in my mind—it was often an awful, crowded, overheated place—but it did serve as a central meeting ground, where many different types of people came, then went, then came again, and I didn't find anything like it in the years after it left.

But New York, like any city, is defined by its upheavals in real estate, and I want to resist sentimentalizing the past since the effort sanitizes—and destroys—my memories of the Spectrum and any number of other bars: their grime, their ugliness, and therefore what made them different from the rest of the city. Nevertheless, I miss them, miss the people who went there, their great anonymous crowds, and as each left—bars, restaurants, clubs that were replaced by other bars, other restaurants, other clubs—I began to better understand what seemed to haunt an older generation of New Yorkers, who often complained about this new New York: namely, the loss of the places that had made them—and their world. And after Sandy, this rapid succession of destruction and construction only seemed to quicken its pace.

That hurricane revealed that the city was close to helpless in the face of disaster, and those of us who lived there were likewise vulnerable against the fickle weather that moved us here and there. And each year, this weather seemed to worsen: summer extended, winter contracted, while fall and spring remained turbulent and ugly, intermixed with storms and heatwaves that were unlike anything I'd known growing up. We were not in our right world—or the world was not right with us. The city was changing because the world was changing, and I could no longer trust this change—and, in many instances, I wanted it to cease altogether, for us to stay still, to slow our forward, indifferent march into a century of climactic calamity that would be a calamity of communities, including mine. One president would depart; an awful president would come. Politics would veer rightward. There were, much of the time, long periods of hopelessness. I saw this time as one of shadows, cast by figures we couldn't always see, but who loomed larger and larger. This was a silly dream.

The Spectrum, for its small part, was not a place that consciously represented any attempt at perfected community but rather one that existed, and thrived on, the contradictions that accompanied the differences of race, class, gender, and identification that were obtained in the faces around me, each a demon unto themselves, an antithesis to anyone who lived their lives on the surface, each an agent that ferried news between these worlds, between office and night club or café and apartment or job and lack of job or sex and sex work and who likely felt that these distinctions were meaningless anyway, at least as they were lived and understood in our own Abaddon, our demon city, of New York.

We were an infernal dictionary, like that of the French occultist Jacques Collin de Plancy, who published his famous demonology *Dictionnaire Infernal* in 1818, which attempts to account for the demons of the world's religions as they were known to de Plancy at the time. De Plancy's book describes those rulers of the various duchies of the netherworld that obsessed him in exacting detail, and when I read about them, I found a curious analog for my own experience of the world: these strange, differing bodies; their freedom from restraint; their nightly doings that textured and shaped their existence. A later edition included illustrations by Louis Le Breton, and his etchings have provided us with many of our popular images of the demons that de Plancy recorded in his anthology, and these drawings likewise provided me with the images I thought might illustrate a book of this city, the city as I lived it, the city of bad weather and bad faith in its fealty to finance and the destructive principles of unyielding American power: Abigor, the Duke of Hell, who carries a lance that he wields over his sixty legions of demons, including Abraxas, Adramlech, Aguares, and Alastor. Breton's drawings mix the anatomy of birds and farm animals into the human form: Siryl, a sleepy-eyed goat who keeps its human hands hidden in its coat pockets. Caim, a crow whose wings end in claws and who carries with it a saber far larger than its body. Amduscias, Amon, Andras, Asmodee, Astaroth, Azazel: an alphabet of bodies in which I saw others and myself. Figures of difference, untouched by the beatific release granted to the saved, and the normal. We, and by we I mean the darkly numinous: Bael, Balan, Barbatos, Behemoth, Belphegor, Belzebuth, Berith, Bhairava, Buer. The removed, the pushed-out, the sidelined, the hellbound, and the damned. Caacrionlaas, Cali, Cerbere, Deimos, Eurynome, Flaga, Flavros, Forcas, Furfur. Ganga, Garuda, Guayota, Gomory. Haborym, also known as Aim, and another great Duke. Ipes. Lamia, Lechies, Leonard, Lucifer, who is well-known. Malphas, Mammon, Marchosias, Melchom, Moloch ("whose poverty is the specter of genius" and "whose name is Mind!"). Nickar and Nybbas. Orobas. Paimon, Picollus, Pruflas. Rahovart and Ribesal and Ronwe. Scox and Stolas. Tap, Torngarsuk. Ukobach. Volac, the dragon-headed boy. Wall. Xaphan. Yan-gant-y-tan. And Zaebos.

I saw them all and wanted to write my own dictionary of them someday. Perhaps that could give my book an arc, the book I was still writing, that was coming along, that had yet to have a title, but had—in the year or so since I'd announced it at Helen's— begun to take shape. This was my world, though it wasn't California, wasn't an inexact history of cults. Instead it was the one that I would make my subject, the way we are bound to one another through place, whether it was the Tom of Finland Foundation or the Spectrum.

"Where have you been?" Stewart asked. He put his hand on my shoulder and squeezed it. "I couldn't find you."

"I was just here, watching them perform." The pageant, or whatever glittery thing it was, was over and the audience had begun to move around again, either to the back or to the exit. A shift in the tenor of the night had taken hold; an after-hours intensity that meant the crowd would divide into those who went home (it was six thirty or so) and those who stayed. Those who stayed would stay for a long time, until well into the morning, even the early afternoon.

"Was it good?"

"It was OK. Where were you? Where's Wolfgang?"

"In the back, talking to people. Not sure where Wolfgang is."

Stewart and I walked around, trying to find him. We circled the main dance floor and peeked into the backroom, but he was nowhere to be found. I hadn't seen him at the performance either.

It was time for me to go home, I told Stewart, who said he would stay longer. He wanted to look for Wolfgang still. Perhaps he had left after he got what he needed. In our final round through the Spectrum I couldn't imagine what they, these people who were beginning to dance again, would look like in photographs, since their presence, not their image, determined the value of this space. Cleaving them from their context, freezing them in a single photo seemed like it would never come close to what I had seen, but whatever, it was his, I thought, the year of his, as the first light crept over the city outside and stragglers began to hail their cabs home. Stewart, who'd followed me out to see me off, waved goodbye. Bye, I said.

Simon's reply to my text reached me when I got service again: "OMG, really. how is he? he doesn't seem to be doing well."

It was early afternoon in Vienna, early morning in New York. I decided to wait to respond to him until I had gotten some sleep, when I could better explain how strange Zachary had seemed to me, how unfamiliar he had become. "just left spectrum. will tell you later."

"k. btw when are you coming to europe??"

I had been invited to give a reading in London on the strength of a chapbook I'd released a few months after I got back from LA, the first time I'd ever been asked to present my work outside the country: "late spring early summer, so a few months? maybe i'll come to Vienna."

I was close enough to my apartment to walk home, so I did, following a few others from the Spectrum who made their way quietly to their apartments across the borough, into the start of morning, when the first Hasidic men began their diligent patrols on Broadway. The Sunday train traffic picked up under the aboveground tracks, with the trains rumbling overhead more frequently as they ferried passengers between Manhattan and Brooklyn.

At the Flushing stop, Julia's café—Donahue's, on Broadway—was close to its opening time. Donahue's occupied a narrow slot in an otherwise nondescript building facing the train tracks, with its name indicated by a neon-pink, sans-serif sign hung on a large, scuffed window. Lit by uncovered incandescent bulbs that dropped from the tin ceiling, Donahue's was decorated to appear older than it was, in an almost nineteenth-century New York style, with faux-antique floral wallpaper upon which the owner had hung old maps of the city, and newly installed, weathered-by-design wood floors. The café conveyed, in a neighborhood of old bodegas and their mangy, commandant cats, beauty salons, and quotidian shops of cheap home and cooking supplies, its status as a forerunner in the gentrification of the area. Donahue's meant the rent was climbing. White kids liked it. I was completely fried, unacceptable in public, but Julia was in, setting up.

She stood at the small counter near the window, fussing impatiently with tins of sugar packets, simple syrup, varieties of stirrers, four metal thermoses of milk. Soy, almond, half and half, organic. She was arranging their color-coded bottles when I knocked on the door. She jumped. "Oh my god, you scared me," she shouted through the glass. We hadn't seen each other in weeks.

"Can I come in?" I said. I must have looked bombed. She nodded, with a look of slight regret. What a mess I was. She liked me but she didn't need me like this.

Opening the door, "Yes, but why are you up so early. It's almost seven."

"I was at the Spectrum."

I reeked of cigarettes and alcohol. She made a face: "I see. How was it?" I was still standing outside, in the doorway of the café. She waited, then: "Well, come in," she said. "I need to get ready."

"The same as ever. It was good."

She went behind the counter to assemble the espresso machine: "Do you want coffee?"

"Maybe a cappuccino, if that's OK. I have, like, two dollars."

She turned around and grinned: "For you, anything."

I took a seat at the counter next to a plastic box of pastries.

"And a croissant, I guess." A hangover began to pulse at my temples, and I was flushed with an alternating cold and hot feeling.

Since we had met, Julia had begun to publish more, including an impressive, dense short story in *Granta*—her favorite magazine, and one that I was envious of her appearance in. She had cut down her meandering novel to a thirty-page meditation on failure and friendship, contriving from the remnants of her book a tightly packed, subtle fiction called "Awful, Internet-Connected Things." "Awful, Internet-Connected Things" was not strictly about awful, internet-connected things, but rather some reverential things—specifically a dead girlfriend's iPhone that might hold the answers to the narrator's questions about her mysterious life outside their romance—that slowly lose their importance to the narrator.

Practically speaking it was about a boy who, after failing to unlock the phone, goes to South Carolina to meet her family. They offer nothing. So, he decides to go on a boating trip to clear his head and, ignoring the advice of experienced sailors, rides into a coming storm. Or something like that. The coast guard rescues him from drowning at sea. After he comes to on deck, all he can say is that he lost her phone in the breakers. It does other, sophisticated things. Julia was very proud of the story. She had done it, after all.

Julia's primary talent as a writer is her ability to transmute the banal into the profoundly meaningful through subtle threads of inquiry. In her spare, hard prose, for example, she manages to weave together a digression on the construction of the phone, its history of upgrades since its introduction to the market in the late 2000s, into a theory of the mind. Or, again, something like that. With Julia's writing it can go many ways. What is plain, historical, even obtuse is otherwise quick-footed and contemporary in her writing, without seeming burdened by the presentness of its present. Her work reminds me of a young Mavis Gallant, but sparer. I was jealous, since, in my writing, the slippery subject often got away from me, became swamped with concerns of the contemporary, and slipped out of sight, into my own spiraling digressions. My own work was about the circles I ran around whatever it was that I wanted to write about. I liked the chase whereas Julia liked to make things sit still, allowing her to describe the contours of their shape, their surfaces, theories, and the varying degrees of emotional meaning to a subject. The subject is the iPhone, the subject is death, the subject is a boy, the subject is the storm. I dislike the fiction of dying, really, but liked Julia's, though hers wasn't about dying so much as it was about the ongoing search for authenticity. In this it closely resembled her life. She wanted reality to feel real, realer than our awful, internet-connected one usually allowed for.

As she busied herself with the espresso machine, I said congratulations on *Granta*. "Did you read it yet?" she asked, pausing to let the coffee drip fill a shot glass.

"I did."

"What did you think?"

"I'm hungover."

"So?"

"I liked it, of course."

"Thank you."

"It's well-written. Are you writing more?"

"Yes. All the time."

"Good." I stuffed the croissant in my mouth.

"Have you heard from Simon?"

Over the sound of her steaming the milk, "Yep."

"How's he?"

"He's the same. He likes Europe better than here."

"Of course."

"I might visit."

She slid me the cappuccino. "Really."

"Probably. I was just talking to him about that."

"Why are you going?"

"I'm doing a reading in London, figured I'd fly out of Vienna."

"Where?"

I explained to her the nature of the reading and the invitation in such a way that I hoped might make her jealous. It was *important*, though I didn't say "important" but rather that "I think it's going to be a big deal"; it was *paid for*, though I didn't say how little I was being paid; it might lead to a British publisher, though I had no reason to believe so, and I blurted that out in such a way that made me feel incredibly silly. Like a boy trying to prove that a lie is true. In any case, she saw through my act, and responded graciously by avoiding calling my attention to its ridiculousness. "I'm happy for you, Nick," she said.

"I don't know. I feel dumb. I guess I'm just coming down."

"From what."

"Everything."

She continued to arrange the counter at Donahue's. She powered on the iPad, which acted as a cash register, and went over to the small stereo system to plug in her phone. She started with a song by Ryan Adams, whose music is the exact sound of a gentrifying coffee shop at seven a.m. in Bushwick. "In your story is the main character based on Simon?"

I'd finished the cappuccino, so Julia refilled my cup with black coffee. "No, why?"

"He reminded me of him. But straight."

"Did the girlfriend remind you of me?"

"She's not in the story, really. So I can't say. Can I have an orange juice?"

"You have to pay for it." But I'm broke. Then no juice.

"I don't think of my characters as 'based on' anyone in particular, though, probably like you, I take here and there from people I know. I'd actually say that the dead girlfriend is based more on you than me," she said. She paused. She hadn't meant to say that. "Well, actually, maybe equal parts me, equal parts you. I figured you'd see that."

"No," I hadn't. "How so?" The girlfriend is hardly in the story, and the few memories the narrator brings up of her seem more like sketches. They are the weakest part of the story, the sections that feel the most labored over, especially given what I had read of the novel version of the story, where the girlfriend is a flutist for an orchestra in New York who doesn't die, but instead breaks her hand and is forced to reconsider her career as she convalesces in her apartment while the Simon character drifts away. Nothing like me. Nothing like Julia.

"I guess I don't see it. But I don't look for fiction to connect characters to real people, even in autobiographical writing."

"Nor do I."

"Then?"

"Then what?"

"Never mind."

"I guess all fiction is about writing. That's what my story is about."

"How so?"

"I mean you read it."

I had, but I guess I hadn't paid close attention. To this, she had no response, so I tried a different subject: "Are you still going to Helen's?" There had been talk, last time we spoke, about her delaying her residency.

"That's the plan, at least. I'm going in June."

"You're quitting?"

"Yes," she said, whispering, "though I'm not telling them."

"Why are you whispering? There's nobody here."

"The owner's this jerk. He probably has some kind of microphone or something." I laughed.

"You've worked here for how long and you haven't figured this out?"

She ignored me. "I'm excited to go to Helen's, in any case." She was rarely excited for anything, but perhaps a stint at a culty art residency where the social stakes seemed abnormally high would grant her some semblance of the authenticity that she was seeking and that city life failed to offer her. Julia liked to not-so-quietly complain that all people wanted to do was go out, and since she didn't drink and didn't feel that drinking allowed for any real connection between people, whatever that meant, there wasn't much else to New York. I couldn't convince her otherwise. Her nostalgia for some other, greener period of arty outings, when the New York literary and art scenes were authenticated by their self-sacrificial pursuit of their work (and by black-and-white photography), seemed forced, and in any case unlived by her. And those artists were always wasted, always on drugs. She hadn't lived in the city even a decade yet—what did she know?

It was not an argument worth having, really. She had fun, just not fun like other people, and any attempt to lure her into nightlife and its recognizable pleasures was wasted on her. "I'm just going to read." Zadie Smith, Henry James, Patrick Modiano, Claudia Rankine. Good for her. I hoped that upstate she'd find what she was looking for: real life.

"It'll be fun."

"Yeah, probably."

There was construction along Broadway, and two workers came in for coffee. They moved me out of the way to order their large, unreasonably priced coffees. "You should get some rest, Nick." She was right. I was awake but crashing, plummeting into sleep even while standing, despite the cappuccino and coffee. Before I left I wanted to insist I wasn't the girlfriend. But she knew that.

18

In Peter Hujar's 1983 portrait of her, Greer Lankton sits in bed, her left arm propped up on her knee, holding her head up as she gives the camera a look of skeptical reserve. Her blankets and pillows are printed with large letters that spell out something interrupted by her body, likely a French phrase (one pillow reads "La" while the other appears to say "Nuit"). Every time I look at the photo I try to piece the letters into a sentence, but can't. Likewise with her sculpture, I can't always put into words what it is I am seeing, despite how instantly recognizable some of her subjects are, from Jesus to Jackie Kennedy. Rather, the dolls seem to follow an unknown grammar of representation, one that insists on its own ineffability, on an otherness that attains familiarity yet remains distant and silent. The dolls, after all, do not speak. *La ... Nu ...*

Born Greg Lankton in Flint, Michigan, in 1958, Lankton transitioned to female in 1979 at age twenty-one, using funds her father collected for her surgery at church. Lankton was "beautiful, glamorous, fragile, with a disarming sweetness and an ironic wit," wrote Nan Goldin, her former New York roommate. She suffered, however, "through her own traumas: the pain from her surgery, her struggle with anorexia, her rejection by lovers, her drug problems." After moving to New York in the late seventies, she began to make large dolls, many of them resembling her diva-heroes like Divine and Candy Darling. Later she exhibited the work around New York, including at Civilian Warfare, a gallery in Alphabet City that included David Wojnarowicz in its roster.

Lankton's dolls are often anatomically unsettled, over-weight or too thin, tattered or shredded apart. They've been painted in a careful, expressionistic manner, one that sometimes verges on the comedic: Jesus, his mouth dripping with blood, is a zombie. They lean on their wire stands or against walls or on tiny furniture Lankton made for them. Their movable bodies appear threadbare, lopsided, sewn together with a provisional craftiness that reflects the fact that Lankton "constantly worked and reworked" them, as Goldin notes, "changing their genders, iden-tities, sizes and clothes." Julia Morton adds that "Greer's dolls, ingeniously constructed out of soda bottles, coat hangers, umbrella hinges, panty hose, layers of paint and glass eyes obtained from a taxidermy shop, have a surreal yet jarring vitality … Some dolls gained or lost weight, others had face-lifts or sex changes, and some were chopped into pieces and left as torsos or heads." As such, they sometimes wear the look of the undead, mixing a peculiar humor with stopgap glamor, effecting a bodily presence in even the smallest of her works. Hilton Als writes that they are "starved for attention." Gary Indiana is more charitable in his 1984 review of Lankton's third Civilian Warfare show: Lankton's dolls "are so charmingly lifelike that their faces catch our attention first; or, in the gymnast pieces, the fluid grace they express in contortion." He continues:

> We do, of course, notice these things *almost* immedi-ately. Not to be funny, but they grow on us. Lankton's creatures live in a psychic interzone where genitals and gender identity are scrambled in the play of appearances, and reveal an exacerbated, possibly mutilated sexuality as the trigger of personality. Like

Theodora Skipitares' housewife automata that vomit and menstruate, Lankton's ambisexual dolls wear faces of crumbling self-assurance, or even moronic friendliness and self-contentment, while breathing pain out through their pores ... They have learned to live with an unalterable strangeness.

I'm not certain I agree that Lankton's work reflects a turbulent or tortured sense of her own body, despite her dolls' sometimes turbulent and tortured nature. Rather, their re-visional quality suggests a distinctly queer and trans experience of the world, one that is attentive to physical mutability and the rotation and flexibility of "roles." Diana Vreeland, Divine, and Candy Darling, to name only a few of Lankton's subjects, are linked thematically in their shared sensibility of the made-up, the invented, and so the changeable. They knew, like Lankton knew, that what was sewn into a boy can be easily cut into a girl, only to be later made into something else altogether.

Writing about the wax dolls of German artist Lotte Pritzel (to whom Lankton's own work bears a strong family resemblance), Rainer Maria Rilke noted: "With the doll we had to assert ourselves, because if we surrendered to it there was nobody there. It made no response, so we got into the habit of doing things for it, splitting our own slowly expanding nature into opposing parts and to some extent using the doll to establish distance between ourselves and the amorphous world pouring into us." This relationship imbues the doll with its "soul," Rilke writes, arguing that it is the extremity of this attachment that leads us to both desire and reject the doll. Unalterable strangeness: Lankton's own work is plotted along the rejection–desire axis, granting the work a peculiar levity of both the fearsome and the friendly.

For Pritzel, working roughly a century before Lankton, this assertion of the self against—and into—dolls alchemized a sculpture of delicate figures infused with Orientalist twinkle, a toy world of near-genderless bodies that, per Rilke, "swarm and fade at the uttermost limit of our vision," safe from any "decline in permanent sensuality." This lends them a particularly dreamy quality, ghostly in the few extant images of them: their skeletal faces yearn "for a beautiful flame, to throw themselves into it like moths." Pritzel's dolls—fragile artifacts of the brief twilight between the gay nineties and the founding of the Weimar Republic—are refugees of art, caught in the difficult obscurity between toy and sculpture.

This tension in Pritzel's work is found in Lankton's own, especially in her bust of Candy Darling, for which she made a glass chest with two fabricated hearts: a naturalistic one and a Valentine's Day card cutout. In setting up this core relationality, Lankton places the correspondence between the literal and symbolic at the figurative heart of her work (and of one of her heroes), laying bare, as it were, her dual impulse toward both. (Julia Morton writes that the two hearts indicate that Lankton was sustained by both "reality and fantasy," though Lankton seems less interested in this binary than in the hallucinatory interrelation of the two.)

Lankton's art is both realistic and unrealistic, a difficult balance that is not unlike Candy Darling's work as an actor, which often operated at the juncture between self-conscious play and unanticipated reality to evoke, again, unalterable strangeness. Following Douglas Crimp's description of the Warhol superstar as someone whose "self ... recognizes otherness already there in itself [and] performs its own self-alienation," Lankton likewise performs the double work of representing bodies (hers and others) while asserting their alienation. Darling rehearsed and played herself in order to be someone else. It might be said that Lankton rehearsed and played others in order to be herself.

Lankton worked on her best-known doll, *Sissy* (1979–96), for most of her career. It has since disappeared. Numerous photos of the doll still exist, providing an elliptical portrait (taken by Lankton) of the doll's progression. In one, perched on a stoop and smoking a cigarette next to a small dog, *Sissy* looks like Joan Crawford. In another, it's broken into pieces, a dislocated and partially skeletal nude descending a staircase. In still another, Sissy is naked, wigless, and with a red heart painted on its chest. Perhaps the most famous image of the doll is of it standing with a skullcap outside the Prince Street N and R train in SoHo. *Sissy*'s pants are pulled down to reveal male genitals. Graffiti on the station reads: Lady. It seems somewhat fitting, however terrible the loss, that *Sissy* disappeared: a translational and transitional object of identity, its continuous shifts—between identities and genders, between the fully formed and the partially skeletal—license an absence that follows Lankton's own. We couldn't know *Sissy*, except in parts, images, remnants, small traces of a figure that slipped, like its maker, above the uttermost limit of vision.

PART FOUR

19

In a pub toilet in Hackney I found a copy of William Blake's poem "The Crystal Cabinet" stapled to the wall. Collaged into newspaper cutouts and photographs, stickers and a half-torn poster for a fag party called Heaven pasted over the shallow toilet, the A4 paper had yellowed with water damage, to the point that some words had nearly faded: "Another England there I saw, / Another London with its tower." With my back against the damp wall I whispered the poem aloud to myself. I'd never encountered English poetry in an English bathroom. This is the Crystal Cabinet: "I strove to seize the inmost form," Blake writes, and I briefly entered it, far from the overcast mid-June afternoon in the city on the Thames. I'd been in London for only four days, really three since I'd lost my first afternoon to a long, jetlag-induced, late-morning nap that slipped well into evening, but in the UK time distended, looped awkwardly, and felt of an entirely different character than New York's speedier cycles. Out of tune with elsewhere, New York or the continent, I rerouted to an epochal London time, which is no time other than its own.

Someone banged on the door. "Hello?"

"Out in a minute," I said and tore the poem off the wall, folding it into a small triangle. It fit snugly in my wallet. I zipped up. Outside the bathroom, a walleyed boy stood anxiously, his doughy face soft in a curtain of yellow light. Musk clung to the air. Desperate to pee, he grabbed at his crotch.

"Excuse me, I have to use this," he said. I stepped aside.

Upstairs, the bar was mostly empty except for two couples sitting at some tables near the door. The wooden, mud-dark interior glowed with the dusk as the late-afternoon light seeped through the scuffed windows. It felt nothing like summer, though I couldn't quite place the season: mornings felt like spring, especially in the pale, brittle light before noon, but the warmer afternoons—enough to pass for mild summer—seemed to belong to some fifth season, a hazy season of rain, defined perpetually by the competition between shadows and the stray sunlight that the cloud cover sometimes permitted to enter the city.

"What can I get you?" the bartender asked.

"What do you recommend?"

He cleared his throat. "What d'ya like?"

"Hmm."

"How about a Pilsner." He poured me a glass and slid it over.

Sipping the lukewarm beer, I reread the water-stained printout of "The Crystal Cabinet":

> The Maiden caught me in the Wild,
> Where I was dancing merrily;
> She put me into her Cabinet,
> And Lockd me up with a golden Key.
>
> This Cabinet is form'd of Gold
> And Pearl & Crystal shining bright
> And within it opens into a World
> And a little lovely Moony Night.
>
> Another England there I saw,
> Another London with its Tower,

Another Thames & other Hills,
And another pleasant Surrey Bower.

Another Maiden like herself
Translucent lovely shining clear
Threefold each in the other clos'd;
O what a pleasant trembling fear!

O what a smile, a threefold Smile
Fill'd me that like a flame I burn'd;
I bent to Kiss the lovely Maid,
And found a Threefold Kiss return'd.

I strove to seize the inmost Form
With ardor fierce & hands of flame
But burst the Crystal Cabinet
And like a weeping Babe became;

A weeping Babe upon the wild
And weeping Woman pale reclin'd
And in the outward Air again
I fill'd with woes the passing Wind.

The city presents itself as a series of cabinets: one after another, room after room, club after club, park after park, pond after pond. Into the passing Wind I had exited the bathroom and entered the bar; both were square with low ceilings, neither was made of gold pearl & crystal shining bright, the patrons were not maidens in the Wild, but let's say the wild's the street and so, finishing the Pilsner, I decided to go outside.

I was already late to meet Phillip, a friend and film curator at one of the museums in the city and with whom I was staying for a few days on my trip. The streets were calm, a little crowded with Saturday shoppers, but far from wild. Or else the Wild's not the England of Blake but the one of global finance, and so a Wild of the Air: an erecter set of cranes and construction sites, the City on the Rise amid the Influx of the international investor class who have flocked to its De-regulated Shores, its Many Towers cutting the long stream of clouds that flow across the countryside, the Shard & Gherkin, the Tower of London & the Walkie Talkie.

Within cabinets: other cabinets. Phillip and I met at the Victorian gardens off the boardwalk in Regent's Park. A sudden bout of humidity deranged the park-goers, and no one strolling among the manicured lawns could keep a straight path. They moved in circles, teetered about among the roses and exotic grasses, almost drunkenly, smelling this and that flowering plant with English whimsy. Caught between a throng of girls goggling at a handsome, shirtless boy with two pugs at his command, Phillip stood near a shapely hedge, distracted from the scene around him by his phone. From any distance I could make him out: brown, tousled hair with a distinct, sharp nose and small lips, and a kind of slumped, bored posture that was somewhat boyish.

"Hey," I said. We kissed hello. "Wanna go for a walk?" Headed north, we came to a bushy, tree-lined wall that sloped down to a fence separating the park from the London Zoo. The zoo was pitiful as all zoos are pitiful: the tanks and exhibits that pin the captive animals together were too small and too narrow, and none of the animals looked very pleased to be stuck in their cages. We could see tropical birds with no business in sopping southern England, caged bands of monkeys off in the distance, and camels chewing dried grass, their huge humps deflated and lying limp across their flanks—what I guessed was a sign of depression or dehydration or both. On the other side of the zoo, a grime-slick pool housed a drowsy family of penguins tanning themselves on a fake rock face over their leaf-choked pool. From the park, the BT Tower broke with the skyline like a grounded rocket, its upper shaft topped with an arachnid's head of eye-like dishes.

"You know I never noticed that tower before," I told Phillip.

"Really?"

The IRA blew up the men's toilet in the rotating restaurant at the top in 1971. Shortly after the bomb exploded at 16:30 GMT, the BT Tower received a telephone call from the group's Kilburn Battalion claiming responsibility for the attack. Damage was extensive, though no one was killed or injured and the tower re-opened a few weeks later. It continues to serve as a television and military broadcast station, but the restaurant at the top remains closed except for private parties. In an image of the floor after the bombing, the foot-thick walls of the restaurant have blown apart and rubble litters the carpet. Investigators stand, hands in their pockets, looking at what remains of the dining room, what shot through glass with ardor fierce and hands of flame, / But burst the Crystal Cabinet, spinning at the Top of the Tower over the gray roofs of central London. Smoke drifts out from the massive hole, a weeping Babe upon the wild, / And weeping Woman pale reclin'd, / And in the outward Air again / I fill'd with woes the passing Wind that blows the hair of those riders on their deathly horses, pitiless at the sight of such disaster hanging grimly on the air.

Phillip and I walked out of the park, toward a bar—the Angel in the Fields—which he said he visited a lot though we wandered among the stately apartments for some time before we found it. "Must not come too often," I joked.

"Right," he said. "Ha." Though it was overcast and somewhat chilly again, the gray promising rain, we took our pints outside, at a table flushed up against the bar's handsome wooden wall. Phillip was reading about the subconscious, he told me. He had just finished a book that argued that eighty percent of our decisions are made without us knowing that we've made them. I wasn't so sure I agreed, though I understood the point. In any case whatever directed me I trusted its prerogatives.

"It's really funny," he said, "that most of what you do in a day isn't done because you thought to do it."

"Right," I echoed him. I thought Phillip was handsome, though his sheepish appeal was somewhat perplexing. Had I invented it for him, and did it matter at all? We invent people all the time. I hesitated to push more on my attraction to him, for whatever reason, and couldn't decide if I wanted to make a move or not (in the end it went nowhere). Mostly, I liked the way he spoke, especially his feathery Scottish accent. He often recalled stories—the bombing of the BT Tower, a bad date, some issue with his job—that were a "complete disaster." It's a punchline that sets him at ease in conversation, and in my few days in London it entered my head like an endless, ever-useful refrain. Missed the train: what a disaster. Got too drunk: what a disaster. Showed up at the Tate right when it had closed: what a disaster!

Sitting outside, two Welsh men passed us with their French bulldog in tow. "I love Welsh," I said, reaching for another subject. "It's so beautiful—and strange."

"I do, too." He told me that once he had been out drinking very late before he had to take the train north to visit his mum. For whatever reason his train veered into Wales while he slept off his long and troubling hangover. When he came to and heard the station announcement and the nearby passengers speaking in Welsh, he didn't recognize the sound of the language and thought he'd had a stroke. "It was a complete disaster."

A drizzle picked up. "Let's go inside," Phillip said.

We found a table in a dark corner. Seeing my empty glass: "What do you want?" he asked.

"Whatever you're having."

Which was a pint of something.

"So what are you working on?" Phillip asked, returning with our drinks. He raised his glass and smiled.

"I've been working on a book." A cabinet into which I'd thrown everything since Helen's, though it had thus far refused to find its ending. In light of this it had become a long, interminable, inconclusive text on weather, not quite fiction or non-fiction, but something else.

"How far are you along? What's it about?"

"You know, I still don't know. But I think I've nearly finished it. It's about the weather, on the one hand, because its genesis was this piece I wrote about Hurricane Sandy. But then it's also about belief, I think, just the idea that, that we sort of live on the cusp of disaster. I thought a lot about the kind of communities that form around disaster."

"Is it a novel?"

"I don't know. I guess so. Then again no. It's like an essay that looks like a novel."

Phillip laughed. "Sounds complicated. How's Simon?"

I told him we broke up last year and that Simon had moved to Vienna. I tried to explain that we had hardly been together, but this didn't make any sense. Of course we had been together, Phillip knew that, but still, I wanted to distance myself from that recent past with him, to push it away, though it was pushing back against me as my trip to Austria drew closer. Simon lingered in my mind despite my attempts to pretend everything was OK. "Well, we were close, but not that close," I said. This surprised Phillip. It was unfair—and untrue. We had been very close, though saying so fit my post-breakup narrative, which required that I get on with my life without feeling abandoned or alone. "We're still friends," I said. "Just not close friends because he's in Vienna. I'm actually going to see him after London though, so next week."

"Good," Phillip said. "But Vienna is boring. Go to the Secession, of course."

"I plan to."

"Will you read from your new book tonight?"

"I think so," I said. "But I have to figure out which section."

The museum had asked me to give a reading on the theme of travel alongside several other writers from Europe and North America at the museum's theater

I had only been to Europe once before and decided to negotiate a longer stay out of the trip. After London I would fly to Vienna … for Simon, though I didn't justify it to myself that way … and return from there to New York.

I'd emailed Simon: "I'm coming to Europe to do some readings for my book that's coming out. Was going to come to Vienna, if you want to hang out."

"Is your book out? Yes, of course! When?"

My book had a shape, an arc—though I was still incapable of describing what that arc plotted or argued for. As a collection of texts, it moved between poetry and fiction, between Los Angeles and New York. The book struggled, self-consciously, with narrative: how to put the things that made up my life, but also the lives of others, into the form of a story. That was all I had. When someone asked me what it was about, I stuck to my line: "The weather." Which weather? It had ceased to mean the state of the atmosphere, the wind, visibility, heat, the chance of rain, and had become instead something far larger, a broader system, one that encompassed our politics, or the politics that had come to encompass us, the politics that were to come.

"OK, well I'm excited to hear it," Phillip said.

He had to run home to accept a delivery for some furniture he was having sent down from Scotland. We decided to split and meet up later at my reading. "If you need any help just let me know," he said. "Is your phone on?" It wasn't—I was trying to save money by living off wi-fi instead of British cellular service—but I told him I'd turn it on since it only cost $10 a day to use and I could afford to have a day with a working phone. The rain had stopped, so I saw him off at the tube, where he descended far below into a burst of hot wind that the train pushed into the station. I wondered what to do with my afternoon. It was one p.m., a whole day's worth of time before the event at the museum later that evening.

"Go to Hampstead Heath," he had said before we separated. "It's just north of here. You can find a bus to Kentish Town. Then you just take another bus or walk up. Go for a swim at the ponds before your reading."

Julia followed the path I'd followed up to Helen's, careful not to squash any of the salamanders that lounged in their neon litany across the cool earth under her worn sneakers. It had rained earlier in the afternoon, but the gray had broken to wide, cloudless, country skies, and the forest up to Helen's smelled sweetly of soaked wood and the mush of upstate dirt that Julia had come to love about rural New York. She had a suitcase with her that she carried by its handle off the ground. It wasn't heavy—all she'd packed were four sets of work clothes, a pair of white pants, and several white t-shirts and white collared shirts for "special events," as described in her acceptance letter—but she was exhausted after spending two days scrubbing Simon's place for him, every inch of the kitchen, the bathroom, even the gunk-ridden stairwell that she was surprised to find was a pale blonde color beneath the layers of brownish grease that had covered it up, so the bag felt twice as heavy as she dragged it up the mountain.

She was already half an hour past her stated arrival time. Simon had been gone for so long she didn't think he'd come back for at least another year, so likely her stay (for two months) before the start of her residency would be the last time anyone would see the house again for quite some time. She had been lonely while living in his cabin, but in isolation her writing had absorbed her, given her focus, and she'd written a novella that she liked, to her surprise, and had started on a collection of short stories. But the hike up to Helen's was the last time she'd have to think about her own work before having three months away from anything other than farming. This, she thought, would clarify her thinking. For now, she would put her writing on hold.

"I can't believe you applied," Simon said in response to her email asking if she could stay at his place beforehand, since her lease was up in the city and she couldn't stand the thought of spending any more time, let alone an entire two months, at the café, or at her apartment in Brooklyn. She had been saving for the better part of a year and, by her calculation, she had enough to live upstate, rent-free, so long as she ate as cheaply as possible and never went out. It would be tight, but she could do it.

"I need to do something else, outside the city."

"Of course you can stay. But won't you get lonely up there?" No more than she was in the city, without Zachary or Simon around to keep her company. With them, she could discuss books and writers. Her other friends, who were really just acquaintances, co-workers at Donahue's, even her sister, who lived uptown, were not the same as those two had been to her. In their absence she had finally fallen out of love with the city, and badly needed time away from it if she was ever going to renew her drive to live there. So she wrote to Helen, who encouraged her to apply for a three-month stint at the project. When she was accepted, she couldn't believe her luck: finally, she could leave the city.

"You've arrived!" Helen said, standing at the entrance to the complex, her mud-stained jeans shredded into makeshift work shorts. She wiped her hands on a towel and beamed at Julia. "Come in. Did you have any trouble? Did you drive?"

"It was no problem. I took a cab."

Helen put her arm around Julia's shoulders and led her inside. "Let's get you settled in. You can leave your things over there." She pointed to an alcove—its walls were lined with rows of crumbling, purely decorative books and black-and-white photographs of New York farmers—that jutted off the hallway toward Helen's bedroom. Julia dumped her bag and backpack onto a red Victorian couch pushed up against a bookshelf. "Come into the kitchen," Helen said. The house had not changed in the three years since Julia had been there. The tables on the porch—two large slabs of wood set on top of metal sawhorses—had the same blue vases filled with sprigs of heather and other wildflowers that she had seen on her first (and only) trip to the project. Back then, she and Simon had sat opposite one another at the end of the table during a large lunch that Helen used to host for her neighbors, sharing a slice of homemade pumpkin pie while Helen sang folk songs with a resident who accompanied her on an acoustic guitar. The same white linen curtains separated the kitchen from the porch.

Helen went around to a rickety, antique island in the middle of the kitchen. A large rack of pots and pans hovered over her newly shaved head. She ducked and wove between them as she rearranged her folders of notes, applications, slips of paper with reminders she'd made for herself, manila envelopes and FedEx boxes of things she needed to review, tax forms, the things she dealt with on Sundays while the other residents were permitted to rest, and found a printout of Julia's application with her notes. Julia sat on a stool opposite her.

"So," she said. "Let's talk about where you'll be staying first. Then we can get to some first tasks that I think it would be good to start you with. We'll do a formal introduction to the farm tomorrow." Helen's cheekbones were higher than Julia remembered, and she looked quite gaunt, almost sullen, especially with her shorn head. She wondered, at first, if she was sick. Simon had warned her that Helen had apparently changed since the book about her had come out in the late fall of last year, but she hadn't expected her to look quite like this. She was thin, and her voice lacked its usual fullness and warmth, replaced instead by a cold monotone. Gone was her cheerfulness, her rosiness. Julia let her memory of the old Helen— the Helen she'd met before Marissa Halpern's book on American "outsider communities," *The Pressure of the Outside*, was published to much acclaim and the embarrassment of Helen Hunley Wright— hang in her mind for a few seconds longer before allowing it to melt away, replaced by this new woman, the new Helen.

Most of the other residents had gone down to the river to swim, Helen said as she flipped through Julia's application, checking the notes she'd made on it. They talked about Julia's strengths, her expectations. From the kitchen's open doors, Julia could see a few residents sunning themselves on the sloping field below.

"So," she said, "Cabin J. I think we should go over there now so that you can let off your things, you can meet your roommates if they're in. Then we can talk about some work later in the afternoon. How does that sound?" While her tone remained flat, the new Helen was at least as friendly to her now as the old one had been. Sounds good.

Julia unloaded her things at Cabin J, the farthest from the complex, right at the western edge of the woods. It was the first place George and Helen had lived in together on the property before they completed the main building a few years later. A remnant of the nineteenth century and the Irish family that had first cleared the land, the cottage's floors sloped unevenly, and two trees had sprouted up close to its front porch and were slowly breaking it apart, as though the forest itself was attempting to tear the house down. Cabin J resisted these efforts with the help of the project, which had cut back and bound the trees while securing the porch as best they could. It was small and could only house three residents, the other two of whom were out somewhere, Helen wasn't quite sure where, on Sundays you can do what you want here. It's a non-religious Sabbath. She sent Julia up to the second floor, where the three would share the entire, undivided level ("A family of eight lived on this floor, all together, if you can believe it"), following her from behind on the ladder that bridged the ground floor to the second. The floorboards ached beneath them as they walked to Julia's cot, a surprisingly comfortable-looking single bed that the other residents had prepared for her. A small note with a chocolate taped to it rested on the pillow. "It isn't much," Helen said, "but it's a good bed. And you'll be working a lot, of course, so you won't be here that often. But when you hit this pillow, you'll be out like a light."

Like a light. Helen asked her if she needed anything else. Julia shook her head no, she wanted to unpack then maybe go out and sun with the other residents, none of whom she knew, if that was OK. "Of course! You'll be living with Lillian and Veronique.

Lillian has red hair," she explained, "and Veronique ... she's black." Helen stuttered with this observation. Julia guessed that she seldom had people of color at the residency. This made Julia uneasy; that the project had mostly appealed to white artists and writers in its history hadn't occurred to her before.

Helen smiled. "They spend a lot of time together—and I think they are on the hill near the river, if you look for them." Helen told her dinner was at eight and that everyone was expected to dine together for each meal (there would be three meals each day with an optional snack time at four thirty p.m. on the porch). Snack time would be a good opportunity to meet the other residents you don't find on the hill, Helen told her. She also explained that Julia didn't have to wear white for the non-public meals, and public events were quite rare now, rarer since Halpern's book had come out last fall, but she didn't mention that, only that "white's not as much of a thing here as it used to be, dear. But anyway, I'll leave you to it," and descended the ladder.

"Thank you," Julia called to her from above.

She had read the book, of course, but had not been persuaded by its portrait of Helen and the community. She had visited before, knew the good that had come out of it and didn't agree with Halpern's view that the project was not so much a residency as it was an unsettling personality cult based around the career of a failed artist. She had liked everything about it when she'd visited the first time, so much so that she had immediately wanted to live there, and had vowed someday to do so—if not for its work ethic, then at least for its promise of a different social experience, one based on "real" (she knew this wasn't quite the word) interactions with people. But Marissa described Helen as an "ego goblin" who fed upon the creative energy of others and who compensated for her own lack of artistic success by luring younger, more talented artists to her cliquish farm, where they would subsequently renounce their artistic practice after an intense period of psychological warfare on their confidence and swear loyalty to her. In her research, Halpern found that few artists returned to their practice after a stint at Helen's. A shame about what some of the residents said about their time, Helen had argued when the fact checkers for Halpern's publisher contacted her about the chapter before publication, but not true that most had renounced their art. Helen submitted many names of former residents who had "returned" to their art after leaving her project, howbeit often quite changed—in temperament and focus—but nevertheless still artists. And Helen had never once demanded that anyone swear loyalty to her. That was not only a ridiculous claim but a bold-faced lie, one that she'd threatened to challenge in court if need be, though she said so without quite knowing libel law. With this threat in mind, and in the absence of any artists who were willing to say, on record, that they had been asked to do so, Halpern had agreed to soften the assertion, though only at the insistence of her publisher, to a lesser accusation: "Many felt that an oath of loyalty was required for their work to be valued by Wright."

Halpern, whom Helen had trusted, had betrayed her. When the book was released it was a success. Many of the "outsider" communities Halpern had written about were inundated with press requests, including Helen's. They had not been prepared for the intense negative scrutiny they received, which culminated when the mayor of the town at the base of the project's hill formally issued a statement condemning "the town cult" while acknowledging that he had no legal power to compel Helen to leave or to close the project. Many of Helen's supporters scoffed at this, but about half of those who were in residence at the time of publication departed immediately, despite Helen's earnest attempts during a bonfire meeting to assuage their concerns about her role in the project. While a few had secretly shared Halpern's concerns about Helen, others hadn't until they read the chapter, after which every move, every word of Helen's seemed to validate Halpern's claims.

After the book came out, and with Sandy only a few years before that, it had been a disappointing, bitter time in Helen's life, one defined by a descent into depression and unfocused anger. In June, she sat down in front of her antique mirror with a trashcan between her knees and shaved her head in some wild attempt at self-therapy. It largely worked: the loss of her hair distracted her from Halpern's book, from that person Halpern wrote about, and when she looked at herself in the mirror she saw someone else, someone who had been inside her but whom she had kept back: a stronger woman, a fiercer, if more guarded advocate for her ideas.

Julia made no mention of the book in her application, of course, except over email, when Helen had asked her if she had read it. (This was a question that Helen posed to all applicants now.) She lied, for whatever reason: "I know about it but didn't read it." After Halpern had so easily infiltrated the community, Helen introduced a new, more intensive application process, adding a required non-disclosure agreement. This secrecy pained her but she felt, at the encouragement of her lawyer, that it was necessary for her and her community's survival. You're alone in this, he had made clear to her, meaning there was nothing George could, or would, do. When the book was published and the first reviews came in, followed by the first press inquiries and subsequent articles about Helen, George had been silent—and refused to comment to any publications, including artnet.com and artforum.com, both of which had asked him for a statement. Helen, in agreeing to speak to both, appeared defensive, while George, "who did not make himself available to comment," luxuriated silently in European isolation.

Julia unfolded the note her roommates had left on her pillow: "Hi Julia, we are so excited to have you with us! xx Lillian and Veronique." She popped the square of chocolate into her mouth and let it dissolve on her tongue.

Most of the other residents lounging on the hill were naked. She could see three, including Veronique and Lillian, sitting under an umbrella nearest her cabin. After unpacking her things, Julia joined them, though she was nervous about the impression she would make, so she decided to wear her dark sunglasses, which always gave her a stroke of confidence among strangers. When she came upon Lillian, Veronique, and a man their age, she stretched out a towel next to Lillian—who was short, with wide, intense eyes—and stripped down to her underwear. "Hi," she said, removing her bra. "I'm Julia."

"Hi," Lillian said.

Jeff raised a hand over his eyes to get a better look at her. She smiled at him. He was beautiful, and he was aware of the immediate, stupefying effect his beauty had on others; even this simple gesture allowed him the opportunity to tighten his abs for everyone's benefit and had a certain cinematic flare in the white-hot afternoon. It projected sex appeal that he knew equated with power. His skin was a golden brown except for his groin and thigh, where his cock was framed by a triangle of only lightly tanned skin. Hidden behind her dark lenses, Julia's eyes wandered down to his substantial member resting between his thighs. "I'm Jeff," he said. He extended his hand to her. Next to him, Veronique nodded. She introduced herself as Julia's new roommate.

"It's nice to meet you!" Julia said, afraid she was too enthusiastic. "Your note was lovely."

Veronique laughed, "So glad you made it!" She was also new, had only arrived three days ago from Vancouver but absolutely loved it. "It's so nice just to be outside, to work with your hands. Get in the dirt."

"It is," Jeff said. "This is my third time here," he explained. "Have you been much before?"

"Once," Julia said. "I was with my friend Simon."

"Nice. Don't think I know him? Did he stay here?" He fell back down on his towel. Julia explained that Simon lived about forty minutes away, but had visited often over the years. "Well, you'll love it here," he said.

Lillian seconded him, "You really will."

After the publication of Halpern's book, Helen scrapped her own memoir. She had only written about fifty pages, so it wasn't as if she'd lost years of time and work, she reasoned, and besides, she needed time to recollect her thoughts anyway in light of this attack on her career and the project. She had had a title for it already—*An Atlas for Us*—and had decided that, too, did not sufficiently convey her position, so she began again, this time with the far simpler, almost contrite, and decidedly generic *Country Days*. She had contacted an agent in New York whom she had known in the late eighties, and they were "in talks" about the book. This agent was convinced that people would want to hear Helen's story now that *The Pressure of the Outside* had become so popular. (When they spoke on the phone it had just received front-page coverage in the *New York Times Book Review*: "The weird American obsession with obsession.") "I think we could get you into airport bookstores, to be honest, maybe even right next to the paperback of *Pressure of the*

Outside when it's out next year. You don't have to go long, you know, it can be short. Your book. Simple. To the point. Your story: where you came from, your marriage to George, what you did. The community. People will want to hear from you. People want to *sympathize*. They want your story."

Standing at the island in the kitchen that one word came to her again, *sympathy*. People want to *sympathize*. A light widened through the western-facing window as the sun began to move down from its station at midday. She highly doubted that people wanted to *sympathize* so much as they wanted to prolong the story of Helen and her freaky little commune. Why, she wondered, had Halpern singled her out? Of all the chapters, including a chapter on a frankly psychotic fitness camp in Arizona based on nutritious popsicles, a chapter on a habitual liar and scam artist from San Francisco who runs a country on an island that sinks half the day, and a chapter on an Ivy League fraternity notorious for its disturbingly elaborate gay sex rituals, all these different and obsessive communities in America, why had Halpern singled her out for particular ire? Certain sentences stood out in her mind, words she couldn't shake no matter how much she tried to forget them: "Wright, who is somewhat overweight despite her daily calls for harder and harder unpaid physical labor, often stood on the porch overlooking her vast property, where she barked orders into a microphone piped into a PA system installed around the complex." She did not bark. She was not overweight. Or worse:

> Obsessed with the intellectual and physical differences between men and women, Wright showed an obvious favoritism toward the men who worked for her, who she seemed to believe were smarter than the women at the project. In conversation, and in her public,

dictatorial speeches, which she often made for the benefit of her tribe, she often presented herself as someone humbly in service to a greater intellectual good (a good seldom defined for me or for anyone who was curious enough to ask her). She downplayed her role in the community by stating that she was simply a servant, here only to teach. At such moments, she often reiterated the point that she learned more from them than they could possibly learn from her. Whatever that meant, I was never very clear myself. But whom, I often wondered, did she serve? And how?

On several evening occasions, she invited male residents to her room for late-night salons, where they would read classic novels. Since I am a woman, I was not invited to this after-hours book club, but one resident confirmed to me that during his stay, which overlapped with my own, they never actually read the books, but rather listened to Helen speechify about their contents and whatever crude arguments she could muster from her mostly cursory readings. My informant had been excited to read *Moby-Dick*, which Helen assigned to them for the month of June, but found that the event was a pretense for Helen to surround herself with boys she could easily impress, some of whom she would ask to stay back at her place for a more intimate conversation after the other residents left. This shocked me, as I could not understand how anyone had the energy to stay up that late and wake early the next morning for the regimen of chores. This possibly explained why some boys had the mornings off in recompense for what Helen said was "night work." I was unable to speak with anyone who enjoyed these more private meetings, but the assumption—widely shared among the residents, particularly the women—was that they were, of course, sexual in nature.

Troubled as she was by Halpern's assertions, Helen ultimately dismissed her claims as baseless, borne of an ignorance of the deliberate ambiguity that the project, like other communities, necessarily rested in. She couldn't dispute her claims about the other places Halpern had written about, the other "obsessives" who had established these maniacal systems to subjugate and control lost men and women in search of a home, because she herself hadn't seen them first-hand. Of her own project, however, she argued, to anyone who would listen, that Halpern's view resulted ultimately from confusion about what community is, rather than a precise, clear-eyed view of the project. Halpern was wrong.

She struggled to work on her own writing after she read *The Pressure of the Outside* because the book largely negated hers. How could she write now without some obligation to respond to Halpern's claims? Had she slept with any male students? Would answering that question in writing, whether it be in her memoir or in some public response to the controversy, matter, would it change any minds? She believed that any answer to this question would be insufficient to her detractors, and would only serve to further muddy their perception of her project.

The arrival of new residents agitated her now, though only for a brief few days usually, but three—the most in some time—had arrived that week alone. She was thus particularly on edge. The idea of another betrayal consumed her. She was always anxious about when the next one would come and this anxiety was accompanied by an immediate distrust for anyone new—all of whom she greeted, against her own wishes, with what she knew was a searching look in case she had missed any telltale signs, like those she had missed in Halpern but had later obsessively recalled: the fact that she was a journalist who had written about *cults*, that she wasn't very clear about the angle she planned to take when she approached Helen about her story, that she always seemed to be biting her tongue when she was witness to an argument or confrontation between Helen and her residents at the time. Helen feared, almost constantly, that some new resident would screw her over, run to some magazine with a fabricated story of emotional and sexual exploitation by way of farming. She had gone into therapy, once a week in the city, which was good for her, to get out every so often, and it had allowed her to reconnect with her apartment and with some friends. Most people were *sympathetic*—that word again—and wanted to see her, wanted to show her that the book had not changed how they viewed her. She reminded herself that these three new girls were nice, for example, had submitted excellent applications and signed NDAs. One, Julia Fitzgerald, was a writer, but mostly of fiction, and nothing she had written that Helen had found online suggested that she would be interested in writing about Helen's project.

A buzzer sounded on her phone. It was four fifteen p.m.: fifteen minutes before snack time. She began to set out bowls of apples and oranges at the tables on the porch. From an industrial-sized refrigerator, she retrieved a few cheese wheels that she arranged on a wooden slab beside a large chunk of honeycomb, some crackers, and grapes that she carried outside and placed beside the bowls of fruit. Earlier in the morning, she had infused several pitchers of water with lemon and cucumber. She set out eight glasses, one for each resident, and eight plates. She handled the snacks every day—it was one way she stayed involved with the project's meals since she played no part in the preparation of breakfast, lunch, or dinner—and used the thirty-minute break to better know the residents as a group. Since she often saw them only individually or in pairs, or at her salons, this time allowed her to observe them more closely, to learn their humor, the various divisions and alliances (all of which she counseled against) that formed among them. At snack time, the map of their lives would arrange itself before her and reveal who was sleeping together, who was jealous, and who had taken the lead among them. Recently that role had been seized by Jeff, of course, her most frequent resident, but his attraction to Veronique opened him up to a challenge from another male since his mind would no longer be solely focused on the work at hand but rather on impressing this new girl. She expected that Mark, a fit but much younger boy from Southern California, would be the one to successfully challenge Jeff for the unspoken leadership role.

For Helen, snack time was an indispensable period in the day that allowed her to identify—and therefore disrupt—the various balances of power that existed between the residents. Knowing that Jeff's attraction to Veronique would present a weakness in the hierarchy that had developed around Helen, she decided that she would exploit it by sitting Mark between herself (snack time was always seat-assigned) and Julia, the new girl. She would then place Jeff with Veronique to further highlight the bond between them for the benefit of the group. This would frustrate the others, she expected, many of whom she suspected had been deprived of intimacy for weeks.

She walked over to the microphone installed at the corner of the porch. Below her, Veronique, Jeff, and Julia sat sunbathing while closer to the river Mark and the other four residents were lounging on rocks. She flipped the speaker system on and leaned in to the microphone. It buzzed as she brought her lips closer: "Folks, would you please join me on the porch?" Her voice echoed throughout the project's grounds, from the speakers installed on Cabins B, C, J, K, and the farm house, startling a few birds in the nearby trees. Helen went back into the kitchen to fetch the silverware and cloth towels for her residents, who would soon arrive, famished from their long morning at play.

The BT Tower burst its side and, lo,
the streets stood in awe.

Is it not a prerequisite of Europe that every tower
must someday fall?

with ardor fierce & hands of flame

I'd never been to the men's pond at the Heath before, but had, of course read about it, the long thread of naked or Speedo-clad English boys that lined its famous dock stretching out over the cold, brown water. People had swum there for more than a century, after London converted the ponds from reservoirs to recreational swimming holes, and ever since that generous civic transformation boys had met one another and later ventured off toward the woodsier side of the Heath, where they'd cruise for trade and fuck in sylvan seclusion. The men's pond sits in quiet privacy behind a long screen of trees. I set down my things on the small, crowded yard at the narrow entrance to the dock, where a sign warned against women bathers (their own pond is adjacent), and changed into swim trunks I'd picked up from a cheap clothing store near the Angel stop off the Northern Line that were not nearly as sexy as the Speedos of the men who hopped along the dock toward the water.

I left my backpack with an older man who said he'd be happy to keep my bag safe with him. He'd been sitting cross-legged beside me, his hands resting on top of his gut, watching me as I undressed in the sun. With a wink, he implored me to go on in after I passed over my bag. All right. I tiptoed along the cold, wet wood toward the water, looked down at the broken surface of the pond, and hesitated a moment—Phillip told me that there were crayfish, or some other hideous freshwater crabs, that pricked your balls and ferried disease-ridden microbes into the bloodstream—before deciding that I wouldn't let this fear take hold of me, and jumped in. I plunged into the cold tonic of mud and rose back up to the surface, to the guffawing and laughing men who were diving off the dock one after the other. They were of all ages and body types, though most were in their late twenties to early forties. Several swans had gathered at the far end of the pond, out of the way of the swimmers and past a buoyed-border rope that none of the men were permitted to cross. Head above the waves, I watched as they flattered one another in the glint of sunlight in their corner of the men's pond. One extended its neck upward, a thin pillar of feathers that flashed neon white in the light, lifting its wings to their full span to beat the water where a clique of mallards had gathered in a circle. What was the occasion of this ceremony of birds I had no idea, but its symbolic order took tentative hold of the afternoon, with the swan serving as some key to an otherwise opaque and dense natural poetry. I could not read it. I paddled among the men who backstroked in the sun. I had heard that the swans of England are protected by decree of the Queen, who alone is permitted to dine upon them.

A young, handsome half-Asian man with long black hair who had been changing near me on the grass kicked past in a quick lap within the pond's perimeter. I swallowed an awful mouthful of water from the wave his legs supplied and spit it back out with a gag at the rank taste of it. The muddy gulp coated my throat and tongue with the taste of England. He stopped swimming and turned back to face me. Wiping his hair from his face so that he could see me, "Hey, sorry about that," and shot me a smile.

"Translucent lovely shining clear," the afternoon light fled when clouds gathered overhead. Regardless of the shadows the boys kept coming, more and more, each as pretty as the last. I swam for about twenty minutes before deciding to get out to ensure that my bag was still with its pudgy guardian. I needed to revise my reading for that night anyway. I dried off on the smaller lawn outside the pond. The sun had emerged again and many of the boys had begun to lie out on the grass, rubbing themselves and one another with lotion. I passed up the distraction and decided to go for a walk.

"Hey, man," the boy who had kicked water in my face said, jogging up from behind. He tapped me on the shoulder. I turned around. He was shirtless, with the tip of his blue Speedo peeking out from the top of fatigue cargo shorts. A thick trail of pubic hair rose from its band toward his outward navel. He had a slightly protuding belly and grabbed at his dick in his shorts as he spoke: "My name's John. Sorry about kicking you back there."

He wrapped his arms around his chest and leaned back, as if to stretch, which made his stomach bulge. I liked his bad posture. "Oh, it's no problem," I said. "Really. I'm Nick."

"Want to go," he started, pulling on a white t-shirt, his head catching in the sleeve, "um, do you want," his head popping through the collar, "to go for a walk." Another grin.

I hesitated. I needed to write, but also a little fun might make it (eventually) easier to concentrate. "Sure," I said.

We made our way out of the ponds toward the west end of the Heath. John told me he was from a small town in the north of England. His father was originally from Tokyo and his mother from Manchester. I told him I was visiting from New York. At this he did that thing, the thing New Yorkers do, but I realized it's what everyone in the world does, and asked me what I did. I don't know, I said, which was true, I write, then decided to say that I was a poet and novelist, even if I feared that sometimes this turned people off. Somehow saying it always made me seem a little aimless or like I was faking it. John said that was cool. What do I write? I told him I was finishing a book that had sort of gotten away from me.

"How do you mean?"

"It's hard to explain."

"I see. Well, I write some."

"You do?"

"Yeah, I'm a poet myself, actually."

"Really? That's cool." I hadn't met a poet in the UK yet, though I expected I would that night at my reading. "Where can I read your poems?" I asked.

"I don't have much published yet, though I've got something out online soon."

"You'll have to send me the link."

We hit the edge of the woods that led to the cruising grounds off in the distance. Public sex wasn't something I'd ever done before—it had always been the purview of Tom of Finland, B-list gay movies, and *other people*, but at this border between the world acceptable to straight people and the one they wouldn't go into, beyond which men were somewhere hunched in the foliage among other men, bent over, or gathering the courage to approach someone they had been spying for a while, I felt a strange, irresistible pull, one that made my stomach drop, like I was flying backwards. "We'll go in?" he asked. I nodded.

We jerked one another off behind a fortress of bushes that formed near a set of scraggly trees, sloppily trading spit in rushed kisses, our tongues colliding with one another in a clumsy effort, far off from the paths that threaded the Heath, and from any of the other boys or men who were searching for a couple to interrupt or join. I pulled down John's shorts along with his Speedo, which was still damp and smelled strongly of the pond, and spread both cheeks to tongue his asshole. He moaned loudly and yanked at his dick in a rush to get hard quickly. My knees dug into the soft earth as I unzipped my own shorts and pulled out my cock. I grew harder as my tongue penetrated deeper into his ass, into its fleshy, pink twist, this tiny keyhole to which I sought entry. It contracted, and then eased open. In that cabinet, my mind wandered beyond John and his ass, to Simon, who always said he liked to hook up outside, though we never did except once or twice on the porch of his cabin. And, unlike at the Heath, those moments felt private since there was no one else around for at least a mile. Both times began like this: me pulling down his pants to lick his ass while he jerked off. In that cabinet I felt love.

Within a few minutes, John was breathing heavily, "I think I'm going to cum," he panted. I pulled back, "Already?" Yes, yes, he said, and went back to jerking himself off with his right hand while he pulled my head closer into his ass with his left, forcing my head up and down into his rear. I disappeared into him, seized the form of our pleasure and inhabited it like a diving suit among the growing waves of pleasure that undulated through him as he came closer and closer to coming. Beams of sunlight pierced the canopy and spiked the ground around us in a definitive syntax of some unknown language that attempted to describe this scene, or at least describe it for me, a crystal grammar in which I saw John, myself, the cruising grounds, all these naked men elsewhere and hidden among the trees and bushes, corralled together into a single sentence, though its precise meaning evaded me when I recognized it in the woods. Cabinets gave forth to more cabinets, and in one, I saw myself going down on John from above, as though shot by a camera hung up from a branch, until that picture gave way to another cabinet, and within that a tiny New York standing on its riparian shelf of concrete and steel, with rooms that opened to Julia sitting on her bed, reading a book; Zachary, Stewart, even Wolfgang at the Spectrum; all these faces glowing in a picture-box New York as my heart pumped faster and faster. In sex my mind tends to go. A breeze rustled the trees and carried a few nearby voices with it. Maybe someone was watching us and was closer than they sounded, but I didn't care to check for any voyeurs. And I didn't mind them. I kept going along with the movement of his hand against the back of my head. Couldn't breathe I was buried so deep between his muscular cheeks that tightened as an electric pulse vibrated through his body and he shot several long, white strands of semen across the forest floor, onto piles of leaves and sticks. They roped in thin loops on the soil. I pulled back to watch him shudder and slackened forward, onto his knees. "Jesus," he said, and turned around to suck me off.

Fill'd me that like a flame I burn'd

John went on his way, whatever way that was (he said something about visiting a pagoda, though I didn't think that I had heard him right), but I didn't follow along despite an invitation to join him. Instead I got his number and promised to text later that night, knowing that I probably wouldn't. I walked back the way we came, passing a few men who eyed me with mild interest, but nobody said a word. My reading was in a few hours.

From a hill in the Heath, London's dimpled skyline broke upwards with its towers and cranes, like spikes on a seismograph. I had ambled up a path toward the lower middle of the Heath, where most of the picnics and couples had grown scarcer as the grass grew taller. At a small hill overlooking the pond and the neighborhoods on the eastern side of the park, I came upon another field, completely empty of any day visitors. The tall wheat-grass, singing with the stereoscopic music of grasshoppers, met the jagged edge of some long-tamed wood about twenty feet away from me, before dropping off into shadows. I spread out my towel in its center. Even lying down I could see the Shard rising up over the tree line, much reduced and recognizable only by its pronged tip, and yet still there, the Tower of Commerce. Above it, tapered clouds moved quickly across the blue, almost whimsically, contracting into various shapes before thinning into white, uncomplicated bands that hurried off toward the countryside.

Another London there I saw

I pulled out my reading from my bag. I was choosing between two pieces: a short essay-fiction about the tides, and one on travel that I had only recently written. A few lines in the tides piece no longer worked, so I struck them from the manuscript and wrote in their replacements, though I was certain that by evening these too would have to be changed. Far off, the city. I tried to concentrate on the page on my lap. I wondered where John's pagoda was, and whether it was real. (Later I learned that there is a pagoda in the Heath, though it is exceptionally difficult to find if you don't already know where it is.) Perhaps he was off to find another boy already, and together they were hidden under the foliage, the smell of dirt and sweat filling their nostrils as one rammed the other from behind. I wanted to be there, but then again I wanted to be everywhere. I cut some more lines from the piece: "~~Like waves in an otherwise still lake.~~" "~~I moved with these disturbances.~~" "~~The catastrophe of his weather.~~" (Whose?) I found the printout of "The Crystal Cabinet" between the pages of the manuscript. It was crumpled, still water-damaged. I re-read it, thinking that perhaps I could open my reading with it, since it was Blake, this was London, the city of the poet's birth, life, and death, and I had found it by chance in a bathroom here. Perhaps I could just read Blake all night instead of my own work, which, looking over it on the Heath, gave me greater pause the more I scanned the inadequate words I'd chosen to describe "the tides."

My phone vibrated in my bag. "when are you in Vienna?" Simon wrote.

I began to type: "in 2 days," then deleted that. "thursday afternoon – early." Which was in two days. His presence, or at least the knowledge that he was somewhere across the gulf of the continent, leaning over his phone and typing, stuttered me. I wrote, "in 2 days."

"cool," he replied. "let's get a drink thursday night. i'll text you then. when is your reading?"

"tonight."

"good luck!!" He sent me an emoji: a yellow face with its palms held up in excitement.

Had George ever loved her? She didn't allow herself to dwell on the thought too often, but at certain late hours it formed somewhere in the back of her head and crept forward, slowly, the longer she stayed awake, drowsy over her Macbook Pro as she typed away at *Country Days*, which she now wondered if she should rename *Falling Away*. By this she meant from the world, at least from the world outside the project (and, for a time, from the world outside her marriage to George). She typed: "We had this notion that we could change people's ideas of art if we showed them that art could be expanded beyond museums and galleries, objects and paintings, into a vaster field—literally, in our case—of work and play." She deleted the word "play," and in doing so that secondary thing trudging up through her mind—had George ever loved her?—inched closer to her mental foreground. Play had been a word of George's. You played with ideas, with things. He described his practice as "playing around." When they first announced their plans to found an artist's colony in upstate New York to a circle of their friends gathered at their apartment, he said that they had been "playing with the idea" for a long time. He did like to play. And no he had not loved her, at least not as she had loved him. She shook her head. He had loved her. Or had he. This back and forth with herself was humiliating, even in private. She wasn't dependent on him, financially or emotionally, and hadn't been for a long time. She had gotten along without him just fine for years. She had even done better for herself now that he wasn't around. She typed: "akldjfklajdglhadlghhewofaaidogj." This fucking book. "This fucking book," she said aloud, though whether she meant *Falling Away* or *The Pressure of the Outside* was unclear even to her. It had been years: and in those years, she had forgotten and forgiven, though Halpern had reinstated her insecurities. She sipped wine.

Outside her bedroom window the moon, a bone-white sliver set deep among its stars, smiled crookedly, even tauntingly at her, almost in confirmation of what was unfolding in her head. It seemed to say, Can you do it? Do what: this? She scrolled through the Word document before her. The opening line: "It was a time of crisis, and we sought to escape." Did the sentiment (or the bad prose) make her a coward? Was it even very interesting? She poured herself another glass and stood up, opened the window to let in the fresh air, and began to undress for the evening.

Under the same moon, Julia sat up in her bed while Lillian and Veronique slept in theirs across the room. Dust motes sparkled in the air over her head, but she'd long gotten used to them, and to the intermittent cough she'd developed despite their daily attempts to wipe Cabin J clean. Her notebook on her lap, she reviewed a few postcards she had written that night to friends back home, including Simon in Austria and her sister in New York. She wrote one to her mother, too, but unlike the other two, her mother would actually respond to her (Simon had replied with a postcard once, admitting in his attenuated scrawl that he was not very good at the post), and frequently, so she found that she was most often writing these little notes to her mother, almost every three or four days, and it was increasingly difficult to keep the pace her mom had set for their correspondence. Dear mom, she began, Thank you for your last postcard. No, things have not changed, at least not significantly, and yes I am still enjoying myself though work, as you can imagine, is quite a challenge given the heat. What else to say? It occurred to her that all she ever wrote about was work rather than what life on the mountain was like. Mostly boring whenever it wasn't extremely difficult. She had gained muscle weight; her arms were toned from shoveling dirt. Would this be of interest to anyone? She hadn't yet let the experience wrap itself in words. Smells, tastes, plants, degrees of light, even the varying kinds of dirt she'd begun to pick up on, had yet to find themselves in her language. She knew she should resist the urge to record it if she could. She spent too much time overthinking her Life, the descriptions that would make her Life—and its Ideas—stick to the page. For once, she needed to live without words cluttering her mind.

She turned a page in her notebook, where she decided she would quietly continue her writing (it had been several weeks since her arrival and she could not stay away from her stories), despite Helen's injunction against "practices." Her mother could wait. She decided, however, to write unsent letters to friends as an exercise in beginning new stories. (That almost everyone communicated by email now, rather than by post, made the form all the more intriguing to her.) They would act as micro-fictions, little stories she could bore herself with. She decided to write another epistolary story to Simon, whom she hoped was still in Vienna. He'd mentioned that he would probably move to Berlin in mid-July (it was early July), finishing his summer in Germany before returning to the US finally, and earlier than he'd planned. This writing rarely amounted to anything more than a few notes:

Dear Simon, I've heard that you dyed your hair blonde—a change from the dark hair I've known to be yours for years. ~~Dear Simon, my hair is still black, so I wonder if your decision to go blonde is, in some small part, an effort to fully cleave yourself from New York and your friends here.~~ Since you are in Vienna, I am thinking of stately European cities on the central European plains.

A city is the way people argue about organization. Streets clean up our lives. But I am most interested in a city's parks, which are the stories cities tell themselves about nature.

In Belgium, there is a park that intersects with one of the largest and oldest forests in Europe, the Bois de la Cambre. It extends down from Brussels to the north of France, beginning—in the Belgian capital—in a subdued park with a small, manmade pond at its center. In the middle of the pond is a small island with a French restaurant that serves raw hamburger. The only way to the island is by a motorized ferry that moves across the water by wire. A round-trip costs a single Euro.

Why Brussels? (It was one of the few European cities she'd been to, so she supposed that was why, but why in relation to Vienna, where she had never been?) She made a note to herself: "Describe parks of Vienna? Or describe them as Simon would describe them." She continued the story on another page:

Memory is non-specific in the way that parks are non-specific.

If the brain is a knowable object within which
unknowable—or mysterious—activity occurs, then
the park is like a brain while the life within it, within
the Bois de la Cambre, is thinking.

This was obtuse, of course. In the margin of her notebook
she wrote:

little girl
in park?

boy says
to girl something
inscrutable. describe
inscrutability
(old eng: not + to search)
of daily conversation?

he has
dark hair
like Simon

What kind of letter looks like this? What kind of story? It was
pretentious, unsuccessful writing, she concluded. She made a
small drawing of herself in the corner of the page, then tore the
page out of her notebook and folded it into a square, stuffing it in
an open copy of *National Geographic*.

She wasn't quite ready to toss the writing, but she didn't
want to see it again either. She was tired, anyway, of her prose and
revising after she'd spent the afternoon digging up a new field for
fall's crops, and so had begun to drift off—

Helen lay on her bed naked, without a blanket, the unexpectedly cool night air prickling her skin, the room lit only by a candle she'd set in the open window. No strong winds blew these late summer days, so the flame didn't go out, but instead burned down to the tin dish she'd placed it on. By August, she could never sleep, even with a pill, which she didn't like to take though her doctor had strongly recommended it. It was usually too hot to do anything but stay up all night. So she lay in bed reading a journal she'd kept in the late eighties (she'd more or less ceased reading anything other than her own journals, those that had survived Sandy, in what had become a contemplative research phase for *Falling Away*).

February 6, 1989

We lost Jim Rhodes our neighbor today to AIDS. Died at home with Frank, who had moved out but often visited and was there with Jim till the end. We went down with Frank to see Jim's body before it was taken away (by who? Jim never mentioned his family before. I wondered but didn't want to ask).

Apartment was full of paintings Jim had done, many of them in the last six months—his best work, George said. I said maybe we can find someone to take these on and Frank was hopeful that a friend at a big gallery (didn't say which) would find them a home, maybe an exhibition. I didn't want to look at his body, but there he was, under covers up to his chin since it was so cold and he was so thin, just like a skeleton. Poor

Jim. He looked starved to death. Starved eyes wide as saucers, with the skin around them very pale and papery, not like his normally full cheeks. Jim wasn't the Jim I knew. I was shocked. I had seen him three weeks ago. He was weak but he looked better than this.

Many others sick of course and no hope of cure but they say they are close.

Several pages covering the rest of that winter and spring were torn out of the notebook, though she couldn't remember why she had removed them. She skipped to June, read a few pages, then stopped at this one:

June 14, 1989

George upset over cancelled show in France but he will be fine. I reminded him it wasn't cancelled, but pushed back and this wasn't really quite enough for him (typical). I bought him used but nice book from the Strand, John Ashbery's *Shadow Train* since he loves poetry & JA, but George reminded me he already had a copy, signed—very emphatically. I read it myself in a single sitting and liked it …

She didn't finish reading this entry since it went on for several pages (the longest—most were quite short) but didn't come to any epiphanic conclusions and didn't include any descriptions of her life then. She flipped to the end of the diary since she'd already gone over that summer several times for anything that might suit *Country Days/Falling Away* (so far, and to her surprise, very little).

September 28, 1989

George and I sat down and formally drew up plans for upstate project. He wants to call it Wright Colony. I think it should be called HG, very modern though also quite pretentious now that I write it down. Other idea is to name it after Irish family's last name: Healy's Hill. We decided to wait on a title—he is very happy, elated even about this, and I am too, so we are getting along very well. The idea of creating a new kind of space w/ a new idea about art thru a new relationship to the land. I agree. He said, "We will change the way things get done here." We both agree that it will be gorgeous. In meantime, we go to France for a month.

Helen opened another leather-bound notebook—this one a gift from her late mother—that continued 1989. Though her slanted handwriting had become larger, more rushed across the page (and with more strikethroughs as she became self-conscious that someone might someday read it), the entries were longer, more philosophical than the previous three journals. Many pages between entries were left inexplicably blank or were filled with *New York Times* and *Village Voice* articles she'd pasted in. She couldn't remember why she had included some of these articles, except for the few about artists she knew and, of course, AIDS. On the front she had written her address: 228 East 11th Street, Apartment 2, NYC.

November 4, 1989

Was so hot late October but quite cool this week in November. Saw Frank this afternoon at funeral for Tim, dancer. He himself has become quite sick, but tells me he is going to fight. Rene Ricard attended, surprisingly (I didn't know he knew Tim), and we realized we hadn't seen each other in maybe 2? years. I sat next to Rene at the service. We both joked it was a terribly black time to reunite. We had been good friends until he fought with George, whom he has never trusted. He said something witty about how wearing black for all these queens was the worst possible tribute—want to kill myself for not being able to remember what he said exactly since approximation would do it NO justice. I laughed, but of course wanted to cry since these are the bad days. George is in France for the show since it wasn't cancelled after all. It opens next week ~~with new "paintings" of his.~~

Helen wasn't sure why this was crossed out, nor could she remember why she'd placed the word "paintings" in scare quotes, since they *were* paintings—or, rather, they were slabs of cheaply painted apartment walls George had cut out of an abandoned building in Chinatown and had framed.

I decided not to go this time. Surprisingly, Rene asked how he was and his question seemed genuine enough. I told him that George was well, but the situation had taken a toll on him, even if he never said so. Like him we had lost many friends. Rene only nodded, at a loss for words?

We decided to get a late lunch afterwards. Rene told me about a new Chinese place on 8th and we went there (great). I asked Rene what he had been doing recently, if he had been writing, and he told me he had two new books this year: a collaboration with

Francesco and another book of poems called *God with Revolver*. I told him I loved this title, and it very much suited our lives in New York. God had his gun to our heads. He's going to send me a copy.

I told him about the colony and invited him to be the first to visit. He said congratulations and laughed but I know he would never be able to drag himself out of the city to come upstate, ~~even if we drove him.~~ I told him I ~~also~~ had a new show of drawings coming up/~~forthcoming?~~ He said he wanted to come by but had a friend's film premiering that night that he couldn't get out of, if he remembered correctly. He promised to check and ring me up if he could come. ~~I understood and said I'd walk him through the show later.~~ He also asked to come by the studio for a visit. We made a date of it.

The drawings: crude mandalas, really, with the faces of dead friends. This is not explicit, at least I don't think it will be, but in them they circle in patterns across the page, like a clock.

In the present, Julia was alternating her notebook entries with fiction and diary accounts of the project. On one page, she wrote,

Two residents finally left after promising all month they were going to go, at least to the others and me. One was my roommate, Veronique, who, it turns out, was half-French, from Paris. We practiced French together, but mine is very rusty now seven (!!!) years after graduating. She left with her boyfriend, Jeff, who had been a resident three summers in a row. That left six of us for the week. Fine—though it meant a lot more work and I've been so tired. One new resident, this boy from Chicago named Mario, arrived today and is extremely nice. Helen introduced us to him at dinner and we sat next to each other and immediately hit it off.

Opposite that she abandoned the form of the journal entry and any pretense to a recognizable form of fiction with a series of observations about cities and parks:

My local radio station in New York reports the temperature in Central Park when it records the weather in the city.

I take this to mean that the urban microclimates constellated across the boroughs diverge from one another too much to reliably record the weather in New York.

On Helen's hill, there is one climate, and I find it difficult to read. Our thermometer is strung to a post near the barn. I imagine the temperature one finds there could be found anywhere in the clearing.

She wrote some dialogue for the scene in Brussels:

"Where are you going?"
"To the beer stand. Do you want any beer?"
"You know

She stopped.

Julia often made lists of etymologies—even the plainest, most obvious ones—to better know their meaning and therefore better understand their (her) usage. She used a dictionary app on her phone:

> constellation = middle English, from the Latin, the arrangement of the stars
> to document = from the Latin *docere*, to teach
> place = old French version of Latin, *platea*, open space
> clearing = who knows

The histories of words mattered to her and didn't matter to her. Knowing them didn't change her prose, but rather informed her sense of her prejudices in word choice. She preferred English words, often with a Latinate root, to the more florid vocabulary of words derived from the French. Did this make her a good writer and did that matter?

December 1, 1989

The show opened two nights ago and I think it was a big success. Many friends came by including someone at the VV, who promised to review it. They sold four drawings already to KB, who always buys my work. George loves the drawings ... he had been hesitant about the photographs before and had encouraged me to draw more, which worked in my favor it seems. Saw Rene again—he came to opening after all since his friend's screening was cancelled or he'd had the wrong day. Just this week I read the new book that he had sent me belatedly (his best). Told him about how much I loved it, especially:

> AND then I tried to put myself at
> a distance from the subject, but the
> distance was just another
> angle on the same subject and
> it was always the same subject, you.

I said this poem described exactly my life. Rene laughed and said, "Of course it does." I also told him that I wanted to steal the line "it was always the same subject" as the title for my next show, whenever that was. At the opening he had that mischievous twinkle I miss about New York. Now it's all rushing out the door for condos. We made another plan for the studio visit since the previous appointment never happened. We talked mostly about Jack, who Rene was very close to. Someone said that the day Jack died a few months ago Rene was the first to know and carried flowers around New York all day.

I showed Rene the photographs in the office of CW but admitted that he felt George was right, that the drawings were much stronger and he was glad I hadn't shown them with the drawings. I told him I agreed. It was cold in the gallery I wondered if he simply didn't have the patience for the photographs.

I said I wanted to come by and see them, so maybe we could do the morning at my place, then afternoon at his. He described them as poems on canvas. I also suggested we do a show together sometime, maybe he'd make some money off them. He said he'd love that. Anyway, otherwise it was the usual crowd. All good friends.

December 12, 1989

Spending a lot of time with Rene. Something few can do for very long and I'm beginning to understand why. Probably won't last, though I hope I'm wrong—if not I will try to keep everything clean, as much as that is possible with him. He got testy at lunch but I didn't mind. George stayed over in France longer—going to London to discuss show there. All fine. He called yesterday and we spoke for an hour (!). Very long for him. Rene said dump him, ha. After lunch, we went to his place, where he showed me some of his paintings. They were strange, somehow very pretty and simple with painted lines from his poems. He had one up that was just an address. I asked him why and he told me I don't remember but I didn't believe it. I bought one painting off him right there. Thought it would look nice in the bedroom. He was totally elated, gave me a nice deal. I think he would have given it to me for free but I wanted to give him money. "You're a good gossip," was his reason for the discount.

Land went through and we start building in the spring. There's already a house on the property—so, so old ... realtor said maybe from late 19th century—and there'll someday be room for visitors ~~since the Big House (as we are calling it)~~ since the main building won't be done till maybe next year or the following, depending on how quickly we can get it all done w/ plans.

259

The house was not completed until 1997.

Rene glazed over, of course. He wanted to talk poetry but I don't read much poetry but George does, and often since he's been a friend to poets forever. Poets like work like his. Told him I had read Ashbery's book I bought for George. Rene said he didn't remember the book very well but had a memory of not liking it. I told him parts of his own work reminded me of Ashbery somewhat and he smirked. I read him my favorite poem, "Drunk Americans":

> I saw the reflection in the mirror
> And it doesn't count, or not enough
> To make a difference, fabricating itself
> Out of the old, average light of a college
>   town,
>
> And afterwards, when the bus trip
> Had depleted my pocket of its few
>   pennies
> He was seen arguing behind steamed
>   glass,
> With an invisible proprietor. What if you
>   can't own
>
> This one either? For it seems that all
> Moments are like this: thin,
>   unsatisfactory
> As gruel, worn away more each time you
>   return to them.

Until one day you rip the canvas from its
frame

And take it home with you. You think the
god-given
Assertiveness in you has triumphed
Over the stingy scenario: these objects
are real as meat,
As tears. We are all soiled with this desire,
at the last moment, the last.

For some reason my reading this aloud annoyed him a great deal and he stood up, set his drink on my table and said, "Look, that is nothing like me and I don't know why you're trying to draw out this comparison."

What a drunk. I tried to tell him I saw it as a poem that really relates to my experience of New York, and that I hadn't meant to say that it sounded like him or that he sounded like the poem. I said, "Look, Rene, what I'm saying is that some of these ideas are there, in both of you." He calmed down a bit but didn't agree in the end. He stuck around for five minutes (an obvious courtesy, which seemed rare for him) and then left in a huff.

Julia wrote:

Two more residents dropped out about a month ago, then a boy came but Helen took a very strong liking to him ... had "private" sessions with him and finally he left. I still can't quite believe that anything weird is happening and even this boy Mario denied it when he packed his things. Lillian was crying as he left. Still he was pretty skitterish. He told me he felt that he couldn't focus here so he's going back to Chicago. It's so incongruous, this weird relationship she has with some people here and her otherwise very professional attitude about everything else. Trying to resist letting that book map onto my experience.

The countryside is no realer than the city.

For a story, compose a list of mistakes, exaggerations, embellishments, falsities made in landscape paintings of real places.

The Hudson River School. Romanticism. Bad maps.

There is Vespucci's map of the world at the Hispanic Society in Washington Heights that is available to see upon request. It is one of two of the earliest maps of the world, both belonging to the King of Spain (CHECK THIS), though one is apparently lost. Three quarters of it are covered with recognizable continents, though all, except for Europe, are severely distorted. Much of North America is Florida. One quadrant, the first, is entirely blank, the space where the west would have been presumably filled in once the mapmaker—or his heir—knew what was there.

Blue flat hills, including the hill where Helen's project now sits, line the sliver of the northeast in Vespucci's picture of America.

She was exhausted from all the work she had put into a project she would never see the end to, and she felt overcome with a deep tiredness that refused to leave her no matter how many hours of sleep she managed to clock, no matter how much rest she took on Sundays. Of course, she had gotten used to this idea: that she was at work on something that she would never enjoy herself, but would instead serve future residents at the project, if it managed to last, though this wasn't sitting well with her anymore either. The future was total crap. And with time, one's commitment begins to falter as the tedium of "service" takes hold. The low, simmering discomfort that pervaded across the property, with Helen cooped up in her room, her T-shaped castle on a hill, had made any commitment to the project nearly unbearable. Why work for her? Why weary myself all day with this bullshit?

As for her postcards, Simon's responses were rare, her sister's rarer, though her mother's never let up, their tone growing more worried as the weeks went by, even after Julia assured her she was leaving soon. Lillian was reading herself to sleep on the other side of the room as Julia finished a letter (her last) to Zachary—who had finally replied to her with a usable address in LA. At the project, nobody talked to anybody—and when they did, they seldom believed what was said. Orders were barked, threats insinuated. Do this, do that. Even she breathed in and out this air of contempt, using any available interaction for some passive-aggressive response to a project leader or to those who were following her. This was not like Julia.

Her clothes sat in a neat pile on a wooden bench across from her bed, pushed up against a wall where she had taped photographs of friends and postcards of artworks she liked, including her favorite painting, Sargent's *El Jaleo* (1882). In the heat, the tape often became unstuck, and she often came home to find these things on the floor, already covered with a thin layer of dust. Dust, dirt, soil, earth, loam, terrain, grass, weeds, sand, leaves, all of it, everywhere, all the time, under her nails, in her bed, clumped to her shoes, in her hair, on her hands, her cheeks, even in the crack of her ass. The stuff upon which this project was built, upon which it pushed forward, ever further into the woods surrounding it, seemed to be at critical odds with everything they were doing, in a once-even battle that was now turning against them. The two trees that had wrought through the porch and that the project vainly attempted to stop from growing into the house would soon need to be sawed down, a pyrrhic victory that unsettled her as they began to mark the places where they would need to be cut. Rocks in the soil where they had been working all summer to lay the foundation for the archive resisted them. Every time they dug, more stone. The land was pushing back, against her, against Helen, and it seemed that the outside world, its "pressure," had entered into an unruly alliance with nature, and was likewise doing what it could to dismantle Helen's project. Helen, sensing this coming defeat, had retreated to her bedroom in preparation for what would be an inevitable anti-climax when fewer and fewer artists applied to live with her and she would have to close down. Work would cease and the woods would begin their long, slow creep back over the property. What had once seemed to Julia a noble project had descended into a narcissistic exercise in the exploitation of young people, with Helen dwelling over them in her tower.

She set her three postcards on the nightstand next to her bed and rose to brush her teeth downstairs, in a little bowl of water they kept near the front door. (There was no proper plumbing in Cabin J.)

"What are you doing?" Lillian asked.

Julia turned to her, to her roommate who rarely spoke to her except to ask what she was doing whenever she moved, whenever she did anything at all, and who had followed Helen into some paranoiac, irritable cognizance of her personal space, and said, "Going out. Is that OK with you?" Lillian shrugged her shoulders. It did bother her. The audience sat in the museum's theater quietly, with a patience I was unaccustomed to at a reading, since typically at events like this one people tended to shift uncomfortably in their seats or to get up to use the bathroom or find more beer or break for a cigarette or do absolutely anything they could to avoid having to listen too closely, so much so that I was nervous at the thought of disappointing them—or failing to excite them into some recognizable reaction to my piece. This audience, unlike any other I'd faced before, composed themselves with the silence of people who were contractually obligated to listen, and when it was finally my turn to read, I tried to ram through the blockade of British propriety that separated them from me with an awkward joke about their captivity as our audience. No one laughed, of course—it was a terrible, awkward joke without a clear punchline, and I delivered it entirely wrong, missing the mark I attempted to hit. Enthusiasm shot out the room like an arrow. This didn't bode well, I thought. I shuffled through the manuscript I gripped helplessly at the podium under the intense klieg lights of the museum's stage. I began to sweat in the heat. "Anyway," starting again, "I'm going to read from a new piece, well, it's somewhat new, but a piece from this new book I'm writing. I wrote it about a year ago. It's an abstract essay, but I think that'll be, that'll be somewhat clear to you. There are about eight or nine sections, so I'm just going to read a few, which, like I said, is pretty new." I began with the first, stuttered through the opening sentences, then picked up steam with the fourth:

> Romantic poetry didn't know what it was missing. At
> Kennedy Airport, I take a seat near a man wearing

shredded jeans and a plaid shirt over a sweat-stained white tee. With his hiking backpack leaned up against the smoked-glass wall next to him, he looks like he's just walked across the country, evidence of a relationship to "nature" that might be truer or deeper than mine. I write this down in a notebook thinking I could use it later: "Is nature true or deep?" Reification of the sublime in his and all those bodies walking about, the airport speakers play Taylor Swift, tuned to those radioed dreams of metropolitan space extorted by global capital for the purpose of ubiquitous homogeneity come true, "Welcome to New York," Taylor sings, "It's been waiting for you," finally risen to the occasion of a world not hers and yet she self-proclaims her kingdom of the very newly saved. The flight attendants circle the smooth floor and the hiker sighs after what must have been a long trip. I covertly photograph him with my iPhone, but the flash goes off and he notices me. He shakes his head, grinding his square jaw in what seems like mild irritation, but doesn't say anything and looks away. I'm grateful he doesn't confront me so I continue to survey him, a little more carefully this time. I turn off the flash and snap another pic. He's pouring over a water-damaged journal in which he seems to have written several formal poems, maybe even sonnets, in an unreadable cursive. Poetry really is everywhere. For something to be everywhere it must now be online. Conveniently, poetry is all over the internet because the web itself achieves a kind of poetry, rendering most online bodies poetic machines and thereby enacting in the proliferation of that messy language the illimitable sense of a socialized network of busy intersections of all discourses that infuses most things written and said with an enhanced vitality, all of it glowing on screens scattered across much of the planet. Or have I been lied to? He closes the notebook when his boarding class is called, it's business so either he's not a hiker or he's a rich hiker, and he pulls up his backpack, slinging it over his shoulder as he crosses the crowd clustered at the narrow gate and slips into it with an ease that suddenly makes me miss him. I forget the feeling once my class is called and I board a jet to London. Later, over the north Atlantic, I wake up at four a.m. East Coast time and see out my window a curvature of gray and blue, bent by a watery, alien light that resembles the flush of the dish water as it finally drains out of the kitchen sink. There can be no alien or otherworldly light on Earth despite any claims that might attempt to release us into some greater fiction. I felt alone and the flight was mostly empty. I have not always been careful. I have been tricked into cheap flights that jumped in cost with hidden fees, a bot has asked me if I wanted to be friends on Facebook and I have accepted its request only to have my account hacked, I've opened an email from an acquaintance with a phishing Google doc attached, I've made dumb admissions of fleeting passwords to scammy sites, unlocked accounts for strangers, signed up for porn only to realize it was a financial trap that partially destroyed my credit, and even accidentally froze my Chase card in Chicago when I withdrew $200 for drugs at a goth club. Quinine water once spilled on my laptop in Bushwick, destroying the hard drive, which I hadn't backed up. Later, on a flight to California, turbulence over Colorado bucked my next computer out of my lap and onto the floor, breaking it, and again I hadn't backed it up. Nothing compares 2 the hike that overlooks LA, nothing compares 2 losing all those files, and nothing compares 2 reading romantic poetry and realizing that much of it is about debt, existential or otherwise. I'm obsessed with debt and the documentary procedures of commerce and our participation in the various markets we rely on, including—and especially—the "job market." I've never kept a job for very long, the preconditions of employment (dedication) being so nearly impossible as to abstract every morning to a timeless, flat plane of actions I can't make any sense of, brushing my teeth and putting on my clothes, maybe jerking off while staring at my face in the mirror, drinking orange juice or coffee, eating a banana, all of it seemingly out of order (or finally pledged to a disorder that overrides the desire to put myself together again), until I'm late and often too late and I'm encouraged to look for a job elsewhere. Regardless of my disinterest in definitive employment the pernicious logic of the market still wields its heavy and not-so-beautiful power over me and everyone else I know, have known, ever will know, despite our concerted efforts to stop it. Pleasures do not accrue with accomplishing any task: your boss is lying to you. I imagine the hiker graduated college and went for a walk, deciding he wouldn't come back. Poems in the cursive of joblessness. To be unemployed is nature.

I finished the last line to polite applause that gave no indication of whether I had succeeded or failed in my effort. Phillip, in the back, gave me an enthusiastic thumbs-up. I wasn't sure about the other sections of this piece, so I moved on and read my essay on the tides.

"It was great," Phillip whispered to me when I joined him in the audience. The other reader, a poet from the Netherlands, approached the podium as tentatively as I had. She offered her own bad joke to excuse the awkwardness she must have felt under the intense gaze of this group of listeners, though it seemed to get lost in her effort to translate the punchline from Dutch to English. Grimacing, she must have realized that she shouldn't have brought along translations of her work and instead stuck to the Dutch originals. The poems would go over better if no one understood her regardless of how wonderful they might have sounded to any other receptive audience.

"This is going to be hard," I whispered to Phillip.

"I know."

So we were stuck at a bad reading, one I was partially responsible for. My solution in a situation like this was usually to concentrate on the back of the head in front of me while resisting the urge to look at my phone. Even at interesting readings my phone begs my attention to it, like a needy child, as in one time, years before, when I attended an Alice Notley reading in New York and I spent the better half of Notley's introduction to her work scrolling through Facebook. At the bar afterward, a woman scolded me for disrespecting Notley on this rare occasion. "You know she lives in Paris, right?" I did. She had said as much in her reading. "You know she never reads here?" I did. "It was really rude of you." It was.

I didn't know what to say. "You could say you're sorry," she said, "It was really distracting for me."

"I'm very sorry." If I have my notebook with me, I'll write over the sound of the reading, since nobody will suspect that I'm not paying attention, even though I find my own writing in those instances equally difficult to pay attention to. At this reading, the poet's work floated over us, but never dropped down onto our laps, struggled to command our ears, and so I played with my hands as the voice kept up in a lilting drone. It wasn't her fault; it was probably very beautiful poetry, what she was saying. I blamed Britain.

"How was the Heath?" Phillip whispered.

"Fun. I'll tell you after."

Staring at the poet wasn't enough to keep my patience. She was already ten minutes in, and seemed to have decided that she would go long despite the mood of the audience, perhaps in defiance of their boredom. I looked around me: mostly young people, though there was a group of elderly men and women clustered in the far right of the theater, near the stage, close to our host, who happened to be sitting next to a head I recognized from behind, but I wasn't sure from where. I stared at his long black hair, trying to remember where I'd seen it before. As though sensing that he was being watched, he turned around to scan the audience: it was John, from the Heath. I hadn't told him I was reading at this event, hadn't even told him my full name. "Believe it or not," I whispered to Phillip. "You see that guy, up to the far right next to the old couple, right near the stage, long hair?"

Phillip craned his neck. "Yes, I think so."

"I actually ate that guy's ass out in the Heath."

Phillip snorted. "Really?"

"Yes, really."

Coincidence is everything. I wondered if he had come straight from the Heath, from the pagoda. I should have gone with him, or invited him to the reading, told him I was performing when he said he was a poet. What had he thought of me while he sat there in the audience? My tongue, my face, my body, my weird omission.

The Dutch poet ended abruptly, her poem trailing off with a line, in English, about "the wind in the economy." She finished with a gracious smile. Our host rose up to the stage to thank the readers. The applause was surprisingly robust, with even a few cheers, as everyone stood up to collect their things and exit to the lobby for beer and wine. "I'll meet you in there," Phillip said, leaving me to a small group that had come to say hello.

I went gray, looked down at my bag as I packed my things. "Hey, that was really great," a stranger said, tapping me on the back. Another joined him: "Yeah, I loved it."

"Thanks," I said, stuffing my reading into my bag.

Another woman said, "That was great." This surprised me because I had specifically noticed, from the podium, that she seemed to not be paying attention to me, as if to prove a point about how awful I was. I smiled. "Thanks." Perhaps I hadn't done so badly after all.

"You were great," John said.

"I didn't know you were coming," I said.

"I didn't know you were reading."

"I know, I should have said something."

He frowned. "I said I was a poet. You should have said who you were."

"I don't know. I didn't, eh, you're right."

"Own it next time."

I nodded, sheepishly. He paused and took me in, as if to say, you should care more about what you do, and who might be interested in it. At least, that's what I expected him to say, what I would have said to me. "Anyway, I like your writing." Thanks, I said. "I'll see you in the lobby?" Definitely.

This was my favorite compliment I'd received, delivered off the cuff and by a stranger I'd met and slept with in a public park. When we had been naked in the bushes I hadn't thought once about writing, my book, but instead had thought of everything else. In my reading all I could think about was us, in the park, on the floor, rolling on the damp ground. During the event they'd become one thing, the reading and the not-reading—a distinction I didn't want to make. At least not then. They were, in that moment, the same.

The curator of the event came over to shake my hand. He said various things about the importance of fiction and poetry occurring in art spaces, how the art world was changing its perspective on literature. I wondered what that perspective had been before now, but decided not to ask. These things change so often. Why catch up. "Thank you for having me," I said, as we moved into the lobby, where wine, beer, and raw vegetables were served alongside cured meats.

Phillip stood in the corner, near the temporary bar, talking to a colleague of his. He opened a beer and they knocked their cans together. I looked around for John, but couldn't find him in the crowd. English faces bobbing in their flatness. A few people smiled sympathetically, not quite ready to say anything to me. I wondered if I had been too dense, too un-poetic? I decided to check the bathroom for John, but he wasn't there; outside, where a few people stood in the warm summer air smoking, he was nowhere to be found. I pulled out my phone and texted him: "hey, sorry if that was awkward. did you leave?"

Phillip joined me outside. "How do you feel?"

"Well, I was nervous."

"I liked it a lot."

"Thanks," I said. "Hold on, let me go get a beer."

In the queue, John texted me back: "Exhausted. Went home.

It was great to meet you. Have a good night."

I felt a fussy sadness, like I had just been dumped. He was a stranger, someone I'd probably never see again, and yet his departure left me with a sludge of indistinct feelings, like I had been asked to remark upon something but had failed to do so, and so I was left with a jumble of impressions, none of which I could shape into an argument. This is what writing, at least my writing, was about: the gulped, imperfect response. I had literally kissed his ass. I'd kiss how many more. I wanted to text back but what a waste of time. Grievances of this kind should not accumulate.

December 18, 1989

At the beach house with George, who arrived yesterday (I've been here all week photographing for new work possibly). Sat down yesterday together and continued to plan the upstate project. George explained our thoughts to an architect two weeks ago and he's going to come up with a few plans for the house. We went over the first sketches that we had talked to him about this morning and all looks good, exciting. Idea is a 3-part house w/ a residential wing, a kitchen, and a large living room/common space to start. We also drew up plans for 2 cabins for guests. Architect says it shouldn't be too much trouble, though from the standpoint of construction it's ambitious—and won't be cheap. George smiled at this. Have to clear a lot of space and get material up the mountain. We waved it off. We have some of the $ at the moment anyway, especially after George's recent shows & somewhat w/

drawing show at CW. It's a start.

Last week Rene came by and asked for his painting back. I thought that was strange but I agreed because arguing with him is exhausting and never worth the headache. He knocked unannounced and was all sweaty even though it was freezing outside. I said, "Rene, I paid for this." And he had the money that I paid him in an envelope and gave it right back. He said he'd realized he wasn't done with it. (I assume someone told him he shouldn't have sold the work—?) He had gone somewhere with a friend and had an idea for it, realizing it wasn't done, but that if I was interested in it again to come back to his studio in the new year.

It was below freezing. I said, "Rene, come up, have some tea, and I'll give you the painting." I didn't want this to turn into a real fight.

"No, I'm going to wait here," he said. Right there on the stoop, Rene in his sweater and not even a proper jacket. I was actually upset about this. "Rene is this about the poem? The comparison?"

"No of course not, Helen, why would it be about the poem?"

"Because you were so upset about it."

"I'm not upset I just want to finish my painting, then you can buy it back?"

He just stood there, with a surprising, begrudging beauty. He looked like the slain hero, his epic poem over. He would have made for such a great photograph. "OK," I said. "I'll get the painting. But give me a second to wrap it up."

He said, "You don't need to wrap it."

I went up to our apartment and pulled the painting off the wall. I held it in front of me at arm's length to get a better look at it. I'd never gone to the address he'd painted and decided I never would. I didn't even bother to make a record of it. I grabbed my camera from a bag by the bed, walked down to Rene leaning there on the stoop and shoved it straight back to him.

"Do me one favor though. Can I take your picture?" I asked.

He thought about it. He was going to say no but I made such a face for him. Then he said Sure Helen and I took his picture, Rene in his red cap, holding this painting on my stoop. A ball of the most furious energy I had ever seen up until then, burning in the cold.

He left, the painting under his arm, my painting. That Ashbery line: "Until one day you rip the canvas from its frame and take it home with you ..." And so it was.

I heard later that B told him not to give paintings away for so cheap. I'm sure he's going to sell it to someone rich. Poets shouldn't make paintings.

In the meantime George and I have our upstate project to look forward to. Get out of New York. Or bring it to us. George even had the idea of making it a retreat where people stayed for a month or more but can't make art while they're there. That's the idea, to get them out of their heads. Rene could use time away from himself. I told George we'd invite him first, even though he'd taken my painting. George said Rene will never come. "You never know," I said. That's true. I don't.

And within it opens into a World

Julia stopped writing fiction or anything for that matter in her note-book in the last week of her stay at the project. She had grown accustomed to its ugly, exhausting imperative to censor her, but knew that it would not rule her forever. She had a new idea for a book: a collection of stories about parks. Then she wrote:

> Set my last day for this Friday. It's Sunday. Had enough
> of this "project." Too much work, no pay, just work
> work work work work work work. Work (of this kind?)
> is despair.

Trained from the airport through the nondescript Viennese sub-urbs along a concrete corridor blitzed with graffiti, into the for-mer seat of an empire that collapsed before its imperial capitol could be finished. Pretty, but too big for its mid-size population, Vienna teeters between Western Europe and the east end of the continent, where the surrounding Slavic cultures turn toward Russia for news of the world. Since I only had about two days there, I planned to spend most of my time at the museums, the houses of Freud and Wittgenstein, and in the cafes, which Stewart, who had spent time in Vienna when he was a student at an art school in Frankfurt, had recommended to me. Vienna twin-kles with nineteenth-century charm, with much of its contemporary design dating to the fifties. It is a stately wedding cake for those dead emperors whose marriages to power always seemed to end badly with a war. Goodbye to Europe.

I knew no one else in Vienna besides Simon, whom I realized as soon as I landed I couldn't rely on as a companion for those forty-eight hours outside of our pre-arranged drink. Of course, I shouldn't have come to Austria. What would I do here? Walk. In crisis resort to basics: one's feet.

From the central train station, I took a street car to the Pension Walzerstadt on Zieglergasse in Neubau, a Wiener-style hotel with a cream-white façade at the corner of an intersection evocative of the new Vienna, with one side of the building facing an English-style pub specializing in brisket, of all things, and two traditional Viennese restaurants, while the other, where my room was located on the second floor, looked down upon a doner stand that became especially popular and rowdy at night, in so far as the Viennese can become rowdy. Two brothers scrambled to greet me at the Pension when I arrived. From the front door to the reception desk, they competed with one another for my attention as I hauled in my suitcase. They wanted to know where I was coming from (London) and how London was (fine) and if I had been to Vienna before (no) and where I lived in the United States (New York) and had I had a nice flight (yes) and if I was hungry (yes, maybe) and if I needed a guidebook (no). "Unfortunately," one brother explained to me with a great theatrical sigh, "you have arrived an hour too early and the room is not yet ready." He frowned.

When I began to say that would be no problem so long as I left my bag with them at the front desk while I went out for lunch, the second brother interrupted me: "However, we could very easily make accommodation for you for ten Euros and allow you into your room early." I considered this. At my hesitation, they insisted the money would go to the maid to speed her along in preparing my room for me, a worthy cause, it seemed to the first brother. "Indeed, sir, it is like a tip?"

I tipped the maid.

The second floor smelled of stale bread and faintly of cheap perfume and I was surprised to find that the high-ceilinged room was especially large for how little I had paid for it, with two double beds pushed together next to a struggling, but effective fan. Between the two windows that opened to the Zieglergasse, the hotel had hung a black-and-white photograph of Franz Josef on horseback in an imperial procession, leading a march through the city, into the new century. Saucer-like streetlights, strung on wires between the buildings, dangled in the air over a few tourists ambling through the neighborhood. The second brother, who had accompanied me to my room, paused in the doorway, waiting for what I assumed was a tip. "Thank you," I said, handing him a Euro, and closed the door.

"we still on for tonight?" I texted Simon. Showered, changed clothes, no reply. Went out since it was still early afternoon and I could catch the Secession, the Kunsthistorisches Museum, the Loos Bar, and a few other museums before we were to meet that evening. I hadn't played the tourist in London but I was happy to in Austria, a country I had never thought to go to until my ex-boy-friend moved there with his boyfriend and I got it into my head that I should visit them, a mistake I had likewise never thought I would make, but here I was on more than just a whim, standing in a hotel room in Vienna with nothing to do but see art and wait for a text message. It finally came after I left my tour of Wittgenstein's house, the last of the day: "hey, omg you're here!!! i totally forgot and i am actually out of town just tonight but back tomorrow if we can see each other then? im so sorrrrrry."

All of Europe with its towers

During the war, the Nazis erected anti-aircraft flak towers (flak-turme) throughout Germany and German-occupied territory. Six concrete structures (in three sets of two, always consisting of a cylindrical L-Tower and rectangular G-Tower roughly fifteen stories high with eleven-foot-thick walls) were built in Vienna. Capped with petal-like platforms that fanned outward from the top, the Towers allowed for a nine-mile defense radius for German guns and doubled as shelters for both the military and civilians during Allied air raids or invasions, including the Soviet assault on Berlin. (Despite repeated Russian bombings, the Berlin Towers were largely unharmed during the final push into the Nazi capitol.) After the war ended in Europe, the British and West German governments destroyed the flakturme of Berlin, but the Austrian government left theirs in place throughout the city, citing both the cost and complexity of demolition. Several were repurposed for public use. In Flakturm V in Mariahilf, G-Tower now serves as a military base for the Austrian Army while L-Tower was permanently refitted as an aquarium, the Haus des Meeres on the Gumpendorfer Strasse, which winds toward the Museumsquartier. In 1991, the Haus commissioned a permanent installation text by the artist Lawrence Weiner for the top of the tower in commemoration of the war. Wrapped around an additional concrete structure placed on top of the V-L, the longer side of the commission reads *SMASHED TO PIECES (IN THE STILL OF THE NIGHT)* while the other revises the first side into *(IN THE STILL OF THE NIGHT)*. In Flakturm VII, located in the Augarten in the Leopoldstat, both the G-Tower, which was partially destroyed by an internal explosion, and the L-Tower have not been reused since the war. In complex VIII, G-Tower is currently used for art storage while L-Tower remains empty.

I passed V's L on the way to the gay clubs after Simon cancelled. The Café Savoy was close to my hotel, and in the general area of a few other bars, none of them very assuring in their names (felixx, Village Bar, Inside Bar) or Yelp reviews. After I left Wittgenstein's, I'd gone back to my hotel for doner, where I ate falafel while staring out the window, wondering what to do in this city, the capital of opera and, in a sense, a certain kind of European conservatism that struck me as incompatible with a robust gay life, Austria being the country of the Freedom Party, an unreconstructed holdover from the fascist period (Austria, unlike Germany, never went through denazification) that would nearly rise to power in a year's time, when the tide would begin to turn against the moderate left throughout the continent and America with the growth of the populist right. But in the Vienna of my summer, there was a cheerfulness bordering on mania. Let me get you this let me get you that. I'd seen half the museums already, all were glamorous and well done, couldn't finish the doner, couldn't stand the thought of staying in a city I'd never been to and wouldn't likely visit again, and so typed "gay bar" into Google Maps on my phone again to see what was around. Several options queued up about a mile or so from me, including the Eagle, a name I at least recognized from New York, San Francisco, and Los Angeles. Finally an America I could find elsewhere, even though I hadn't been looking for it. The Yelp review promised a dark room. Another cabinet. I put on a jacket and left.

I smoked a cigarette outside the Eagle, near the back entrance to the Estherhazypark that surrounds L-Tower. Up above, two of the four petals cast long shadows over the street that cut between the tower and a police station. The shouts of rival gangs of teens rose up over the fence that wrapped around the elevated park, lit dimly by the aquarium's spotlights, until the sound of a shattered bottle broke them up and a few kids fled down the street. It was still early for a Thursday night. I linked to the bar's open wi-fi. A suite of texts I'd received since I left the hotel buzzed my phone, including a couple by Simon:

00:23, ten minutes ago: "sorry about tonight."

It's OK.

00:24: "anyway if you can meet tomorrow that would be cool. you're only here for a few days?"

00:36: "ya. tomorrow is my last night," I replied.

00:37: "ok, can you meet at the museumsquartier at 21:45 tomorrow. it's late but im having dinner w my roommates and want to be sure for time with u :)."

"works for me," I wrote.

00:41: "till tomorrow."

Then I went into the Eagle, where I undressed with several men in the dark.

I wasn't sure how to kill the hour until I would see Simon. We had agreed to meet in the courtyard of the Kunsthalle Wien, about a fifteen-minute walk from my hotel. I was anxious, edging toward some low-grade panic no amount of impromptu meditation could remedy. Finally, we would come face to face, after all this time apart. I wasn't even sure why, at this point, seeing one another mattered all that much, what difference it might make between us. Probably none. Eye contact and small talk about travels and who's-up-to-what-back-home wouldn't restore even tentative peace between us, those feelings that had brought us together in the first place and that I belatedly missed, and it wasn't like we even needed to make "peace," the terms of which would be ambiguous to me anyway. I needed something but what. At least rapprochement. On my gut I said do it.

I showered, unloaded my bowels in the German-style toilet. Paced. Forty-five minutes to go. Really, fifty-five. I needed to be late, late with purpose, of course: "Sorry. I was having dinner with a friend." The room's yellow almost-malarial light, emitted from thumb-like bulbs encased in a cheap floral chandelier, was wrong, the bed stiff, and I couldn't get comfortable at the small desk to read—or write. I didn't want to do either. Sitting down I tapped my fingers on the wooden surface. I did a round of push-ups instead. Up and down, up and down: the tip of my nose grazing one unit of the carpet's pattern of pointillist flowers in a kind of meditative operation, nose to flower, nose to flower, nose to flower. The room smelled of old tennis shoes, dirt tracked in from a field, infused with the sour but distant fragrance of dried sweat. I got up on my knees and breathed, checked my phone. Nothing. The old fan, set to its highest level at three, turned in the corner near the window, pushing the stale hotel air around in a chore of summer. It wheezed with the difficulty of making the room somewhat bearable. I put on a light jacket and left the room.

Warm-up to round two: on Zieglergasse toward Burgasse, I stopped at the Restaurant Neubauschenke for an Aperol Spritz on an outdoor deck that jutted off the sidewalk and into the street. The restaurant served traditional Austrian food: sausages, boiled meats, and vegetables, amid candlelight and small potted plants from countries far beyond Central Europe. Mostly palms that came to about my waist, a difficult plant to maintain in the shade. An elderly German waiter, his skeletal face the color of chalk, asked if

I wanted anything to eat but I shook my head no. "OK, sir," he replied and snapped shut the menu. It is traditional for Viennese waiters to express their contempt for diners who don't spend any money. That made sense. I appreciated it after years of faking it in restaurants myself, as a server who smiled under threat of dismissal from various managers. "One Aperol Spritz," sibilant emphasis on the z. With a tsk of disappointment. As I liked it.

It hadn't become dark yet, though the light was beginning to dim to blue overhead. Across the deck a man sat with his legs propped up on a chair, a cigarette dangling from his mouth as he talked into his phone. He was in his mid-forties, with cold blue eyes and a thin, sharp nose, giving him a canine symmetry. I read the news on my phone but occasionally looked up in his direction. His eyes narrowed on the cigarette in his mouth as he sucked in smoke. "Nein," he kept saying—the only word I could recognize in his frustrated monologue, a soup of choppy German with occasional flecks of English—to whoever was on the other side of the line. He was movie-star-like in his performative gestures, hands looping in the air as he explained things and argued whatever case he was trying to make (now in American-accented English, as the conversation had apparently progressed to a more complicated subject and one outside the reach of his low-level German), and he acted like he knew he was always being watched. He even extended a pinky on his right hand when he lifted his glass of wine. It was an awkward gesture but one I recognized as conveying some knowledge of an elite code he'd established in a posher world than this palm-besotted one we found ourselves in. Suddenly, he was frozen in a look of boredom, his lips in perpetual purse: "And what would you have me do," he said. "What would you have me do exactly?" He set the phone down while a male voice continued to shout through its speakers, in garbled speech. He looked away, toward the sky, and dragged on his cigarette, then turned to me and winked.

When his cigarette burned down to its filter (the voice, growing angrier the less he responded to it, continued in its crackly rant), he put it out in a tin dish like it was an insect whose buzzing nuisance he'd finally crushed. He leaned over the phone lying on the table as the voice was saying something in English about his time in Chicago and pressed the end-call button. The voice cut out. Was none of my business, of course, but I was curious to know what and why. I sipped my Aperol Spritz without looking away from him, this man in the final act of an art-house film about the listless *fin* to our respective romantic dramas, if it was romance that was his problem. I let the dumb question as to why I was in Vienna pass through my head again, written out in huge bold letters on a banner rippling off the back of an airplane bumping over whatever mental vista passed for the interior landscape of my desires, *What are you doing?* I knew why I was in Vienna.

It was 21:25, twenty minutes plus ten until I would see Simon again.

I ordered another Aperol Spritz. Pleased that I was spending more than five Euros, the waiter was friendlier this time and asked if I wanted a glass of water, "Yes," I said. "Thank you."

"Nooooo … problem," he twirled. He took the man across the way's order—another glass of white, he said in English—as he lit up another cigarette: the chain-smoker's melancholy gathered around him in a gray halo of smoke amid the plants and lights strung around the deck railing. The wanderer. He inhaled, exhaled. Sucked up the smoke through his nose.

The waiter returned with our drinks on the same tray. Where was the dinner crowd? I wondered. Is the Neubauschenke so awful? or had our shared gloom, if it was gloom, poisoned the atmosphere for any passing diner? Everyone who went by was laughing, happy to be out on a warm, early-summer night.

"Where are you from?" he called over to me.

"New York," I said.

"Me too. To that." He raised his glass.

"To that," I repeated after him. Fifteen years must have separated us, but we found ourselves equalized in our respective blue moods.

"Want to join me?" he asked.

I considered it. Had the Maiden caught me in the Wild.

"Sure," I said. "For a minute. I have to meet a friend."

The man took his feet off the chair opposite him and I took a seat. "I'm Mark," he said, extending his hand across the table.

"Nick," I said. "What brings you to Vienna?"

"Work." He paused. "Well, not work. I'm a reporter—and I'm on my way back from Egypt, but I wanted to have a few days to myself. I was in Vienna for a semester in college … and I needed to see it again."

"What kind of reporting do you do?" He told me he was a tv reporter and worked for CNN. "Are you one of the talking heads," I joked.

"In a way," he said.

"How's it being on tv?"

"Lonely. Sometimes you have to talk to people you don't want to talk to."

"Does it make you sad?"

"It doesn't make me sad, no. The secret is you learn to split your life between what you're saying on air and off. A lot of the guys I get into it with are my friends outside the studio."

I nodded along. I hadn't seen him on CNN, but I didn't watch CNN. He asked me what I did. I said I bounce around. "So," he said, "when are you seeing your friend?"

"Soon. We're supposed to meet at the Kunsthalle. But he

keeps cancelling."

Mark swirled the last of the wine in his glass. We knew something about one another, sure, that we belonged to the same tribe, the markings of which were always visible to those who belong, even if they were invisible to outsiders. "Have you been to the Kaiserbrundl?" I hadn't—nor did I know what it was. "It's this gorgeous old sauna about a twenty-minute walk from here, just past the museums. I was thinking of going. It's stunning: a big, nineteenth-century Turkish bath, with these great pools and steam rooms. It's a little scummy, but I love it. Or used to. I haven't been in twenty years."

It hadn't come up on my list of things to do, but Mark assured me I couldn't miss it, it's been the best part of Vienna for centuries.

He said the fey brother of the long dead emperor, Ludwig Viktor, was a well-known fag who used to go there in the nine-teenth century to fetch easy trade. "His excuse was that the pal-ace didn't have a pool. They called him Luzi-Wuzi." The first German gay periodical, *Der Eigene*, noted that he had "precious grace." On the flat Central European plain of mute glamor his charm was special, an acceptable face that hustled between the surface world and its bathhouse underground. After years of dal-liances among Vienna's ornate pools and saunas, his reputation came to its bad end when he made unwanted advances on a young, middle-class man who, not sharing the emperor's broth-er's predilection for cock (or at least imperial cock), rejected him. Viktor would not accept no, there was no no, could be no no, and there would never be a no to the brother of the emperor, and so he tried his luck with the trick again. This time, the man slapped Luzi to the ground, leaving him stunned among the gawking, unkind bathers who recognized him, of course, as the *warmer bruder* of Franz Josef.

Rebuffed in the nude among the subjects, Viktor had the man arrested on the spot, in the dark, blue-tiled corridors of the baths, though he was cleared of any wrongdoing after the police determined that, despite his royal station, Viktor could not force men to fuck him. Even the brother of the emperor can be refused. Franz Josef, who had long tolerated his brother's open homosexuality, was embarrassed that he had acted so foolishly in public, disgracing himself and by extension the emperor and his family and their collective power, which was sexless and unsullied by the banality of such base and misguided desires, was the desire to which all other desires were to submit, and so he banished him from the city to the family's summer palace in Salzburg, where Viktor lived until the mid-1870s as a "patron of the arts," stripped of his titles.

Mark wanted to know if I'd join him at the Kaiserbrundl. Its name means the Emperor's Well, he said. I told him I still had to meet my friend. I was already late. He stood up and said that it was on the way. "It's history," he added. Yes, I nodded. But whose? Like I said, I was already late.

ACKNOWLEDGMENTS

I owe a debt to several historians and researchers in writing this book, especially Mike Davis (*Ecology of Fear, City of Quartz*), Elizabeth Kolbert (*Field Notes from a Catastrophe, The Sixth Extinction*, "The Siege of Miami"), Carey McWilliams (*Southern California: An Island on the Land*), Rebecca Solnit (*Storming the Gates of Paradise: Landscapes for Politics*), and Kevin Starr (his *Americans and the California Dream* series).

Selections of this book appeared (often in a different or excerpted form) in *BOMB, Document, Flash Art, Lit Hub*, and in the anthology *Transactions of Desire* (Cornerhouse, 2015). Kenning Editions published several chapters as a pamphlet in December 2015.

I am very grateful to Asad Raza and the Boghossian Foundation for housing me in Brussels, London, and Vienna for summer 2016.

Stefan Kalmár introduced me to the Tom of Finland Foundation and made sure I found what I was looking for in LA on a trip that prompted this book. I'm always thankful for the long nights and early mornings of our friendship.

Finally, many friends read and guided this book from its beginning, but I am most thankful to Brandon Brown, Kevin Champoux, Stuart Comer, Ben Fama, Richard Hawkins, Kevin Killian, Charlie Kuder, Jacolby Satterwhite, Stewart Uoo, and Steve Zultanski. Lastly, I am grateful to Stephen Motika and Lindsey Boldt of Nightboat and Carl Williamson of Familiar Studio for their support, faith, and patience. This book would not be here without them.

ABOUT NIGHTBOAT BOOKS

Nightboat Books, a nonprofit organization, seeks to develop audiences for writers whose work resists convention and transcends boundaries. We publish books rich with poignancy, intelligence, and risk. Please visit nightboat.org to learn about our titles and how you can support our future publications.

This book has been made possible by grants from the National Endowment for the Arts and the New York State Council on the Arts Literature Program.

National
Endowment
for the Arts
arts.gov